LIES RUN DEEP

THE PREDATOR / PREY THRILLER SERIES
BOOK 2

VALERIE BRANDY

Published by: Emerald Lion Press

23901 Calabasas Rd., Ste 2088, Calabasas, CA 91302

emeraldlionpress@gmail.com

ISBN 978-1-964161-04-4

Cover design by Stuart Bache. Copy Editing provided by Sharon Lennon-Mehlschau and Linda Triol. Photo of the author by David Mueller. French to English Translations provided by Analiesmarry.

Printed in the United States of America.

🌸 Created with Vellum

CONTENTS

FACT.

~

The word "honeymoon" is derived from an old Northern European custom in which newlyweds consume a daily cup of mead— made with fermented honey— for a month.

This custom would not be possible without bees.

1

ZOE

Our wedding is simple.

Pink and beige crepe-paper folded into petals and stars, hung in tree branches with invisible fishing line. Lights curled in mason jars, twinkling like fireflies. An empty shadowbox with a slot on top serves as our guest book— it's a cross between a piggy bank and a picture frame. Mike carved pieces of balsa wood into circles. A sharpie sits nearby, so guests can write their well-wishes on the round, wooden shards before dropping them through the slot. When the visual guest book is done, it'll be a piece of art. We'll hang it in the living room, above the couch.

Our venue is nothing.

An open hillside out in Simi Valley. It has a name, but I can't remember it— and I prefer it that way. The man who owns the land has a small house over the ridge. When I knocked on his door and explained what I wanted to use his property for, he shrugged his shoulders and said, "Who'd wanna get married here?"

"Me, I guess," I answered back, watching as the lines

between his ginger eyebrows deepened, as if concerned for my mental health. "I can pay you," I added, pulling out my check book. "Not much, but a couple hundred, maybe, for the trouble?"

He waved a hand at me and looked over his shoulder, where a TV blared. An episode of Dr. Phil was reaching its climax, its unlucky guest awaiting the results of a paternity test.

"Nah, don't worry about that," the man shook his head, his eyes still fixated on the screen in the other room. "Just try to keep the noise down, alright?"

"The wedding's June 22nd," I told him. "At night. We might come by a couple days before, to set everything up."

"Sure, sure," he nodded, making no effort to record the date. "I'll be visiting my cousin up North then, anyways."

"I'm sure he'll be thrilled," I told him.

"The groom?"

"Your cousin."

He nodded, then took my pen from my hand without asking me, scribbling down his phone number on the back of my checkbook.

"Nothin' out there. You'll have to bring your own light," he said before closing the door.

And just like that, we had a venue. Towering oak trees with bark sloughing off their sides, reaching their long branches toward each other, as if waiting for a hug. Brown grass growing knee-high in some places. And best of all: the view at sundown.

It was the view that made me know I wanted to get married, here. I was driving down a side road, running out of light, when I rounded a corner and the sky opened up. Blood-orange paint dripped down the golden hill, reds and oranges burning. It's something to do with the angle of the mountain: the ridge kisses the sky at the perfect point. Mike and I sat out one night and timed it. At 7:55pm sharp, the sun's edge sinks beneath the ridge, coloring the hill all red and yellow.

Now, it's 7:45pm, and I'm standing at the top of that same ridge, wearing a white dress. It's sleeveless, with thin spaghetti straps, a wisp of a thing. A cotton-candy skirt bells out at the bottom— whimsical, flighty. But the top is all structure and neat lines, restrained and aloof. When I tried it on, my Mom said, "It's sugar and spice, just like you."

She's standing beside me, holding my arm, ready to walk me down the aisle, which is really just a long stretch of grassless earth that Mike mowed clean. We laid a tan runner on top, with a crunchy plastic underside to keep the dew from leaking through.

The sound of a single violin plucks its way over the hillside.

"Ready?" my Mom asks.

I nod, and we make our way down the hill. One hundred eyes stare. Everyone stands, rising from the white plastic chairs we rented. My stomach churns. We sent out too many invitations, expecting most of them to be returned with a "Not available," RSVP. There wasn't much notice, and the venue is in the middle of nowhere. Looking out at the crowd, I'm taken aback. Maybe we underestimated how much everyone loves us.

Lanterns bob in the trees, helping us find our way toward the carved pergola that Mike built, which serves as an altar. The wind blows, hiking up my dress, and I know it's the Great Everything, moving me forward, telling me that I'm right where I'm supposed to be.

Mike comes into view, looking way too good in his charcoal tux. I'm always surprised by how well he wears one. Some men put on a suit and immediately look lost, like a kid who was forced to dress up for church. With his usual uniform of ripped t-shirts and old jeans— stained with varnish— Mike's a prime candidate for this category. But somehow, he pulls it off. Maybe it's an extension of his ability to be comfortable in all situations, with all different kinds of people. Mike *wears* the suit: he doesn't let it wear him.

He smiles at me, and suddenly I'm not concerned about how many guests we invited. Mike is my safe place. The world could crumble, the skies could fall— if Mike is there, we'll be alright.

My Mom gives me away. Mike looks at her, and when he takes her hand, he whispers something in her ear. I can't catch what he says, but I think I hear the words "take care of," and "always."

My maid of honor— Tori— smiles at me, her eyes tearing up a little. She mouths the word "twenty." It's how many years we've known each other. She touches the sash on the waistband of her dress. We had the number sewn on the inside. It's our secret.

Rick— Mike's best man— nods at the officiant as if to say, "Let's do this, already." Rick is a somber, lanky investment banker, and the closest thing Mike has to family. Mike calls Rick his brother.

The officiant says some words about love, but the wind is blowing again, so I don't listen. Instead, I focus on the sound of the leaves rattling, the melody of our future riding on the wind's back. It promises me decades of slow dances on our patio, breakfasts in bed, cold winters spent by the fireplace, and warm summer nights laying hand-in-hand beneath the stars, silently wondering how we got so lucky but not daring to ask it aloud.

It's time for Mike's vows. He wrote some himself. He promised to keep it short, so that I wouldn't look out of place having not written my own. He knows I'm not a great public speaker. I'm better with actions than with words.

"I didn't know what 'home' was," he says, quietly, "until I met you."

He takes my hand and slides the wedding band onto my finger, repeating the traditional vows line by line.

It's my turn, now. I hear myself say, "As long as we both shall live," before sliding the ring onto Mike's left ring finger. It's the hand that's missing a pinky, now. He makes jokes about the missing digit, but I've noticed he hides the hand in his pocket, especially around strangers. The terrible thing that happened to us in the dark, vast wilderness of Yosemite pushes at the edges of my mind. I try not to think about it, but it pops up when I least expect it. But not now. Not here. I won't let anything ruin this moment.

That's it. We're married. The sun sinks below the mountains with a final defiant flash, and the night sky blankets the hillside. Mike beams, his eyes reflecting back the moonlight, looking at me like I'm all he's ever wanted.

I remember what the man who owns this property told me.

"You'll have to bring your own light," he'd said.

I hold Mike's hand in mine.

As I look into his eyes, counting the stars, the moons, the infinite universes there, all of them glittering with the light that holds my world together— I know that we did.

2

CASSANDRA

The venue they've chosen is dark— too dark.

It makes it easy to hide.

If Mike were still talking to me, I'd warn him about choosing to host a wedding in such a remote location. A pitch black field in the middle of nowhere screams "horror film," not "marry me." Not that I mind their choice. It's great, for me. I do well in darkness, where you never know what's going to happen next. I enjoy the unpredictable. Sometimes, when things get too boring, I'll smash something in my apartment, just to create a mess that needs cleaning.

I sink deeper into my hiding spot in the living room of the house at the top of the hill, unnoticed by all. The house smells like rotting vegetable soup, and there's five seasons of Dr. Phil queued up on the Tivo. The owner couldn't have been more careless in the way he positioned the hide-a-key. He left it on the back stoop, sitting right next to the door. The hide-a-key itself wasn't even convincing: just a faux-rock made from an unnatural-looking plastic. He didn't put much effort into security, but I understand why— he doesn't have much to lose.

The house creaks as I adjust my footing, staying as close to the dusty wall as I can, imagining that I'm one of its bare wooden planks.

I clutch the splintering window-frame, peeking over its edge. Zoe and Mike exchange their rings. It makes me want to cry out— watching Mike marry someone else— but I stay silent, biting my tongue until I start to taste blood. I want to light the house on fire, burn the whole thing down, just to make them look this way.

There's a plan, I remind myself. *Stick to the plan.*

I am here to procure four items:

The sash. The wallet. The necklace. The gun.

My task is to steal these small objects. Not to cause a scene at the wedding, although I would like to. Not to flip over tables. Not to set the hillside on fire, watching the dry grass burn. I wouldn't create a scene to hurt anyone. I would just want them to notice me. I would make just enough fuss that they wouldn't be able to deny my presence. "Hello, Cassandra," they'd say, and I'd quiet immediately, just happy to be acknowledged. That's all I ever really want. Is to be noticed.

No. My purpose tonight is not to be seen. I am to get in, and get out. I am to resist my own impulses in order to serve the long-term plan, which Logan has promised me will prove much more satisfying.

"If you do this," Logan told me when he first recruited me to his cause. "Mike will be forced to notice you. You can have him, alone in a room, and he won't be able to look away."

I repeat the list to myself like a mantra: *The sash. The wallet. The necklace. The gun.*

Outside the window, everyone cheers, snapping me back to reality. It's done. They're married. A woman— Zoe's Mom — motions down the hillside to a flat area, where huge tents have been set up to create an indoor-outdoor experience for the reception. The guests stumble their way down the makeshift path, using their cellphones to light their footsteps.

I shake my head, crouching out of sight. I imagine how easy it would be to push Zoe down the hill and watch her tumble to the bottom, bones snapping all the way down. Is she were out of the way, maybe Mike would look at me again.

Help is so very far away, and who knows what could happen. What on Earth were Zoe and Mike thinking, getting married way out here?

There's a lot of crazy people in the world. You can't be too careful, nowadays.

3
____

ZOE

Our first dance is under the stars.

It's a warm night. Crickets sing, and the trees in the valley are dotted with little pastel flowers.

I never thought I'd get here. There was a time when finding a man I loved enough to marry seemed impossible.

We're on a flat plastic dance floor, brought in by a party supply company. We ordered everything from one place, including the white billowing event tents at the base of the mountain. I wanted the entire evening to be spent outside under the stars, but Mike and my Mom pointed out that our guests might not be as comfortable in the elements as I am.

"What if it rains?!" my Mom asked during one of our many wedding-planning sessions, looking across the dinner table at Mike for support. He nodded. I shrugged.

"Then everyone will get a little wet."

"What about Tori's Nana?!" my Mom pushed, rolling her eyes. "Do you really want Bam-Bam to catch hypothermia?"

"Zoe..." Mike added, "You *love* Bam-Bam."

Eventually, they talked me into the tents by pointing out that my perception of the outdoors has been forever changed. It's true. I survived a week in the harsh Yosemite backcountry, in the middle of winter, stalked by a killer. In order to survive, I became a part of the forest, as much as any animal. Being exposed in nature doesn't scare me now. I've left the woods, but they haven't left me.

Mike spins me around. It's too advanced a move— one I'd barely pull off gracefully in ordinary sneakers. In these shoes, it's impossible. My hand returns to Mike's shoulder just in time, right before I'm about to fall. He catches me. He always catches me.

Mike smiles at me. We're the only ones who know I was about to fall. Another secret we share; another addition to our private little world.

The strangeness of tonight makes me sigh. I'm wearing a dress I never thought I'd wear, living a life I didn't think I deserved, dancing with a man better than anyone I ever imagined. I'm happier than I've ever been, but there's a sticky bit of sadness underneath it. Finding my happy ending means letting go of a struggle I've grown accustomed to. I've spent a decade defining myself as single, doomed to be alone forever. Now, I have to let go of that old image of myself— the first edition of Zoe— and embrace something new.

"Husband," I say quietly, so no one else can hear.

"Still trying out the word?" Mike laughs.

"It's too strange. Maybe I'll call you my life partner."

The music stops, the last note on that lone violin fading into the valley. Our first dance ends, and two caterers pull open the entrance to the tents, urging everyone inside for warm food, good company, and a celebration.

I watch our nearest and dearest float into the tents, and suddenly I'm glad we ordered them. I really *do* love Bam-Bam.

4

CASSANDRA

I'm wearing a caterer's uniform— one I stole from the van parked out back. The company is called "Lavender & Sage," as if the owners thought naming their business after herbs would disguise the fact that it's just another basic enterprise in the food industry. Generic dishes like chicken and fish, ordered in bulk— served always with cheap potatoes— keep their margins down. Using a temp service to hire their wait staff means they don't have to provide health insurance. Everyone working for them is a contractor. They won't look twice at an unfamiliar face like mine.

I keep my head down as I lift up a corner of the white event tent, making sure I hold it high enough that it covers my face. No one will expect to see me, here, but still— I must be cautious. The majority of these guests are unfamiliar to me, but there's a few who I've met before. They're the ones who knew Mike in another life.

A life he shared with me.

Mike's lack of family is a benefit in this case. During our relationship, I only met his Aunt and Uncle a few times, as we preferred to spend holidays on our own. Their names are Donald and Alicia. They're a disinterested pair, unlikely to recognize me given how little we interacted.

I watch as they scoot inside the tent. Donald checks his watch, like he has somewhere better to be than at his nephew's wedding. They practically raised him, but they never treated him like a son. Their lack of attention is probably what led Mike to date inappropriate partners. Partners like me.

Right behind them is Mike's best-man— Rick. I need to stay as far away from him as possible. Rick is shrewd. He's a micro-manager with an eye for detail. He always pays close attention, especially when it involves Mike. He'll recognize me in a second if I let myself get in his line of sight. I'll have to avoid him at all costs.

The last of the guests flood into the tents, focused on the hot food that awaits them. Everyone is inside now. I lower the edge of the entrance and stay to the fringes, examining the crowd, hundreds of them buzzing about.

In the far corner, a bartender wearing suspenders zests an orange peel before combining it with some bitters using a mortar and pestle. He lights a cedar plank on fire with a small torch, wafting the smoke over a cocktail glass filled with whiskey. I'll give Zoe and Mike some credit. They may have missed the mark with the food, but they splurged on the cocktails.

I push past the crowds as I make my way toward the bar. I'm swimming in a stream of hungry ants, eager and insistent. Their voices grate against the quiet of the night, insulting its silence with snippets of useless commentary.

"...and her dress, it's just perfect!"

"...loves her so much. You've heard then, about how they survived up North, in Yosemite? Stalked by a maniac."

"... he's missing a finger from the frost bite. Don't stare, just glance, when you can."

I try to tune them out, but it's impossible. Zoe may not like much fuss made over her, but she should have realized: no matter how remote the location, no matter how minimalist the decorations, their wedding is the event of the year. I'm surprised there's no press here.

I can't help but grimace: so many people in one place.

They're all bugs to me.

Every guest is a different kind of insect, burrowing themselves into the fabric of Mike and Zoe's story, taking up spaces I might have filled. They swarm about, itchy and twitching, making homes where they shouldn't. Entitled. That's what they are.

I have a peculiar hobby. I like to look at a person, and try to guess what kind of insect they'd be if they'd been born a bug. It's like identifying someone's personality type, only nastier.

Scientists have discovered almost one million species of bug in the world, and by some estimates, there's as many as twenty-nine million still waiting to be found.

I guess what I'm saying is there's a lot to choose from.

The man in the black suit with a plate in hand? He's a termite. The woman in the yellow dress who talks with her hands? A caterpillar.

I adjust my caterer's uniform, making sure my hair is tucked under the white, fluffy cap. I have to make sure Mike doesn't notice me, and my hair could give me away. It's a unique shade of blonde; not mousey, but a rich caramel with lighter ribbons running through. My hair is my single remarkable feature. It's the only thing people ever comment on, besides how rickety I am. Not skinny— rickety. All elbows and edges, sharp lines where there should be curves. That's me.

I reach the bar and lean up against a bussing station, where other waitstaff are picking up trays. I grab one for myself. Nearby, the bartender is pre-pouring shots. When he's not looking, I take one of those, too, and toss it back.

Revenge is best served drunk.

I circle the party, starting with the outside edge. I'm careful to stay away from those who might recognize me. Zoe and Mike are at a table in the front, reserved for the bride, the groom, and their families. Zoe's Mom is there, along with Mike's Aunt and Uncle. I try not to stare, but make a mental note that Rick— Mike's best man— is also at the family table, a beautiful redhead clutching his arm, wearing a mermaid-style formal that makes her look like she's stepped straight out of a black-and-white movie.

It's not long before someone takes an appetizer off my plate. It's a tiny pastry wrapped around itself, with some kind of creamy filling in the middle.

"French onion?" the woman asks me before biting into the pastry. For a moment, I'm speechless, because I realize she's one of the targets on my list.

Tori. Zoe's Maid of Honor.

Her long black hair is pinned back in a bun. In the photos Logan showed me, it was loose, cascading past her shoulders in an uneven pattern, wavy in some places and curly in others. Now that it's pulled back, her round face is easier to see. Her cheeks are full, and her jaw barely narrows, settling instead into a semi-circle. She looks bigger than she did in the photos, and I wonder if it has to do with the straight-up-and-down bridesmaid's dress she's wearing. She's not overweight— just built wider, shaped like a circle instead of an hourglass. Her eyes are dark— bottomless and thoughtful.

If Tori were a bug, she'd be a beetle. All round edges and slow movements; harmless, and a little lost most of the time. I feel sorry for her. Being friends with Zoe must be terrible. While stalking Mike, I've learned a lot about Zoe, too. Zoe is athletic and quick-witted. She's the kind of person who always knows what to do. Tori must feel insecure around her. I would.

"Good?" I ask her, motioning to the pastry in her hand. She's already grabbed a second one.

Tori nods, her eyes darting across the party, searching for something, filled with an unnamed longing. The ice in the cocktail glass she's holding clinks against the glass's empty edges. Ten minutes into the reception and she's already downed her drink. A girl after my own heart. Even though the glass is empty, she tips it back anyway, letting one of the ice cubes slide into her mouth.

"How do you handle it?" she asks without looking at me, still focused on something across the room. "Seeing so many weddings?" She sways a little. The drink is already having an effect. She must not hit the bottle as often as I do. The key is to drink one sip of water for every three sips of liquor. Keeps your feet steady but your face numb.

Another waiter passes by, and I wave at him like I know him. I hold up my empty tray, motioning at his, which is filled with drinks.

"She wants another one," I tell him, winking at Tori. He shrugs, passes her a drink before moving on.

"Thanks," she smiles at me.

"No problem," I say, careful not to make any kind of impression whatsoever. During our training sessions, Logan emphasized the importance of not being memorable.

"People only remember what stands out," he said, leaning toward me, a secret in his eyes. "Keep your words vague, your personality unremarkable. You're nothing more than a mirror. Reflect."

Reflect, I think, offering Tori another pastry, which she accepts without question.

"Do *you* like weddings?" I ask. She sighs, her eyes welling up a bit.

"More than anything," she answers, and now I know she's a liar. No one likes weddings, unless it's their own. "I'm the bride's best friend. We've known each other since we were kids. Twenty years of friendship."

She pulls at the sash tied around the waist of her dress, untying the bow. She lays it on the table and flips it over. There's a tiny number "20" embroidered into the corner in black thread. My heart races. I'm so close— I can't blow this.

"It must be amazing to see your best friend get everything she's ever wanted. I bet you're really happy for her."

"*So* happy," Tori lies again. She's looking at the bar, wistful. I've got about ten seconds.

"Right," I continue, searching for the words I need to push her to the edge. "Are you married?"

She shakes her head, pointing across the tent to a tall guy in his mid-twenties, a DSLR camera strapped to his hand. His hair is perfectly coifed, sweeping across his forehead in an elegant swoop that should qualify him for membership in a boy-band.

"Jason's my boyfriend," Tori says, watching as he chats up a group of three bridesmaids, all wearing the same pink dress as her. "He's really popular on Youtube."

"Those girls sure seem excited to see him. He must be *super*-famous," I add, praying she'll take the bait.

"He is," she nods, looking concerned. As if he can read

my mind and wants to help me achieve my goal, Jason chooses that exact moment to reach out and touch one of the bridesmaid's arms. His hair may be stupid, but the guy has great timing.

"I'll be right back," Tori says before disappearing into the crowd, moving as fast as her little beetle legs will take her. She's determined to check on her famous boyfriend before he becomes her famous *ex-boyfriend.*

I wait until I'm sure she's out of sight, then I slide the pink, gossamer sash off the table, stuffing it into the waist band of my pants. The embroidered number "20" disappears from view.

Thank you, Tori, I think to myself, trying hard not to smile.

The sash. The wallet. The necklace. The gun.

One down, three to go, and the evening's only just begun.

Tori's unfinished drink sits on the table, and when I'm sure no one is looking, I grab it and toss it back. A reward for a job well-done.

I smile to myself. Maybe Tori was right. Maybe I *do* like weddings.

5
___

ZOE

"Rick's wasted," I whisper in Mike's ear, pointing across the table. Rick has his arm around Lana, but his hand keeps slipping off her shoulder. She's beautiful. There's a timeless quality about Lana that makes her seem ageless, but if I had to guess, I'd say she's in her early forties. They've only been married six months, and it was a whirlwind courtship. We've had dinner with them every couple weeks since they met, but the woman is still a mystery.

Mike shakes his head, whispering back at me, "It takes exactly five drinks before he does something stupid. How far in are we?"

"Three shots, one cocktail, and most of the bread," my Mom answers. She's sitting to my left with her new boyfriend, Oliver. He's a retired pilot who used to fly for major airlines. When his vision quit, so did he. Now, he wears thick glasses to help him see two feet in front of him, and spends his time sharing stories about being up in the air. When he tells his tales about the *good old days*, his British accent makes it sound like he was following

Churchill into World War Two, not flying for Virgin Atlantic.

Oliver leans in, watching as Rick downs the rest of his cocktail. Rick slams down the empty glass and heads for the bar. "Does he always look quite this—"

"Sad?" I finish Oliver's sentence for him, because I've noticed it too. Rick is a brooding type on any given day—the kind of person who mulls things over, beating them to death with his thoughts. He can hold a grudge like a champ, and his disposition isn't particularly sunny. But tonight, it's different. This is more than his grumpy status quo. He isn't just surly. He isn't just cynical. He's depressed.

"Rick is an investment banker," Mike shrugs. "Are they ever happy? I warned him in college that basing his life on the market would ruin it."

"How so?" Oliver asks.

"Market's up, he's happy. Market's down, he's sad. The way I see it, the stock market isn't even real. It's an idea. It's invisible."

"That's why Mike keeps his money in empty cereal boxes," I tease.

Mike laughs, "Babe. Don't give away my hiding spots."

"That isn't— you're not— serious?" my Mom asks, mildly horrified. My Mom is a retired nurse who happens to be great with money. She never made much in terms of salary, but she socked away what she could, year after year. Now, she's financially set for the rest of her life. She owns three rental properties in Arizona that no one even knows about. She's one of those quiet, unassuming investors who played the long-game and came out ahead.

I can already see her wheels spinning, thinking of possible investments that offer more return than a cereal box.

"There's so many other things you could do with it!" she sighs.

"We're okay, Mom," I reassure her. "It's not *really* in a cereal box."

Mike raises his eyebrows. It's true, we don't *technically* keep money in a cereal box, but Mike does own a wooden puzzle box he stocked with a couple thousand dollars cash for emergencies. He carved the pattern himself, and showed me how to open it so we could both access it in a worst-case scenario. We call it our apocalypse money. It's enough for tickets to Canada in case something terrible happens.

Mike looks down at his hand— the one that's missing a pinky finger— then tucks it under the table. I take it in mine, squeezing gently to let him know he's not alone. We've both learned that impossible disasters happen every day. Now, we prepare.

"Anyway," Mike continues, "point is, I don't think life should revolve around money. The best things in life are the things you can't buy."

He kisses me, and it takes me by surprise. Mike's love is so earnest, so easy. Even now, I'm always taken aback by how simple it is for him to express affection.

A clanging noise rings out from the end of the table, snapping me back to Earth. Mike and I separate, seeking the source of the sound.

Rick's returned from the bar; he finished his new drink as soon as he ordered it. Now, he's clutching an empty champagne glass in his right hand, beating it with a knife. Lana looks away, biting her bottom lip.

"It's about time," Rick slurs loud enough that the other guests can hear, "for a speech!"

The room quiets. Everyone stares.

"Bud, we're not doing speeches until after dinner," Mike

motions for Rick to sit down, but he doesn't. My stomach flips over.

Lana pulls on the edge of Rick's blazer, whispering, "The food! You should eat something—"

Rick bats her hand away. Lana looks like she wants to crawl under the table and disappear.

"When Mike and I were in college," Rick launches into his speech, swaying a little. "The girls loved him. No, no, it's hard to believe, looking at him now, but I promise you, the guy was a real ladies man."

Mike smiles outwardly, but I can tell, he's uncomfortable. Chuckles pepper the room, all of them good-natured.

I notice someone weaving through the tables, camera in hand, trying to get a better angle. It's Tori's boyfriend, Jason. He's a pretty-boy YouTuber, who never goes anywhere without his DSLR. For some reason, people care about what he has to say.

He stops when he reaches Tori. She smacks his arm, trying to get him to put the camera down. He refuses. Jason follows drama like a shark hunts fish, and tonight, there's blood in the water.

Rick continues his speech, louder, more boisterous than before. "Back then, Mike was only interested in the furniture he built. Kitchen tables, coffee tables, what's the... honey, can you remind me, whaddaya call the table that goes by the couch?"

Lana shakes her head. She wants no part in this. Rick presses her anyway. "You know, the short ones we have on either side. There's two of them?"

"End tables!" someone calls out from the back of the tent.

"Right, end tables! Like I was saying..." Rick clears his throat, continuing. "All these years, I think 'Mike's never gonna get married, cuz there's no way he'll meet a girl he likes better than furniture.' And then..." Rick looks at me, his eyes hardening. "*She* comes along."

He steps forward, scanning my face for hidden information. "And suddenly, Mike's a different guy. And I'm left thinking... okay... what does this girl have that a coffee table doesn't?"

Murmurs echo across the tent. Someone gasps. My cheeks flush, and I hope the makeup I'm wearing hides it.

"Excuse me!" my Mom is on her feet, ready to tell Rick off, but Rick moves to the other side of the table to avoid her, talking faster as he goes. Mike is frozen. He looks like someone whose favorite pet dog just bit him.

"Alright, sure, she's got an okay face, but the legs, I mean, I've seen Mike carve better legs in an hour! And the finish! She's a bit plain, isn't she? Where's the *shine*..."

I'm about to interrupt. To make a joke, to shake this off and tell everyone I'm not sure why Mike married me either. But before I can, Rick is side-swiped. A figure comes out of nowhere, tackling him like a linebacker.

Mike.

The room gasps. Rick almost falls over, but manages to use the shoulder of an empty chair to stay upright. When he recovers, he pulls back an arm, winding up a right hook. The look on his face is one I've never seen him wear before: calm, icy Rick has suddenly turned into a snarling, red-faced grizzly bear.

He's bursting with rage, but the alcohol has made him slow. Too slow. Mike blocks his punch and catches him in the chin with an upper cut. Rick's lip busts open, spraying the floor with red. He covers his mouth with a shaking hand, staring at Mike, betrayed.

Rick tries to strike back, but Oliver pulls them apart. They stand across from each other, restrained, seething.

Eventually, Rick fills the silence.

"So that's it, then."

He turns on his heel, exiting the tent without another word.

Lana is still seated at our table. She doesn't look at me. Instead, she picks up her white linen napkin, folding it over in triangles. She smooths the creases with one of her long, manicured nails.

"Lana..." I start the sentence without knowing what I'm going to say.

"If you'll excuse me," she says to nobody in particular, "I'd like some air."

She gets up, a hundred eyes following her as she floats toward the exit, holding her head high, big, salty tears threatening to spill onto her perfectly sculpted cheekbones.

6

CASSANDRA

Thank you, Rick, for the perfect distraction, I think as I weave around the outskirts of the party. He's making a speech, launching off about Mike and how all the girls loved him in college. He's not wrong. I'm tempted to stop, to listen, to see if he mentions *me*, but of course he won't. My name is a dirty word, now.

I mentally repeat the list of items I've yet to procure:

The wallet. The necklace. The gun.

Jason— Tori's boyfriend— has abandoned the troupe of women he was talking to, and is pushing through the throngs of people by the bar, camera in hand. He's only a few feet away from me.

I adjust course and bump into him at the perfect moment. "Excuse me," I start to say, but he doesn't even look at me.

"Sorry, I'm just..." he answers, holding his camera higher, trying to get the perfect angle of Rick's speech.

As he reaches up, my hand slips into the pocket of his pants. My fingers touch the edge of his wallet. It's one of those stupid ones made only from cords that snap together to keep cards and bills in place. There's no weight to it, so it's easy to lift. This is his punishment for not investing in a decent leather wallet, like all grown-people should.

"Don't worry about it," I tell him. He nods, disappearing into the crowd. I quietly pocket the sad excuse for a wallet, tucking it under my catering apron. Between the wallet and the sash, I'm two items down. This is easier than I'd expected it would be. Logan underestimated me. The instructions he gave were detailed— too meticulous— to be applicable in a real-world scenario, which is always-changing and evolving.

"Just drug them at the proper moment," he said two weeks ago, passing me some powder the color of death. He slid it across my kitchen counter in a plastic bag. "Make sure you do it when they've already been drinking. They'll think it was the worst hangover of their lives."

I sat cross-legged by the coffee-maker, wearing nothing but panties and Logan's over-sized t-shirt. I loved that our plans were made this way. Like heathens.

"You look like a kitchen appliance," Logan said, scowling. He hates when I sit on the counters. But they're mine, so I do it anyway. If he had his way, the entire world would fall into line just the way he likes it. He gets what he wants, most of the time. But I secretly relish the moments when he doesn't. It's fun to watch his discomfort when faced with things he can't control.

"What'll it do to them?" I asked, turning the powder over in my hands, wondering if I should put a little in my morning coffee, just to try it out.

"It'll make them sleepy," he answered. "Wait until you see them moving slow, then take what's on the list."

Now that I've gotten to know Logan better, I think this might be his biggest weakness. He's strategic, but he doesn't think well on his feet. He's a chess player, not a tennis player. He's always five moves ahead, which gives him an advantage in some scenarios, but also means he lacks the ability to improvise.

It's his greatest flaw.

I reach into my pocket and touch the edge of the tiny bag, filled with the powder. I haven't used it once tonight and I don't plan to.

Logan will be angry when he learns I've thrown out the plan. I look forward to it. Ever since Mike and I broke up, I've looked for ways to hurt myself. Logan is the perfect choice. He causes me nothing but pain.

I risk a glance at the couple's table just to see Mike's face again, but he's not there. He's standing, rushing toward Rick, arms out in front of him.

He tackles Rick, and all hell breaks loose. Guests swarm toward the feuding men, like so many bugs descending on a breadcrumb. A few people pull them apart. Mike throws a punch. Rick's lip is bleeding.

Chaos. My speciality. Within its infinite folds, I see only opportunity.

Zoe's Mom— Rachel— is standing behind her, hands on Zoe's shoulders. I rush to the bar, picking up a silver bucket filled with ice.

I make my way toward Rachel with the ice-bucket in hand, my heart-pounding. Zoe won't recognize my voice, but I'm sure she's seen pictures of me and could recognize my face, if she were looking for it. I need to be quick. Careful. *Invisible.* It shouldn't be a problem. People ignore me all the time.

Rachel's boyfriend is beside her, looking absolutely flabbergasted at the behavior he's just witnessed. He's probably wondering if all Americans are this rowdy.

Wait until you see what comes next, I want to tell him.

I tap Rachel on the shoulder, holding out the ice bucket.

"Ma'am?" I say, my voice higher than normal. "For his hand," I nod at Mike like I don't know him. He's about fifteen feet away— too far to hear my voice. He's shaking out his fist, loosening the clenched fingers, wiping blood from his knuckles.

"Thank you," Rachel sighs, taking the bucket. It's now or never. I have to make this as normal as possible.

"I'm so sorry," I say, trying to sound as if I really mean it.

I pull her into a hug, and at first her body feels stiff, withdrawn. But then she relaxes, hugging me back. I'm careful to make it seem like an accident as I let my fingers slip over the edge of her necklace, squeezing hard on the ridge of its clasp. I can feel it open, and I wind it around my finger, making sure not to let it fall.

It's mine now. I slip it into my pocket, giving Rachel one last, sorry look before moving across the room, out of sight, impossible to catch.

I feel weightless, like the wind. My body soars across the tent, seeking an exit. The white fabric barely makes a sound as I push it back, exiting the tent and inhaling the sweet, cool night air.

The sash. The necklace. The wallet.

There's one more item I need— *the gun*— and now, I know exactly how I'm going to get it. I run down the hill toward the gravel parking lot where the mountain meets the street. Cars are parked tight together. I crouch between them, a tiger stalking prey, keeping my head down as I check the license plates.

I stop when I find one with the digits Logan made me memorize. TFJ388. It's a New York plate. The car is a black Hyundai.

"Use the master key," Logan told me during one of planning sessions. "You get in, you get out— no one knows you were there."

"How'd you get it?" I asked him. He didn't answer.

The master key is hidden in my pocket, next to all my new treasures. I could use it so easily. Instead, I head back to the hill and scour the ground for the biggest rock I can find. I pick one that's twice the size of my hand. It's light enough to lift, but heavy enough to do the job.

Rock in hand, I return to the car. One deep breath, and I chuck it through the window.

Glass shatters. The car alarm blares.

I open the glove box, and there it is— the gun. But not just any gun. This gun belongs to a particular person. And that makes it special. It's unique, too, by virtue of its color. It's a soft, bubblegum pink shade. A strange choice for a deadly weapon.

After tucking the gun into the waistband of my pants, I route through the glove box, looking for a permit. When I find it, I double-check to make sure the numbers on the permit match the serial numbers carved onto the side of the gun. They do.

I've done it. I run down the street with both the gun and the permit safely out of sight, staying close to the edge of the road even though there's no cars coming. When I get to the bottom of the hill, Logan will be waiting to pick me up.

My breath crystallizes in the cold air, but I'm warm inside, like I've come down with a fever. I can still hear that car alarm screaming in the distance, and it makes me feel so alive. *I'm* the one that made the car cry. *I'm* the woman who made it scream.

I've spent so much of my life seeing myself as a victim.

I could get used to being the bad guy.

7

ZOE

The airport is quiet. Mike and I wheel our suitcases through the automatic double-doors, listening to the way their wheels click-clack on the tile floor. Airports are too sterile for my taste. It wouldn't take much to warm them up. A couple of plants. Some pieces of art.

"Do you want to call him one more time?" I ask Mike, trying not to say Rick's name aloud. Every time he hears it, Mike gets a heavy look in his eyes.

"If he hasn't answered by now, he won't answer at all," Mike says, sighing. "*He* should be the one apologizing to us, anyway. He publicly insulted my wife. I'm not sure where we go from there."

"Sometimes people make mistakes," I start to rehash the same conversation we've had every hour since the wedding ended. A never-ending debate. Do we call Rick, or let him come to us? Does one mistake negate years of friendship? With some prompting from me, Mike decided to be the bigger person and call first. So far, no answer.

We pass a store that sells *Los Angeles* souvenirs. Mike stops to look at a circular rack of knick-knacks, spinning through plastic academy award keychains and tacky aluminum palm trees.

"I thought he was happy for me. If I'd known, I'd never have invited him."

"Don't give up on him," I tell Mike. I'm not Rick's biggest fan, but I know how amazing Mike is, and it's hard not to feel sympathy for a person who might lose him forever. "He's practically your brother. He'll come around."

"He *was* my brother," Mike says, emphasizing the word "was." He pulls me toward him, tucking a stray piece of hair behind my ear. "It's me and you against the world, Zoe. If Rick has a problem with you, he has a problem with me."

Mike takes a pink baseball cap off the rack. There's a flamingo on the front. The bird is wearing a pair of converse. Mike rips off the tag, then puts it on my head.

"Ready?"

"Where's yours?" I ask him. He shrugs. I pick out a pale blue cap with a picture of a dolphin on its front. The back reads "*Santa Monica Pier.*"

"Why is the dolphin wearing sunglasses?" Mike asks me as we head to the cashier. He passes her his credit card, along with the price-tags we've removed.

"I don't know, but shouldn't we be buying souvenirs on arrival, not departure?" I nod at the price on the screen— thirty dollars for two baseball caps. We're definitely still in LA.

"It tax free! Besides," Mike Mutters, "Considering how our last trip went, I think we should live it up now, while we still can."

The room spins. Suddenly, I can't breathe. Images flash through my mind— things I saw, and have tried to forget. My own blood on the snow. An open gash in my leg that has since become a scar, a piece of me, as immovable as skin itself. The look in my tormentor's eyes as he asked me to make a choice between what I want, and what I fear.

I've never left the forest. Not really. Mike and I try not to talk about it, but every now and then, something will remind me of what's happened. A simple word. A glance. The build of a stranger's body, reminding me of *him.* Throughout all of our honeymoon preparation— the packing, the planning, the purchasing of tickets, the booking of tours— one question has simmered in my stomach, rising up like acid. I've ignored it, but now, it burns a hole in my throat, forcing me to wonder:

Are we going back?

"Shit, Zoe," Mike says. I'm frozen, unable to breathe. "Zoe, I'm sorry. Hang on..."

I'm running out of the store. I've left my suitcase behind. I'm not sure where I'm going, but I know I need to get there immediately. I spill out into the terminal, looking for safety. Finally, I find it. There's a fabric bench, pushed against a wall, unoccupied. I sit down and put my head between my knees.

My eyes close, shutting out the world around me. A soft pressure on the seat next to me is followed by a familiar arm around my shoulder.

"Zoe, I'm sorry," Mike says. "I didn't..." he pauses, trying to pick the right words. "I was just thinking out loud."

I inhale for four seconds, the exhale for ten.

"Do you get it too?" I ask him, finally opening my eyes. "The feeling?"

"All the time," he admits. He tucks his left hand in his pocket, as if catching a glance at his missing finger might send us both over the edge.

"It's different, now," I say, assuring myself it's true. "Isn't it?"

"You were alone out there. You were alone," Mike says in his thoughtful, earnest way. "And you survived. Now, we're together. This is a new trip..."

"It's a different place," I say, repeating the lines we've practiced.

"And we can't stop living..." Mike responds, waiting for me to fill in the rest.

"... because if we stop living, he's won."

"If you don't want to go," Mike says, holding me close, "We can cancel. It's really alright."

I consider it, but decide against cancelling. If we don't go on our honeymoon— if we *don't* celebrate our love— Logan really *has* won.

After Yosemite, the FBI searched for him, but they weren't able to find him. The agent in charge of our case called him a ghost. He's a person with no identity, someone so off the map they can't trace him. But he's on their radar now. He's in hiding, and he won't risk coming out. The truth is, Logan isn't a threat anymore. There's still a battle going on, but it isn't with him. It's inside me, between the old me that entered the forest, and the new me that left it.

"We can't cancel," I say to Mike, serious, "I promised you we'd go somewhere tropical next time, remember?"

Mike smiles at me. "Let's track down your suitcase. Hope it hasn't been stolen," he says, lowering his tone in that way he does when he's about to make a joke. "None of my bikinis will fit you."

"Thank you for that visual," I say, rolling my eyes.

"You've got a lot of trauma stored up there," he points at my forehead, turning my baseball cap around. "Thought you could use some more."

We walk back to the store. My breath returns to normal, but the feeling lingers. It isn't real. It's only in my mind— a ghost of a memory, a fleeting, temporary thing, soft and cold, just like the snow that fell that week in the valley. It won't last forever. One day, this feeling will melt away, leaving me warm, safe, and at home with myself.

One day, I'll leave the valley. And I'm taking the first step, right now, by getting on that plane.

8

———

CASSANDRA

A musty smell wafts through the airplane hanger. It's smooth and satisfying when I inhale, a cross between gasoline and sawdust. Above my head, metal rafters are supported by wide beams, sad lightbulbs dangling off their edges.

"Don't touch anything," Logan says, tying a bandana around the bottom of his face. He's wearing sunglasses even though it's dark in here.

I take my hand off the side of the wall. I've never been in a private hanger before. It's hard to resist exploring. Logan wipes the aluminum down with the edge of his flannel shirt.

"Fingerprints," he says.

He starts to walk away, but I grab the edge of his shirt, pulling him toward me. He's disgusting. A terrible person, inside and out. He's not even physically attractive. His skin is always red. His eyes are not warm. His teeth aren't straight. There's something about his round jawline that's eternally young, but not in an appealing way. His face looks like he's always on the verge of a tantrum.

There's absolutely nothing to like about him.

But that's why I play with him. He provides me with one thing, and one thing only: the feeling of being seen. Sure, he doesn't see the best in me. He doesn't notice my strengths—only my weakness. But he pays attention to me, and that's what I need. It's what I want so badly from Mike. Just a look my way. Just a nod in my direction.

"Almost sounds like you're worried about me," I smile, winding the edge of his shirt around my fingers.

"If the FBI finds you, they might find me," he answers, grabbing my wrist to stop my hand from wandering.

"But aren't you an evil computer genius?" I tease, happy I've upset him. "Couldn't you disappear if you wanted to?"

"Sure," he says, returning to a black SUV that's parked in the middle of the hanger. It's the car we arrived in, and the license plate on its rear bumper is a fake. Logan said he bought it from a friend. He has a lot of "friends," but no one who calls on holidays. He works with them, but in what capacity, he won't say. "I could disappear in a thousand different ways."

He bends down and unscrews the plate, revealing a second plate underneath. I wonder if there's another license plate beneath that one, and another, and another. It wouldn't surprise me. This is how Logan operates: a plan within a plan within a plan.

"I could also make *you* disappear if I needed to." He doesn't look at me when he says it. It bothers me. I want him to look at me. I need to be noticed.

"Probably," I answer, turning in place, my eyes still glued to the ceiling like a kid seeing a museum for the first time. "But who would be around to annoy you then?"

Logan finishes with the car, stuffing the plate into a large grey gym bag he carries with him everywhere we go. As he unzips it, he turns the opening away from me, concealing what's inside from view. When it's securely fastened, he clips a Masterlock between the zippers, securing them together so the bag can't be opened. Then, he stands, walking toward me. Good. Some attention, finally.

He takes my face between his hands, squeezing too hard. "Never forget how replaceable you are," he snarls. He tells me this all the time. Out of all the mean things he says, this is the only one that really hurts my feelings, if only because I think it might be true.

I'm about to respond, but his phone rings before I can say anything. He answers, whispering into the receiver at some shadow of a person on the other line.

"Stay outside," he says into the phone. "I'll come to you."

So far, I only know three things about Logan's work:

1. His job involves computers.

2. Whatever he does is illegal.

3. He feels deeply inferior to whoever he works for.

He didn't tell me the last one, of course. Logan would never admit to that kind of weakness. I figured it out myself. It's a subtle thing, but easy to see for someone like me, who spends her time buzzing around others. I notice things things about other people because I've centered my existence around them. It's easy to judge me for the way I live my life, but at least I know what kind of insect I am.

I am a bee.

I buzz around the center of another person, treating their whims like nectar, their wants like petals. In the sweltering heat of a summer afternoon, their lives become my own. My wings trace zig-zag patterns, always seeking stamen, the buttery pollen that makes more flowers, in the attention of another person. More to have, more to hold. Black and yellow stripes color all my conversations, inserting themselves in the most casual of settings, making me ask again and again: "Will you notice me? Do you hear me buzzing?"

By buzzing around others, I take back some control. I answer the question, "Will you notice me?" by forcing them to look my way. I become so intrusive I'm a force they can't ignore.

I've had almost thirty years of life to find my own center, but it never came. Instead, I orbit around others letting them serve as gravity. Even when they don't want me, I'm still drawn toward them by some intangible natural pull, the desire to turn yellow dust into honey. Logan is just another flower to me. I don't love him. But I need him. Sometimes I imagine the rooms of my apartment as pieces of a hive, carpeted floors and eggshell walls turned into honeycombs, empty and craving other bees.

And before you feel pity for me, know this: I'm not the only bug in the room. Anywhere I go, I recognize fellow insects all around me. They don't know that they're insects — not yet, anyway. But I see them and recognize them for what they are.

A woman in the grocery store wrangles the kids, reaches for a box of cereal, pushes the cart, all while her bored husband with two free hands plays a game on his cell phone. "Shhh," she tells her youngest, as the little boy pulls on the edge of his father's shirt. "Don't bother Daddy."

She makes it alright for her husband, sheltering him from the burden of love. She packages love on a platter so he can have it in the way that suits him. Most days, she floats around him in spirals, but every now and then she snaps at him— an unexpected bite, the diffusion of tension. She lets off just enough steam to keep herself satiated, then returns to business as usual. I see her as a mosquito— harmless most days, but bites can be fatal.

Then there's the flies. They're worse than me. I see them often, equal parts men and women, the saddest of all. I noticed at the cafe outside the retail shop I work at. It's a part time gig. They let me run the registers. I like talking to the customers, even though so few of them make eye contact. After my shift is over, I sit alone sometimes at that cafe for dinner. Twice a week, this man is there too. He's in his late forties, always wears a suit that doesn't fit quite right. Usually, he's alone, but a few weeks ago, he was holding the hand of a beautiful woman who looked utterly, totally disinterested in him. He tried to engage her in conversation: what did she think of the movie last night? Did she like the food here? Her answers were minimal, her smile as forced as it was radiant. But he buzzed around her anyway, hoping for attention and finding only unrequited love.

When I watched the exchange, I felt superior to him. At least bees can sting. I'm not the saddest of all bugs.

I watch Logan as he types on his cell phone, trying to decide what kind of bug he might be. I finally settle on a tick. He is a blood-sucking parasite who attaches himself to his prey, sinking his teeth in and never letting go. By the time they note his presence, he's already bled them dry.

"He's here," Logan sighs, tossing me a black bandana. "Don't take it off."

I tie the bandana around my face, feeling a little ridiculous.

"I thought you said we could trust the pilot?" I ask.

Logan shakes his head. "He's a ferry pilot. He'll do his job, but that's it," he nods at the trunk of the SUV. "We need to unload 'em before he gets here. Put the sheet over the top. If he asks, it's just 'cargo,' nothing else."

He gets in the SUV and starts the engine, backing it up toward the rear-end of a small, private plane. The plane is so much smaller than a jet that the effect is shocking. It's like being asked to ride in a Fiat after you've just returned from a monster truck rally.

When the SUV'S trunk is lined up with the tail of the plane, he shuts off the engine and gets out, opening the hatch.

"Can this thing really make it across the Atlantic?" I ask, motioning to the plane and noting the paper-thin wings. It reminds of pictures I've seen of the first plane the Wright Brothers flew, all sticks and canvas.

"If it couldn't, someone would've been *fired* a long time ago," he smiles, and I get the impression being fired in Logan's world means something different than it does in mine. "We'll have to stop to refuel, and it won't be a comfortable ride. Don't expect an inflight meal."

This is bad news as I'm actually really hungry, but I don't say anything.

Logan stretches like he's limbering up for a football game. Together, we unload the "cargo," moving it from the SUV into the plane. It's a two person job.

When we're done, we stand back and look at our work.

There they are, lined up foot to foot, head to head: a handful of bodies. People, carted around like luggage.

For a second, they look dead to me, and my lungs flood with panic. As much as I enjoy setting my madness free, I never signed up to kill anyone. I only wanted somebody to look at me, to be forced to glance my way.

I lean in, and I can see their chests rising and falling. Their lips flutter with every exhale, eyelids heavy with slumber.

"What if one of them wakes up while we're in the air?" I ask Logan, worried.

"Then it's onto plan B," he shrugs. I shudder, wondering

what Plan B is. That's the thing about Logan's plans: each one is meaner than the last.

He grabs a thin sheet and tosses it over the bodies, making them look more like crates of apples, or piles of oranges— not human beings. Then, he glances at the hangar door. The pilot is waiting for us on the other side. Once we let him in, this is real and final. There's no turning back.

Logan holds his hand out like he's asking me to dance. "Shall we?" he grins. It's nice, to be invited into someone's space. It makes me feel whole, like I'm not some invisible spirit orbiting around the lives of others, but a real person worth looking at.

I slide my hand into his, shaking off the strange feeling that I'm about explore some new version of myself— an alternate me who's always been inside, hidden under my skin like those bodies under the sheet, sound asleep, just waiting to wake up.

9

ZOE

Twenty-one hours and a single layover bring us to our destination. The Seychelles is a tropical island nation, a paradise just off the coast of Madagascar, East of Africa but South of India. It's a network of islands hidden in the middle of the Indian Ocean, a location some have called the most beautiful place on Earth. Now that I'm here— sitting in the back of a shuttle-bus from the airpot, watching an aquamarine ocean lap against the shore— I can see why.

"Careful," our bus driver says when he catches me staring out the window, watching palm trees whip past. "The Seychelles will keep you if you let them. It's so beautiful on the islands, some people never leave."

"You've seen it happen, huh?" Mike smiles, his hand on my knee.

"Sure have," the driver nods. "Those people that never leave? I'm one of them."

"A good choice, overall?" Mike asks.

"Better than my office at an insurance company in Canada."

The truck careens around another bend. The coastline splits open, revealing a white beach, grains of sand ground so fine they look soft as powder. Crystal blue water splashes onto the shore, kept free from sediment by temperate weather. The ocean is clear enough that you can see straight to the bottom— even from afar— and it goes on for miles, like it won't give up its spread until it catches the horizon. This is probably what heaven looks like.

Our driver points out the window a tall church tower, its spindly peaked roof reaching for the sun. "That's where you'll meet your guide tomorrow."

"Is he good?" Mike asks. We went out of our way to pick an expert. The tour was expensive— more than our budget warranted— but we were promised we'd be given a once-in-a-lifetime look at the true history of the islands.

"Francois is best," our driver nods. "He's a full-fledged archeologist. Got his degree from one of those fancy colleges, an Oxford or a Cambridge. He's a little..." he pauses. "*Eccentric*, to be sure. But he knows the islands better than anyone. His family has been here for generations. He's as close as you can get to a local."

"What do you mean?" I say, confused by the wording. "If he's born here, isn't he a local?"

"Well, sure, technically," our driver confirms. "But no one can trace their lineage back too many centuries. There *is* no population native to the Seychelles. The islands are so far out at sea that human life had to find it on a boat. And the boats came from all over."

The engine quiets as we pull up to the front of our hotel, "*The Grand Constance*." It's a sprawling, beautiful establishment with individual suites that line the coast, backing up to the ocean and a private beach. The lobby sits in the center, its exterior featuring a thatched roof and glass windows that let in light from every angle. It's one of the most glamorous hotels I've ever seen. The thought brings with it a wave of guilt— like I'm cheating on the hotel I manage back home.

"Have fun tomorrow," the driver says as we roll our luggage down the steps to the asphalt. "Just don't get Francois started on pirates."

"I'll keep that in mind," Mike laughs. As the bus pulls away, he leans over and whispers in my ear, "Now we *definitely* have to ask him about Pirates."

We wheel our suitcases into the hotel. It's a quick process at check-in. The concierge gives us our keys, and it isn't long before we're unlocking the door to our own private suite. It's at the end of the row, far enough from others that it feels like our own section of paradise. The ceilings are tall and vaulted, with warm Edison lights dripping downward. Rose petals dot the bed and a bottle of champagne sits on the bedside table— the staff must know we're honeymooners.

I open the sliding doors to the balcony, which extends over the water. Mike wraps his hands around my waist, whispering in my ear, "What are you thinking?"

"I was just thinking," I say, taking in the view. The clear sky bumps up against the vast endless sea, two blue universes meeting. I once wondered how Mike and I would make a home when we are so different from each other. He is a fish, and I am a bird, and here we are— together— finally in the place where the Earth meets the sky. "I'm glad we didn't cancel."

10

CASSANDRA

Vomit splashes over the dirt runway. It's mine, and I'm not proud of it. I wipe the edge my mouth, resenting the acidic, metallic burn in the back of my throat. Throwing up makes me look weak.

"You didn't say we'd be in the air so long."

Logan shrugs. "You knew where we were going. Next time, get a map."

We're on a small island, one of more than one hundred in this area. Logan selected it after hours of extensive research spent pouring over topographical maps that outline the geography. The chosen island needed to have a long enough strip to facilitate landing the plane. We also required something far enough away from the main islands to avoid discovery, but close enough to allow for the importation of resources.

After eliminating dozens of possibilities, we settled on this God-forsaken rock. Don't get me wrong— it's beautiful. I only hate it because I know what's going to happen, here.

Logan slips the pilot some cash, and asks him to wait behind a cluster of boulders. The pilot just shrugs, like he's used to odd requests. As he walks away, he lights up a cigarette.

Once the pilot is out of sight, Logan and I get to work unloading the bodies. He takes the shoulders, and I take the feet. We painstakingly haul them into the shelter of palm trees, the beginning of a dense tropical forest that spans the center of the island. We arrange them in a circle, head to head. The pattern they make looks like a star, or a flower.

When we're done, Logan takes the Masterlock off his super-secret gym bag. He pulls out a syringe and some vials.

"Again?" I ask him, wondering what will happen if any one of these people gets too big a dose.

"Do you want them to wake up too soon?"

"No," I tell him.

"Then yes, again."

He gives each one an injection. I half-except someone to wake up— to shout at him— but nobody does.

"I'm going to build the campsite," Logan says. He disappears into the trees, and I know it will be a long time before he returns. Logan said he wanted to build the site far enough away that the walk would weaken them, make them tired.

While he's away, I sit next to the group, watching their chests rise and fall. Watching is what I'm good at it. It's comforting, for awhile, but then I start to feel anxious that they don't know I'm there. When I watch Mike and Zoe, I try to leave little clues to let him know I've been by. I'll move a flower pot, or take the mail out of the box. Just so that I feel acknowledged. I wish there were a similar way I could make everyone in the circle see me. For a second, I imagine pulling up their eyelids, but I know it won't help— they're completely unconscious. I think about leaving notes in their pockets that say "Cassandra was here," but of course, that will ruin Logan's plan.

Before I can decide exactly what to do, Logan returns, beckoning me back to the plane. The job is done.

Logan whistles at the pilot, who's still taking a smoke break behind a rock formation on the beach. He puts out his cigarette, wiping his nose with the back of his hand. We pile back into the plane. It feels empty now that our sleeping cargo has been unloaded. I didn't realize how much I depended on them to fill the space between Logan and me.

WE'RE ONLY in the air for a couple minutes before we're landing again, this time on a neighboring island. It's bigger than the one we left behind, which is still visible on the horizon. It's close enough that I think I could swim there, if I weren't so hungry.

"Do you think it's too close?" I ask Logan.

"It's in range of the equipment. I need to be able to tap into the nearest satellite image to make sure they're still there. That's all that matters."

Logan pays the pilot one last time, giving him something wrapped in a black cloth. "Make sure they use it, and that it's seen," he says. The pilot nods, and I notice the cloth slipping aside long enough to reveal a familiar shade of bubblegum pink.

The gun.

"Have them hide it when they drop off the cargo. You have the coordinates," he adds seriously.

The pilot counts his money, then takes off into the sky, leaving us behind.

"You trust him to make sure that gun gets to where it

needs to be, but you won't fill *me* in on your plan?" I ask, feeling frustrated and invisible once again.

"Everybody gets to know something, but no one knows everything."

"What if we need to leave in an emergency? Will he come back?" I ask, feeling trapped by how irreversible my path has become.

Logan points to the edge of the beach, where a rickety dock juts out into the sea. It's missing planks in all the wrong places, left to wither from a lack of care. At the end of the dock sits a small speedboat, sleek and shiny.

"That's for me. As for you, hope you can swim," he says. I know he's kidding, but in that moment: I hate him.

We make our way past the beach, finally arriving at an abandoned old house. It's the only building on the island, and it hasn't been lived in for years. Logan said he purchased it from a group of investors in a blind sale. I wonder what it cost. It's not much to look at.

Logan kicks in the door. I expect to see a cobweb-ridden, decrepit interior, but instead, it's immaculate inside. The house has been swept clean, not a speck of dust to be found. A massive desk takes up an entire wall, three desktop computers pinging on its surface. Some kind of receiver buzzes, and an old H.A.M. radio sits next to it. On the far wall, a kitchenette gleams, brand new appliances looking like they were just installed yesterday. The double-door refrigerator smiles at me, and I open it up, praying it's fully stocked. It is. The motion sickness has passed, leaving a terrible, rumbling hunger in its wake. I go straight for the cheese drawer, unwrapping a block of cheddar and biting into it whole.

"That's disgusting," Logan says, sitting in front of the computers. I ignore him.

"How did you do all this?"

"As I said," Logan smiles. "I have friends who owe me."

A telescope points out the window, calling me. I bend over it, positioning my eye over the tiny hole. The horizon comes into focus, and I scan the edge of the Earth, looking for the island we just left.

It appears so quickly that at first, I pass it, doubling back until it manifests again, magnified a hundred times, so close I can almost reach out and touch it. For a second, I think about it what it would be like to see Mike standing on that island, staring back at me through a telescope of his own. It would be nice, if he were watching me too. Looking at me through a piece of glass, magnifying all the things he never noticed about me— all the pieces he never appreciated.

11

ZOE

When I wake up the next morning, it's not to the blare of an alarm clock, but to the sound of plates clinking. Mike's already ordered room service for us. The smell of French toast, eggs, orange juice, and strong coffee wafts across the room.

I rise from the bed, zombie-like, hair a mess.

"Thought this might be the only way to get you up before eight," Mike laughs, passing me a coffee.

We eat breakfast on our balcony, silently taking in the ocean. The tides are low, the waves quiet. They trundle onto the shore like they don't want to disturb us. Warm, tropical sun beats down on my face, sinking deep into my bones, warming me from the inside out.

"We could move here," I say, only half-kidding. "You don't have to make furniture in Silverlake. You could make it here."

Mike swallows the piece of toast he's eating, seriously considering the point. "The supplies might be cheaper, and the warehouse space, too. The shipping would be an added cost, but I could offset it."

"There, it's settled then," I tell him, leaning back, letting the sunshine drip through my hair, sticky and gleaming.

"What about your hotel?"

"What about it?" I say, trying to keep the edge out of my voice. "It's not really mine."

"It's as close as it can be, without you owning it," Mike argues.

"Tell that to the real owners."

The truth is, I love my hotel. It saved me when I was a lost graduate, looking for a purpose in life. It became my project, and— when I was eventually put in charge of the entire operation— my identity. I nurture it like a child, and I care about how it grows. I have a vision for its future. In my opinion, it's one remodel away from becoming a destination, the premiere hospitality joint South of the Santa Monica mountains. But the owners— a brother and sister pair who inherited the place from a deceased relative— disagree with my grand plans. They would rather let it operate in disrepair.

Plumbing backs up. Door hinges squeak. Musty carpets gather more dirt. The walls creak. Ceilings sag. With each passing year, the hotel disintegrates just a little more. The staff and I do what we can to band-aid the problems. We hand-wash the giant rugs in the lobby, hanging them outside to dry, trying to lift ancient stains and rearranging furniture over the spots we can't fix. We buy eggshell white paint to patch the ceilings, plastering over the places that are peeling. Holes in the drapes are concealed by tying them back. We do our best to hide the problems, but the guests are starting to notice.

"It's going to end up with a developer," I say, shaking my head because I can't bear the thought. The hotel is a piece of living history, and it just needs someone who appreciate its charm to invest in it. There's a way to fix it without destroying its character. But if things keep going this way, the attendance will fall, and the siblings who own it will sell. A developer will tear it down, and replace it with a Holiday Inn.

Mike is silent for a moment, then says casually, as if anything is possible, "What if *we* could buy it?"

"Did you win a lotto you didn't tell me about?"

"I'm saying..." Mike looks at out at the horizon, searching. "We could make it a goal. Maybe not this year, and maybe not the next. But in the long-term, we could try to buy it for you. Then it would really be yours, Zoe. You could re-model it the way you want."

I follow Mike's gaze toward the sea, watching how the tips of the waves change from blue to white. A soft breeze rustles the tops of the palm trees, chattering to the sky as if making it promises.

"Is that possible?"

Mike leans over and kisses me. His hand slips around my waist, and he pulls me into his lap. When we break apart, he smiles at me.

"Anything's possible. It's us against the world, now."

"We'll just keep hiding money in the puzzle box then?" I say, running my hands through his hair.

"Exactly. A dollar a day. It adds up."

LATER, we head to the lobby, where the concierge gives us a paper map featuring a cartoon drawing of the city center. She takes a red pen and sketches a walking route to the clock tower, the place where we'll meet our guide.

As we stroll through the island's capital of Victoria hand-in-hand, we take note of the architecture. The buildings are painted in pale pastel shades of pink and yellow, stucco exteriors making for a light, airy feel. Arches frame windows with curved edges on the trim. It's a whimsical, fairytale town, influenced by so many different styles of construction it's easy to feel you've toured the world in a single, brief walk.

We reach the clocktower, which marks the town's center, its hands so high up they catch the sun's glare. Francois is waiting for us, wearing loose khaki shorts, face devoid of a smile. He's in his early fourties and still holding onto his hair, which has gone all salt and pepper at the edges. He's shrewd and expressive, with the careful, calculating expression of a person who is too smart for his job. There's a permanent far-away look on his face, like there's something else on his mind— some place he'd rather be. I can see it in his eyes when he moves to shake our hands. "Nice to meet you," he says, with a tone that says it's not nice at all. "You're late."

"We got lost," Mike lies. We weren't lost. We're just honeymooners. "Confusing place. Sorry about that."

"Hmm," Francois murmurs with a skepticism that says he doesn't believe us. "Best to get started then, no?"

We follow Francois into the curving streets of Victoria, where he leads us through a walking tour of the city center. He may not love being a tour guide, but his passion seeps through as we weave through narrow cobblestone streets. His knowledge of the country is so thorough that he makes the place come to life.

"There is no indigenous population in the Seychelles," Francois says, leading us through one of the winding pedestrian alleys between store-fronts. "The islands were too remote to support life, and remained uninhabited until the first sailors from France arrived in the lated 1700s."

"That's why the architecture looks..." I try to find the words.

"Parisian, in some places, yes," Francois nods. "The islands were eventually populated not just by the French, but by people from all neighboring countries, including East Africa and Asia, whether through immigration or the terrible slave trade. My own family can trace our lineage back to both. The official language today is Seychelles Creole. A nod to our history."

"How long have you lived here?" Mike asks.

"Born and raised," Francois says, his voice souring. "I know *almost* all her secrets." He hits the word "almost" a little too hard, like the islands are an ex-girlfriend who won't answer his calls.

When we finish the tour of Victoria, Francois drops us off at a tortoise sanctuary. "The Aldabra tortoise is the largest tortoise in the world, and lives to be one-hundred-and-twenty years old," he says, yawning as we feed the tortoises— who look like large, moving boulders— pieces of cabbage.

"They're dinosaurs!" Mike exclaims, laughing as a rogue tortoise tries to nibble on the edge of my shirt.

"Yes," Francois almost rolls his eyes, but manages to resist. "The tourists always say so. I'll return in an hour." He walks off into the distance, relieved to be rid of us, like we are small children he's been tasked to watch.

As I watch Francois amble away from the sanctuary, I wonder what his story is. The bus driver told us he's a brilliant man, and his knowledge of the island's history is par none. He claims multiple degrees from top universities, and could probably make a living doing almost anything. Why is he employed in an industry he appears to despise?

· · ·

OUR STOMACHS ARE RUMBLING by the time we leave the tortoises behind. Francois meets us down the street at a cafe he recommended. It's walking distance from the tortoise preserve and— according to Francois— serves the best food on the island.

"I haven't asked him about pirates," Mike whispers as we head toward the restaurant, an anxious edge to his voice.

"Now's your chance," I laugh, happy to encourage him. There's a mystery around Francois. I'd love to solve it.

The restaurant is a small establishment, tables set outside in a little row, with the kind of indoor-outdoor kitchen that's arranged in a galley formation.

"The coconut curry. You must try it," Francois points at the menu. We're seated at a table on the back patio. The restaurant doesn't offer any indoor seating at all— a testament to the island's good weather.

When the food is ordered, we raise our glasses in a toast — three beers, courtesy of Mike and me.

"To a beautiful island," Mike says. Everyone drinks. Francois lets out a sigh.

"She is beautiful, yes," he says, sounding like there's something else he wants to say.

Mike glances at me. This is his opening.

"A place like this," he says casually, "Must have a history of piracy."

"What would make you say that?" Francois asks, suddenly suspicious.

"Nothing, just..." Mike backs off, noticing he's offended but unsure of how. "I only figured, because of the location..." Mike changes course, trying to recover. "It's fine if you don't know anything.

Francois slams his hands on the table, scooting his chair back as he rises. His breath comes out in a hot, heavy vapor.

"Who are you with?" He snarls. "Arcadia? The Venture Project?"

"We're not with anyone," I say, but Francois acts as if he doesn't hear me. He starts to pace, moving in a strange sort of spiral across the ground.

"Plying me with alcohol, pretending to be tourists," he says more to himself than to us. "There is no limit to the lows they will take."

"We're not with anyone," Mike says with a firm tone, trying to diffuse the situation, which has escalated in a matter of moments. He puts a hand in front of me, moving forward like he's worried he might have to protect me from our tour guide. "We're just on our honeymoon."

Francois pauses, as if our innocence is a strange idea that hasn't occurred to him.

"What did you say you both did?" Francois asks.

"I make furniture," Mike tells him. "Zoe's in hospitality. She manages a hotel."

"Ah," Francois nods, considering. "Do you do well?"

"Sometimes," Mike shrugs, not admitting that he does better than people think. Custom furniture carved by artisans doesn't sell as often as cookie-cutter pieces from Living Spaces, but when it does, it's expensive.

"And you?" Francois asks me, frowning.

"I do just fine, thanks," I say, annoyed at the invasive line of questioning. "Why does it matter?"

"You would have no need then, to accept a bribe for information?"

"None," Mike shakes his head.

"Why did you ask about pirates?"

"Our bus driver told us *not* to ask you about them," Mike says earnestly.

"So obviously, he had to," I sigh, rolling my eyes. "We

shouldn't have. We didn't know it would upset you. We're very sorry."

"We were just curious," Mike adds, relieved Francois has stopped pacing.

"I'm happy to tell," Francois sinks into his chair, looking desperate and lost. "But I am tired of sharing with those who have no imagination." He scans the pair of us, trying to decide if we're worth betting on. Mike, with his gentle eyes, is the kind of person others like immediately. I'm a harder sell, with my aloof nature and overt skepticism. The contrast between us is not lost on Francois.

Mike waves at the waitress, holding up his empty glass and three fingers, signaling for another round.

"I happen to have a great imagination," Mike smiles.

12

CASSANDRA

Logan stands in front of a map of the islands. Pins and strategy notes are taped to various locations. Logan has a knife in his hand, and he's carving lines between areas. Whether this is actually helpful, or just an emotional release, I can't say.

"It's going to work this time," Logan whispers beneath his breath, praising his own plan.

I quietly stir my Fruit Loops with the back of my spoon. I've added whipped cream on top, letting it soak into the milk for a thicker experience.

"What if it doesn't go the way you want?" I ask, genuinely curious.

Logan doesn't answer. The knife stops its slow journey across the map. The sound of its blade carving into paper disappears. There's a moment of silence. Then, he turns, rushing across the room, knocking the bowl of cereal from my hands and letting it smash against the floor. He grabs my hair and pulls me up from the table, pushing me up against the wall, knife in hand, pressing it into my neck.

"Things always go the way I want," he snarls. "Are you insulting my intelligence?"

I don't answer him.

"Are you afraid of losing an ear?" He moves the knife, tracing a line around the edge of my hairline.

"Would I still be able to hear my own thoughts?" I say, as if I'm seriously considering it. "If so, I'm indifferent."

Logan lowers his knife, looking at me like he's never really understood me before now. I know what's happening. I've seen this expression before, on the faces of others who have spent extended time in my atmosphere. Logan is finally realizing how messed up I am inside.

His analysis— the careful scanning of my expression for normalcy without finding any— should make me feel naked, but it doesn't. It's worse when people try to convince me I'm fine. At least when someone finally understands how twisted I am, I feel *seen*.

"You're such an asshole," I say, not worried about offending him. Logan knows what he is. "Why am I here?" I whisper, wondering at myself.

Logan shakes his head. "Because you want him to notice you, and you know I can make that happen."

"I don't want him to get hurt," I say, repeating myself for the thousandth time.

"He won't," Logan shrugs. "You do what I've asked you do on that island, and I promise you, once the game is over, he'll be delivered to you in a place you can contain him."

The truth is, I have plans for Mike, but not to hurt him. My plan— when Logan gives him to me, is simply this: I want to tape Mike to a chair and make him listen— really *listen*— to everything that happened in our relationship, as I see it.

It's an image that dominates my day-dreams: wrapping

silver duct tape around Mike's wrists. Lashing him to a hard-backed chair in some dusty warehouse, far away from anyone who would respond to his cries for help. I lecture him for hours, saying everything he never let me say, making him understand what I went through when he left me. I want him to walk in my shoes, to see how he hurt me, to let me tell my side of the story. I'll tell him what happened and how it felt, again and again, until the message sinks deep into his brain. Sure, I'll have to keep him restrained for a few days. But he'll leaving noticing that I'm a person worth talking to. A person with all the same feelings as him. Someone just as valuable.

I don't expect reconciliation. I'm just tired of being ignored. If I can get Mike alone in a room, he'll be forced to see me. He'll be forced to *notice* me. My buzzing won't go ignored, with no response. It will be the sound that makes him sit upright and take note.

All I want is to finally be *seen* by the man who was supposed to know me better than anyone. To be understood in my glorious brokeness, my lack, my shattered, messy, raging self. All I want is justice, in the form of recognition. Is that so much to ask?

"What are you going to do with Zoe?" I ask Logan, suddenly nervous for her. I hate that she takes Mike's attention away from me, but I don't necessarily want her dead.

"Zoe lives on the border between optimist and cynic," Logan says, simply. "She is, to me, a symbol of a bigger debate about the essence of human nature." He scans me, up and down. "It's nothing you would understand."

"What do you mean?" I ask, pushing.

"Zoe's refusal to believe in universal self-interest is what keeps her from embracing her full power," Logan answers.

"Universal self-interest?" I ask, trying to sound stupider

than I am. The only way to get into Logan's head is to make him believe he's smarter than you, and give him the chance to prove it.

He sighs, annoyed. "For example, you are using me, and I am using you."

Logan isn't wrong about us using each other. He is using me to accomplish his plan, and I am using him to accomplish mine.

"All people are, at the end of the day, most interested in their own survival over all other things."

"That's incredibly pessimistic," I tell him.

"Like I said, you wouldn't understand," he sneers. "Last time, I asked Zoe to make a choice. This time, I'll teach her. The game I've created will help her see."

He pauses. "It's time."

Logan might be right about the connection between him and me, but he's wrong about love, and about selflessness. Mike showed me what that looks like when he put up with me for years, no matter how bad it got. He stuck it out, until he didn't anymore.

But still, I want my chance to talk to him. I want my turn to be noticed.

"Make the call," I say, and Logan reaches for his phone.

13

ZOE

Francois' home is a cement block at the edge of Victoria. Here, the buildings are grey, made with utility in mind. The pastel architecture we enjoyed in the town center is gone. Francois' apartment is on the third floor. There's no elevator, so we climbed the narrow stairwell to get here, metal steps creaking under our feet.

During the walk to his place, I tried to keep track of how it all happened. It started with the second round of beers. The beers turned into cocktails. Mike and Francois had a shot. The conversation ebbed and flowed with the liquor, and ended with Mike telling Francois he should have been best man at our wedding.

"You would have been great," I remember agreeing, taken, for once, by Francois' sudden openness, his desperation to be believed. "Better than Rick."

We became friends. It happened so fast.

Now, we're sitting in Francois' one room studio. A bed has been pushed into the corner, messy sheets piling over each other. A table with a coffee maker and microwave on top serves as a kitchen. There's no stove, but there's a sink, and a bathroom.

Francois is making tea, warming water in the microwave. Mike and I sit together on a worn-out loveseat.

"Is this insane?" I whisper to Mike, suddenly realizing that we've ended up in a stranger's apartment. The liquor is wearing off. I'm one step ahead because I refused to take a shot.

"He's licensed and bonded. I checked before we left," Mike says, but there's a question mark in his voice. He looks over his shoulder at the front door, as if making sure it's still there.

Francois brings us two steaming mugs, each with a tea bag inside. He sits down and nods at our expressions.

"You don't believe me."

Back at the restaurant, under the cloak of night and after too many beers, Francois told us about his family legacy. It's a tall tale of hidden treasure, the kind of thing passed from parent to child over many years, warping over time in a game of generational telephone. No one could blame us for being skeptical.

"It's alright," he waves a hand, tipping slightly. He's still off balance from the drinks. We'll all be sick tomorrow.

"Anything is possible," Mike answers fairly. "But if it's really been there three hundred years, wouldn't someone have stumbled on it and dug it up?"

"And if someone *did* find the treasure," I add, "Why would he bother to say anything publicly? How do you know someone didn't find the treasure and sell it off quietly on the black market in pieces?"

"You misunderstand," Francois shakes his head, frustrated with our unwillingness to believe. "These items are so rare— so precious— they could never circulate unseen. The stir such objects would make would ripple across the international marketplace. We would know."

He pauses, walking across the room to a desk on the far wall. He removes a key from his pocket, then unlocks the top drawer, pulling out a file that must be five hundred pages thick. He leafs through it, searching.

"To understand why this treasure has not been found, you must first understand the man who hid it, Olivier Le Vasseur."

He pulls a sketch from the file and lays it on the table in front of us. It's of a man wearing a feathered hat, and a dapper vest. His long, dark hair falls in waves toward his shoulders. His expression is stalwart, but his eyes are soft. There's a rough edge to his exterior, but a gentle inner life that peaks through.

"He looks..." I pause, trying to find the right word. "Complicated."

"Yes, he was," Francois says, as if he's met the man himself. "Vasseur was nicknamed *La Buse*— in English you would say, *The Buzzard*— because of the speed with which he attacked his enemies. He was a pirate by choice. He was given the opportunity to become a merchant, and instead chose a life of crime."

Francois leafs through the file, finding another image of Vasseur, this time surrounded by a crew of hard-lived men.

"He was an excellent Captain, but had one great weakness."

"What was it?" I ask, taking the sketch in my hands. The ink used to make the sketch is a tawny bronze color that blends into the page, making it look like the sailors are fading into the parchment, struggling to stay remembered.

"He never trusted his crew."

Francois pauses, letting this sink in. Then, he passes us

another image. This one is of a ship, its name carved into the side of the hull.

"'*Nossa Senhora do Cabo?*'" Mike reads the ship's name aloud.

"Yes. The ship was a Portugese Galleon, carrying treasure unlike any other on the seas at the time. Hundreds of diamonds. Precious gemstones. Gold. Silver. And most importantly, the cross of Goa," Francois pulls another image from the stack. It's a sketch of an ornate cross.

"It was said to be over seven feet high," Francois continues. "Made from solid gold. Encrusted with rubies and pearls. It was priceless back then. Today, it would be worth..."

"How much?" Mike asks, his eyes lighting up.

"At least one hundred million," Francois says, confident. "The problem, of course, is finding it. Which brings us back to *La Buse...*"

Francois stares at the sketch like he's willing La Buse to speak to him. "After La Buse and his men commandeered the treasure, they sped across the seas, the Royal Navy in pursuit. La Buse, I believe, found himself in quite a dilemma. His crew consisted of seven-hundred-and-fifty men, separated between three separate ships. If La Buse had trusted his men, he could have placed the treasure on one ship alone, and sent it in another direction, allowing the other two to serve as decoys, essentially leading the Royal Navy on a wild goose chase. In this scenario, he might have reunited with his men later, and divided the treasure equally."

"But he didn't," I say, looking at the picture in my hands, noting a coldness in La Buse's eyes. "He couldn't trust them not to run away with it."

"I'm afraid not," Francois answers. "Instead, La Buse

weighed anchor off the first patch of land he encountered. Can you guess where?"

"The Seychelles," Mike says.

"Yes."

"On Mahé?" Mike lifts up his feet a little, like the treasure might be buried in the floorboards.

"Not on Mahé," Francois smiles. "The big island is surrounded by many archipelagos, and La Buse would have likely encountered one of the hundreds of smaller islands before reaching Mahé."

"What did he do when he found land?" I ask, trying to imagine myself on an empty island with no cell phone, no restaurants, no one but myself and my crew.

"He ordered three of his best sailors to help him carry the treasure. They loaded it into tiny row boats, making their way ashore one haul at a time. They painstakingly carried it across the island, searching for a spot to hide it, far away from prying eyes. When they ultimately found a safe spot, they concealed it."

"Wasn't La Buse concerned the three sailors would come back later without him to claim the treasure?" Mike asks.

"He most certainly was," Francois smiles. "That's why he shot them."

"He let them do the work and then *shot* them?!" I exclaim, angry on their behalf.

"He was a pirate, my dear," Francois laughs. "They were not known for their sense of righteousness. As I said before, La Buse's greatest weakness was that he did not trust his men. When he arrived back at the ship— alone— the crew was outraged. They turned him over to the Royal Navy to be hung. On his execution day, however, he appeared to have a change of heart."

Francois removes a photocopy of a hand-written document from the file. It's an assortment of strange symbols—squares and triangles, ancient gibberish.

"Just before they hung him, La Buse did something remarkable. His neck was in the noose. A crowd had gathered, some of his crew present in the throngs of people there. When the final moment was about to arrive, La Buse tossed this parchment into the air and said, *'J'ai posé un lapin.'*"

"Which means?" Mike asks.

"It's a French idiom. The direct translation is 'I put a rabbit to it.' But its metaphorical meaning is 'I stood someone up,' or 'I did not keep a date.' It was La Buse's way of acknowledging that he failed to keep his commitment to his men."

"And you believe the parchment he threw in the air leads to the treasure?" I say, connecting the dots.

"I do," Francois says. "And so did my Mother, who was given the paper by her father, who received it from his father, and so on. For many years, my family has believed that this moment was La Buse's final act of reparation."

"But what if it wasn't?!" I cry out, too invested in the story at this point to remain impartial. "What if La Buse was a monster? Maybe he just wanted to drive his men crazy with this," I pick up the parchment with the code on it, "Gibberish."

"I believe they are not alphabetical, but directional. If I can only find the island on which he concealed the treasure, I believe these symbols will show me which way to go."

"I think he did it to drive everyone crazy looking."

"You don't have much belief in a man's ability to redeem his soul, do you?" Francois asks me.

"Not when they've done as much wrong as him," I say. "Why should I believe he changed?"

"Nothing changes a man like staring down death," Francois answers, simply.

"At the restaurant, you thought we were up to something," Mike asks, suddenly nervous. "Why?"

Francois sighs. "I am close, I believe, to finding the treasure's location. I've narrowed possible islands La Buse could have chosen based on the direction his ship was known to be sailing. But I am not the only one looking."

"Treasure hunters?" I gasp, enthralled by the idea. I can't help but imagine Indiana Jones, his hat tilted to the side. Francois frowns like he can read my mind, and disapproves.

"Do not glamorize," he says. "They are thieves! They search the world for its most precious artifacts, then take them away from their country of origin. They place them in museums in the west, instead of leaving them in their homes. It's robbery."

Images of all the museums I've walked through in my life flood my body with shame. The permanent exhibits of items from far away places, their outlines feasted on by hundreds of eyes. Suddenly, it all takes on new meaning.

"You mean there's people looking for the treasure who would move it off the islands?"

Francois stirs his tea again, staring into the bottom of the mug like he hopes to find answers there. "They possess more funds than I do. Expensive equipment. Already, they dredge the sea by the Western Archipelago. If they succeed, it will be the greatest find since the Titanic." He sinks back into his chair, cradling the mug like its a life preserver. "I would like for it to stay here. Those artifacts and the press from the discovery would bring more tourism, more money into the Seychelles, but only if the items are allowed to remain in their home."

"They *can't*."

"Can't they?" Francois answers, throwing his hands in the air. "Greece has been pillaged. The statues from the Acropalis were promised to be returned upon the construction of a museum. The Greeks built a beautiful museum, but have yet to see a single statue make its way home. Plaster casts fill its halls."

"So if we go to Greece to see the ruins..."

"You may see the ruins in Greece, but the statues are in the British Museum. They are separated. There are thousands of other examples. Paintings won through wars. Pillaging by the Nazis in WWII. Very rarely do items find their way home."

"Isn't there a legal process? A way to make sure that doesn't happen?"

"The only way," he says, "Is to make sure I find the treasure first. A feat looking more and more unlikely with every day that passes." He folds the paper with the symbols on it into an origami square, passing it to Mike and I. "Keep it," he says. "It's a photocopy of the original. One of many." He pauses, like there's something more important he wants to say. "When you go to a museum back home, think about where the items came from. And, if you feel so inclined, petition that they be returned."

"Thank you," Mike says to Francois, shaking his head. "For sharing the story with us. Not an experience we were expecting, but a cool one to tell our family at home ab—"

Before Mike can finish his sentence, the door blasts open. The sound of the bolt shattering echoes across the room. Wood splinters, causing particles to fly into the air. Two men stand in the entryway, guns in hand. They're wearing camo gear, their faces covered by ski masks.

Their uniforms are dark, neutral-colored, but I notice something strange about the weapon in the hands of the biggest man. It's a pink gun. Not a black gun. Not an assault rifle. A pink, ladylike handgun.

There's a moment where we all look at each other. Mike and I stare at Francois. He gazes back at us. Our mouths hang open in three directions, everyone wondering which party betrayed the other.

The silence is broken when Mike whispers at me, "Zoe. *Run.*"

Then, the two strangers enter Francois' apartment, and everything turns upside-down.

The world moves in slow motion. I duck under an arm. Mike flips over a table. It shoots across the room, blocking the path of one of the men. I slide past the other, and now my feet are on the stairs.

I take them three at a time, noting the footsteps behind me. I look over my shoulder, expecting to see one of the masked intruders, but there's only Francois, behind me in the stairwell.

Mike is alone up there.

I want to turn around, but I know our only chance is to get help.

The sound of glass shattering fills the stairwell, and I look upward, covering my face just in time to avoid the shards dropping from the level above. The man in the ski mask wrenches a fire extinguisher from the wall. He hits Francois over the head with it. Francois' eyes rolled backward. He collapses like a puppet, strings cut.

I run faster, taking four steps at a time. I leap down the stairwell. I'm finally at the bottom. My fingers wrap around the handle to the exterior door. Strobes of sunlight flood the landing. I pour onto the street.

I've made it.

Then, a vice slips around my throat. It's an arm around

my neck, holding me in a barchoke. I struggle to find some way out, to escape, but I'm trapped. The sound of my own choking fills my ears. I reach behind me, searching for an eye to gouge, or an ear to rip. Nothing comes.

Nothing but a tunnel of darkness, growing thinner with every passing second.

As I fade away, I glance one more time at the waistband of the man who's choking me to death. There, in a holster on the side of his belt, sits that pink gun. It's a strange shade of bubblegum, mocking me with its bright, happy disposition.

What kind of a kidnapper chooses a pink gun?

Before an answer comes, the world turns to black.

14

CASSANDRA

Logan and I sit on the beach, barefoot and waiting. We're side by side, feet pulled up to our chests. Our toes dig into the sand, leaving indentations— little beige mountains. In the distance, the motorboat bobs on the water, inviting me to take a ride. It's powerful enough to navigate between islands, and I almost suggest we move to a different location. It's hard to sit still. Waiting makes me antsy.

Everything we've done so far has led us to this moment. If this part of the plan doesn't work, we've gone to all of this trouble for nothing.

Finally, Logan's cell phone rings. He answers. "Well?"

My heart pounds. A low murmur emerges from the phone's receiver— the person on the other end is speaking, but I can't make out the words. My tongue sits in my throat, dry and heavy, suddenly rendered useless.

Logan hangs up. He slides the phone back in his pocket. I'm worried he's about to give me bad news, but then he looks over at me, smiling.

"They're on their way." He pauses, scanning me like he's memorizing my body. Maybe he's going to miss me. Idiot.

"This merits a drink," he says, standing up with a stretch. He heads for our tiny headquarters and I follow him, heart still racing because the fun part is about to begin.

He pops open a bottle of Champagne and pours it into two skinny flutes. It looks expensive, but it's not dry enough for my taste. I prefer the cheap stuff.

"You're sure you can do this?" Logan peers at me over the edge of his glass.

"Of course," I tell him, annoyed that he has to ask. "I've been looking forward to it."

"I'm sure you have," he lowers the glass. "You're massively screwed up, you know that? Wired all wrong."

"Sure," I shrug. He's not telling me anything I don't know.

"Be prepared for anything," Logan continues. "Whatever you do, stick to the plan, even if something happens that you don't expect. What's your main objective?"

"Create discord," I recite. "Make them hate each other."

"And?" Logan asks, impatient. He doesn't trust me at all.

"Make sure they find the clues," I say.

"That's right. If she misses even one, she won't learn."

"It's strange," I ask, shaking my head. "You *want* her to get the riddle right. To win the game."

Logan smiles. "Yes, I do. I'm teaching her a lesson. It's nothing you would understand."

"Don't you think I should know what the puzzle is?"

"You don't need to," he bristles at the question, finishing off his champagne.

"Not even the answer, at least?" I ask, pushing the issue. "What if she's not getting it right? If I knew what the puzzle was and had the answer, I could push her in the right direction."

"It's not your concern. I've designed it for her, and her only. She'll get it." He stands, stretching his arms long, expanding his ribcage wide. He starts to head for his bed, but pauses, thinking better of it. He pushes the Champagne bottle toward me, sliding it across the table. "You should celebrate. Live it up while you can."

"What's that supposed to mean?"

"Only that you have a big job ahead of you."

Something in his choice of words gives me pause, but I take the bottle anyway, drinking straight from the neck. It's not the cheap stuff, but it'll do.

"Hey, Cassandra?" Logan asks, looking sorry for me as I chug from the bottle. Condescending asshole.

"Yeah?"

"Remember out there: you've gotta play to win."

With that, he climbs into bed, flicking off the lights behind him.

15

———————

ZOE

When I wake up, the first thing I notice is the smell. Crisp and fragile, it rides light on the air, signaling that we're not on Mahé anymore. Despite its idyllic appearance, Mahé couldn't escape the side effects of human presence: the scent of Creole food cooking, oil burning, engines back-firing. Wherever I am now, the air is pure. It smells like coconut water and some fragrant flower I can't name.

I'm on my back, staring up at a clear, lilac sky. The sun flashes in my eyes. Confusion. I try to remember how I got here. My fingers curl under at the memory of what happened, scraping against soft, familiar sand. I roll over, not ready to sit up yet.

I touch my neck. It's sore.

"Mike—" I try to shout, but my voice comes out as a whisper. Something is wrong with my vocal chords. I hope it's not permanent.

I move to my hands and knees, sitting back on my thighs, trying to get a sense of location.

An ocean in front of me. A rock formation behind me. A beach on either side. No sign of life. No sign of others.

Slowly, I rise, swaying like a boxer in the final round of a fight. I take in my surroundings.

I'm on an island. The ocean stretches out in front of me, so much uninterrupted blue.

If I'm here alone, I'm as good as dead. Very few castaways survive long stranded alone, and I've already beat the odds once. I need to find people. But which direction to go?

The rocks behind me are steep. They would make for a difficult climb. To my left, the coastline narrows. Eventually, I'd have to swim to see what's beyond the edge of the coast. To my right, the beach extends onward, then curves out of view. Any number of things could wait for me on the other side, but it's my safest bet.

I walk for what feels like hours. The sun beats down on my back. The scenery grows so familiar it feels as if I'm barely moving. Palm trees. Clouds. So much sand. The beach becomes paradise made banal through repetition. It's surreal in its presentation, a movie set on a lazy-susan, rotating around and around with the same trees, the same rocks, the same plain, blue sky

Finally, a figure appears in the distance. It grows bigger, taller, wider, as it runs toward me.

"Mike!" I try to shout again, but his name comes out hoarse. My feet take over, and suddenly I'm moving faster, clumsy in the sand but determined just the same.

The figure stumbles toward me, and as his face comes into view, I realize: it isn't Mike.

It's Francois. He's waving at me, arms in the air like a castaway signaling a ship, expecting rescue.

My body takes over. Rage ripples through my limbs, hot and hungry, requiring action. I pick up my pace and run as fast as I can. At first, Francois looks confused, but then he realizes what I'm about to do. He tries to change course, but it's too late.

I ram straight into him, taking him down. His head hits the sand, and then I'm on top of him. He's pinned, unable to move. He tries to roll me over, but I'm already striking at his face, fingers scratching, seeking vengeance.

"Where's Mike?!" I scream. The sound comes our like a croak, my broken vocal chords creating a new language that's impossible to understand. The intention, however, is clear: I'm ready to destroy this man. "You did this to us!"

Two strong arms wrap around my waist, and suddenly someone's lifting me in the air, legs kicking.

"Zoe!" Mike shouts, trying to calm me down. "It's okay. I'm here."

Once I realize it's Mike lifting me off my target, I stop struggling, but my heart is still pounding. Mike sets me down on the sand, and I fall into his arms, furious, burying my rage into his chest. The anger melts, turning into relief that he's alive. Hot tears threaten to spill over the edge of my eyes, but I won't let them fall.

"He set us up!" I whisper urgently, turning away from Francois, who's peeling himself off the sand.

Mike sighs, breath heavy. "It wasn't him, Zoe. He woke up farther down the beach, just like I did. Come with me, we'll show you."

We separate, and Mike takes my hand in his, pausing for a moment when he notices my throat. He touches my neck, gentle, eyes-widening at whatever he sees there. I don't know what it looks like, but it must be bad. Anger flashes across his face.

"What did they do to you?"

I want to ask him the same thing. Mike's right eye is

surrounded by a black circle. His top lip is swollen. If I look half as bad as he does, I look terrible.

"I don't rem—" I start to say, but my voice won't cooperate. Mike shakes his head.

"Does it hurt to talk?"

I nod.

"It'll get better," he says, trying to sound certain even though he isn't. "Your voice will come back. Right now we just need to stay alive."

"Pink gun, he had—"

Mike cuts me off, so I don't have to speak. "I saw it too. It was strange. Almost made me laugh."

I reach up, running a finger over Mike's busted lip, wishing I could heal it with just a touch. Behind us, Francois sighs, irritated.

"Yes, so romantic, don't mind me," he says, kicking the sand about with the heel of his shoe. "I'll dip my head in saltwater to sanitize the wounds, please ignore my screams. Don't let them ruin your lovers' vacation!"

"This is as much of a shock to us as it is to you," Mike says.

"Yes, except you two have each other, and I am here alone. So if we could, please, move it along." There's a sadness in his voice that makes me want to hug him. I wonder what Francois has given up in his pursuit to protect an invisible treasure, and if it was worth it.

Mike nods, agreeing. "Zoe, you need to see something."

Francois glares at me. I've left a bright, red scratch on his cheek.

"Keep her away from me," Francois says to Mike. Mike doesn't answer, but he walks in-between us as we head across the beach. The three of us push through the sand. This end of the beach is more of the same, until we reach another rock formation. We stop, shoulder to shoulder, looking up at what's written there.

"Look," Mike points at the rocks.

There a single word, written in blood-red paint on the formation's surface.

It says: "UP."

Beneath it sits a red arrow, painted in the same fashion.

My knees sink into the sand, because this is confirmation of the truth I've been dreading. It's *him* again.

Logan.

Up until now I've lied to myself, pretending our kidnapping was some random act of chaotic evil connected to Francois. But it isn't. No one except Logan would send us on a hunt, or make us solve a puzzle. No one.

My whole body shakes, bones trembling with all the things I can't say. My eyes close as I fold into myself, avoiding the thought: *it's happening again.*

Mike sits beside me. He holds my face in his hands.

"It's different this time, Zoe. You have to look at me."

My eyes open.

"We can't panic. We have to hold it together. My whole life I've known that bad things happen, but you know what got me through?"

I shake my head.

He exhales, saying what comes next not just for me, but for both of us. "I might not be able to control what bad shit comes my way. But I can choose who I tackle it with. And I choose you."

He helps me stand. We face the rock, eyes turned upward.

"You're not alone," Mike whispers. "Not this time, Zoe."

Francois clears his throat.

"I'm sorry," I say, referencing my earlier behavior. If he accepts my apology, he doesn't say so.

"Never forget," Francois says, his eyes burning, "that I am not an accessory to your journey. I am not here to help you. I owe you nothing. It is your fault I am tangled up in this. It is me who should be attacking you."

"You're right," I say. "It's our fault you're here. If we'd thought there was any chance he would do something like this, we would never have come to the islands."

"I will work with you, only because we are more likely to find rescue together. But never forget I am doing it for my own benefit. If the time comes to leave you and save myself, I will."

"I can't honestly blame you," I say.

"Good. If this man is, as you say, so very dangerous, perhaps we should not climb?" Francois looks across the ocean, trying to place our location. "Some of the islands are visited by researchers and tourists. Perhaps this is not one of the most remote."

"He'll have thought of that," I say, my voice weak but sharp. It's hard to speak, so I choose my words carefully.

"This man— Logan— he's strategic," Mike finishes the explanation for me. "He would have researched every island and picked the one with the least likelihood of rescue."

Francois huffs, skeptical. "So be it."

Left without options, Francois steps toward the rock, one hand reaching. It's not a completely vertical climb, but it's steep enough that it requires both hands and legs.

I follow Francois, Mike right behind me, the three of us inching up the rock formation with no idea what dangers will greet us at the top.

16

CASSANDRA

What will Mike think, when he finds me here? It was hard to watch the motorboat ride away. Logan didn't even look back after he dropped me on the island. He stepped on shore just long enough to make sure all the pieces were still in place for the game he won't tell me about. When it was done, he came back to the circle and made sure everyone was in position. Then, he hopped back in the boat and disappeared into the distance, getting smaller and smaller. He didn't even look over his shoulder to wave goodbye.

Now, I'm the only fully-conscious person here. A circle of bodies is sprawled in front of me, the outlines of their arms making a strange star shape. Logan's left me with a raggedy medical kit, and tasked me with doing something I hate. Still, there's no time to waste.

Hurry, Cass.

The medical-kit's zipper gets stuck halfway around, and I end up having to rip it apart with my bare hands. I don't have much time to execute. If I'm caught in the act, everything will be ruined.

One by one, I inject each person with the adrenaline, moving quickly so I'm out of the way before they wake up. Logan says it has a five minute delay, but I'm not betting on it.

When I'm finished, I bury the kit under the sand at the base of a nearby bush, making sure it's out of sight.

I step into the circle of bodies, laying down in a blank spot that's been left especially for me. My eyes close, and now I look like the rest of them, a completely innocent person caught somewhere between asleep and awake.

What will Mike think, when he sees me again?

He won't suspect my involvement, that's for sure. I've listened to his conversations with Zoe in the early hours of the evening, hiding outside the kitchen window they like to leave open while they cook. He blamed me for what happened in Yosemite when I had absolutely nothing to do with it. If he tries to blame me again, Zoe won't believe him.

I'll make him see me. Make him hear me. Make myself impossible to ignore. I'll buzz around him in a place he can't run from me, and my reward will be time alone with him in some abandoned warehouse on Logan's radar.

Mike will notice me, whether he likes it or not.

17

ZOE

My fingers are raw, stripped bare by the rocks. They're so tired that— mere inches from the top— I miss the final hold. The mistake causes me to slide backward, but Mike is behind me. He catches me with one hand, slowing my fall long enough for me to regain my footing.

Francois is already at the top of the rock formation, exhausted and breathing heavy. With a final, determined heave, I pull myself over the rock formation, landing on a patch of ankle-high grass. Mike lands beside me just seconds later.

The three of us rest in the grass, catching our breath.

"I can't believe we're doing this again," I say. The words still come out like a croak, but my voice is getting stronger. It's a good sign. I haven't been rendered permanently mute. "I should have killed him when I had the chance."

I wait for Mike to say something, but his usual inspirational speech doesn't come. All he does is gasp; a choking, tortured sound. He sees something terrible.

Francois sees what Mike sees, and says something in a

language that I don't understand. From the tone, it sounds like a curse word.

I'm afraid to know what he sees, but I follow his gaze anyway. About fifty feet away, opposite the direction we came, the trees create a frame for a horrible picture. Between a handful of broken palm trees lay human figures, prostrate, exposed to the elements.

The bodies are arranged in a circle, their feet at the center, heads facing out.

But that's not the worst part.

The worst part is that we know these people.

"Mom!" I cry out, and this time the emotion overrides my crushed vocal chords.

"Oh God, please no," Mike says. He's usually the more composed one. It terrifies me to hear the panic in his voice.

We half-run, half-crawl across the grass, stumbling toward the macabre work of art. We stand over the strange collection of friends and family, taking inventory of who's there.

My Mom, curled beside her boyfriend Oliver, his glasses hanging off his cheek. Rick, his face still bruised from where Mike punched him just an evening ago. Lana, laying next to him, her classic red hair spilling over her shoulders in perfect waves. Tori, my best friend, her mouth open, drool dripping down her chin. Beside her lies Jason, her boyfriend, a camera still in hand. Mike's aunt and uncle— Donald and Alicia— are side by side, aloof even when they're not awake. Another woman I don't recognize completes the circle, although there's something vaguely familiar in her features, like I've met her in another life.

It's as if someone took our wedding party and dropped them on this island as collectibles, toys on a shelf.

"You know these people?" Francois asks, aghast. Neither one of us answers.

"Are they..." Mike's voice cracks. He can't bring himself to ask.

I kneel beside my Mom's form, heart pounding. Mike does the same. "Rachel?" he asks. She doesn't stir.

But then, her chest rises and falls.

"She's breathing," I say, relieved.

"I'll check the rest of them," Mike gets up, moving from person to person, checking their pulses. Francois stands apart, looking shocked, like he's been dropped into a nightmare.

The grass rustles to my left. It's Oliver. He turns on his side. His eyes flutter open. He's confused. He pushes his glasses back into the correct position.

"Zoe," the words come out in a slur. He hasn't escaped the influence of whatever sedative knocked him out. "Where —" before he can finish the sentence, he notices my Mom, lying beside him.

"Rachel!" He tries to shake her awake.

"It's okay, she's alright!" I tell him, although I'm not sure any of us are alright.

My Mom's eyes open and she looks up at me like I'm ten years old, waking her up too early on Christmas morning. She reaches up, laying a hand on my face. "Sweetie," she says seriously, sounding dreamy and far away. "Shouldn't you be on your honeymoon?"

"I am, Mom," I'm laughing and crying at the same time, because I'm so relieved she's here, but also wish she were back home, safe and far away from Logan's reach.

"It's happening again," I say, rambling. "It's him. He didn't stay hidden. This time he brought all of you and I feel terrible. It's my fault we're all here."

My Mom makes the sign for *shh* and pats my cheek twice, as if I've just given her a bad weather report. "Not to worry," she sighs. "We'll deal with it as it comes." She lays back down, stretching her arms upward like she's on a wonderful vacation.

Whatever drugs Logan gave them must be good.

A shout from across the circle. It's Mike, wrestling with Rick, who's just woken up.

"Watch her, okay?" I tell Oliver, pointing at my Mom. He nods, and I run toward Mike, who's restrained Rick as best he can.

"Let me explain!" Mike's shouting to be heard over Rick's protests.

"You'll hear from my lawyers," Rick screams, trying to force his way to freedom. "I won't be had! I won't be extorted! I've left specific instructions on what to do in the event of my disappearance and you won't get a dime."

Mike looks at me, wondering what we should do.

"It's the drugs. My Mom was out of it, too."

I lean down, making eye contact with Rick. "You're okay," I tell him. It seems to settle him down, so I keep going. "You're alright. Take a deep breath. We're not kidnappers. That's right..."

Rick inhales, looking around. When he glances at Mike his eyes soften, signaling he finally recognizes him. Rick reaches up and puts a hand on Mike's shoulder.

"It's you," he says, gentle. Something about it makes me want to look away.

"That's right, buddy," Mike smiles, encouraging. "How's the fat lip?"

Rick blinks. The change in his expression says he remembers what happened at our wedding. He removes his hand from Mike's shoulder.

"Not great," he answers, a little colder.

"Guess now I know why you didn't answer our calls."

"You called?" Rick asks, hopeful. He pats his pockets, looking for his cellphone. His search comes up empty.

"Rick, what's the last thing you remember?" I ask, stepping back into his field of vision. He scowls at my appearance.

"I left the wedding. Lana came after me. She bitched at me on the car ride home. She said I was a fool who should be ashamed. She said I embarrassed her."

"Good," shouts a voice behind me. It's my Mom, arms crossed, being supported by Oliver. She's sobering up, becoming more and more herself with each passing moment. "Because your behavior that evening was completely inappropriate!"

"I agree," says Lana. She's awake now, laying beside Rick, still in her dress from the wedding. She sits up, shaking pieces of grass from her perfect head of hair. "Thank you, darling, for asking if I'm alright."

"I was a little busy," Rick mutters, and Mike steps back, surprised. We've never seen Rick show such disregard for Lana in public. It makes me wonder what he's like when they're at home alone.

"Baby! Oh my God, Jason! Baby!" Tori's sobs fill the air. I run to her side. She's awake and leaning over Jason, shaking his body, knocking the videocamera out of his hand.

"He's going to wake up," I tell her, holding her arms back to keep her from shaking him. "He's been drugged, but he'll wake up."

"These men— they came with black ski masks," she tells me in a hushed, low voice, as if someone might be listening. "It was right after the wedding. We had just gotten home and Jason said he was going to get a shower, and then 'boom!'" She claps her hands together, illustrating the point. "The door broke open and there they were."

She's wearing pajamas, a matching set with a plaid top and shorts. It corroborates the timeline. I shudder, realizing Logan must have kept them all asleep for two days.

Next to Tori sit Mike's Uncle and Aunt, Donald and Alicia. Their eyes are open and they're sitting up, listening, but they haven't said a word.

"Donald?" I ask, trying to see if he's realized where he is.

"What on Earth have you gotten us into?" he says, but not to me. Mike's come to check on them. Donald stares right through him, ice in his eyes.

Alicia bursts into tears. "The boys have a tennis match on Friday," she cries, chest heaving. "We'll miss it! They'll be so disappointed."

"A tennis match?" Tori whispers at me. "Never-mind we've been kidnapped..."

"I know," I whisper back, making sure we won't be over-heard. "That's Alicia for you."

"Tell her I'm *so sorry* our life or death situation inter-rupted her children's recreational sports schedule," Tori smirks, rolling her eyes.

"And it's the finals!" Alicia rages, still venting out loud. "Their coach won't move them to Junior Varsity unless we're actively involved in each game. This is terribly selfish of you, Michael."

"Look what you've done to your aunt!" He shouts at Mike, face turning red. "You've gotten mixed up in some-thing? What is it?! Drugs?"

"After everything we've done!" Alicia wails.

"It's not..." Mike starts to say, but he stops in his tracks.

He's staring at the woman laying next to Alicia. She's

still flat on her back, but her eyes are open and she's looking up at the sky.

I swear I see a smile pulling at the corner of her lips.

She's the woman I recognized, but couldn't place. A second glance is all it takes to jog the memory. It's her pretty, caramel hair that gives her away. I've only seen it in pictures, but it's a unique color— one that's in-between all of the others, a shade that's hard to forget.

Mike steps back like he's been stung.

Someone has to say her name, and it might as well be me. It comes out soft and familiar, like I'm meeting an old friend.

"Hello, Cassandra."

18

CASSANDRA

Zoe says my name like she knows me. What a stupid thing to do. She would have notice me to know who I am, and absolutely nobody— *nobody*— notices me.

"M-M-Mike," I stutter, eyelashes fluttering. I try not to go overboard with it. If I seem too confused, it'll be a giveaway. "Why are we here?" I ask, looking around.

"A better question is why are *you* here?" Mike answers, his hands clenching into fists. Crap. I didn't expect him to be so hostile. You follow a guy for a couple years just to get some closure and suddenly you're not to be trusted. Fine. I see how it is. Two can play that game.

"Did *you* bring me here?" I ask, eyes widening. They start to water because the sun is so damn bright here. Another reason I hate nature. It's too abrasive. Oh well. I use the inconvenience to my advantage and try to make it look like I'm crying. "Someone knocked me out. I was at home." I feign a struggle to remember, "And then I felt a prick in the back of my neck."

"Bullshit," Mike says, rolling his eyes. "You followed us here, didn't you?! You were probably on the plane with us!"

He's not far off.

"Mike," Zoe says, touching his arm. "Look around. She didn't follow us. She's here because Logan picked people who are in our lives."

"She's *not* in our lives!" Mike shouts, practically tearing his hair out. "I've worked very hard to make it that way."

"She didn't choose to be here. We can't blame this on her."

"For fuck's sake," Mike sighs, rubbing his eyes. He shouts across the circle, "Rick!"

"Yeah?" Rick answers.

"Got a smoke?"

Rick pats his jacket pocket. He pulls out some cigarettes and a lighter, waving them in the air like a flag at the end of a race. Mike marches off, grabbing the cigarettes as he goes.

It's just Zoe and me now. She stares at me, not sure what to make of it. I blink, innocent, just another victim.

"Didn't he quit smoking?" I inquire.

"He did," Zoe says.

"It was when he met *you*," I continue, testing the waters. I want to know how she feels about me, if she hates me or not. "I saw him go to the drugstore, and he came out with nicotine patches."

Zoe visibly shudders.

That's right, I think. *I know everything.* I like how in control it makes me feel to reveal myself. The best part about being a bee is when others notice the buzzing, notice the trails you carve in the air. I wait for her to walk away, but instead she sinks down to my level, looking me straight in the eyes.

"I'm so sorry," she says, and the words threaten to rip me

apart from the inside out, because the worst thing anyone could feel for me is pity.

She stands, wiping grass stains off her jeans.

"Let's get this over with."

She strides across the group, helping the others stand as the drugs wear off. Tori straightens the bottoms on her plaid pajamas, looking at me twice. For a moment, I'm afraid she recognizes me as the waitress at the wedding, but I'm hoping she was enough drinks in that she won't make the connection. She leans over to Zoe and asks a question. Zoe whispers something in her ear. She nods, understanding.

Clearly, Zoe has told her I'm Mike's unstable ex. With any luck, she won't connect that we've met.

Rick calls out to me, perfectly timed, "Hey, Cass! Bet you're happy to be here, huh? Doesn't matter if it's in the middle of the ocean, as long as Mike is around." I can feel my cheeks flush, but not with embarrassment. I'm honored, actually, that Rick remembers me. He knows I've been following Mike. That means they've talked about me. Without another word, he lights up a cigarette, heading off in the direction Mike went, presumably to share a smoke.

I know what I have to do, now. I need to lead them through the forest without appearing like I'm behind it. I need to make sure they find the boat, and the surprise that's waiting for them within.

It should be easy for them to overlook my nudges, my quiet, helpful directions. For once, being invisible will help me get exactly what I want.

19

———

ZOE

We follow another red arrow, painted on a fallen palm tree that borders the clearing. It leads us across the island; towards what, no one knows. Progress is slow. Every now and then we find another red arrow, positioned to adjust our direction.

I thought being stranded alone was a bad thing, but after a couple hours with our wedding party, I'm starting to wonder if I'd do better on my own. Our group complains the entire time.

"And everyone is *sure* they don't have a cellphone?" Rick asks for the third time, repeating himself yet again. "All pockets have been checked?"

"Nothing, chap," Oliver answers for the group as a whole.

"What if we missed an arrow?" Tori asks. We've been walking about forty minutes without stumbling across another sign. She wipes her brow. Beads of sweat have accumulated on her top lip. "Maybe we should veer left a little."

"I'd stay straight," Cassandra says, quiet and mousy. "Just an opinion, though."

"Yeah, but how will we *know* if we've gone too far?" Tori

asks aloud. Beside her, Jason has the camcorder turned toward himself, a small, extendable screen flipped in a way that allows him to look at his image as he records it.

"We may be lost," he says seriously. "But please, know, Jason Gems. My will to survive is all about coming home to you!"

"Jason *gems?*" my Mom asks. Oliver helps her step through some fallen branches, her arm intertwined with his.

"That's what I call my fans," Jason beams at her. Her mouth falls into a tight line. I'm familiar with this face. It's the one my Mom makes when she's literally biting her tongue.

"We're stranded in the middle of nowhere and he's live-streaming?" Donald mutters to Alicia. They've fallen behind, mainly because Alicia's walk has been plagued by a myriad of mysterious illnesses. First, her stomach was upset. Then, she tripped and scraped her knee. But her main affliction is a desperate need to be the center of attention at all times.

"It's not live-streaming if there's no signal, actually," Lana says practically as she ties her hair in a messy bun with one hand. Alicia glares at her. If looks could kill, Lana would have died a thousand times over.

"And how would *you* know?" Alicia asks.

"I'm the head of a news network," Lana answers. "Learned a little something about broadcasts along the way."

Alicia grimaces. She's used to being the most beautiful woman in any room, but her good looks are purchased. Lana is the real deal; naturally stunning, and incredibly successful. Donald's been looking at her wistfully since they woke up on that beach, and his roaming gaze hasn't escaped Alicia.

"Fascinating," she snarls, waving off Donald's hand as a

wayward palm leaf hits her in the face. Its sharp tendrils poke at her skin. "My eyes!" she cries, stopping yet again to address what is definitely not an emergency medical problem.

"Found another!" Rick shouts. He points at another red arrow, painted on a tree. We adjust course accordingly. Rick beams at Mike, pleased with himself. "You have to look *past* the color pattern," he says. "It's easy to miss things out in the wild. There's a natural camouflage that happens."

Rick is at the front of the pack, and he's spent the last hour talking Mike's ear off about next steps and survival strategy. Mike is still cold toward him, but on Rick's end, it's as if the fight at the wedding never happened. I want to remind Rick that I'm the only person here who's survived in the wilderness alone and without aid, but it wouldn't matter. Rick is part of that group of men that relies exclusively on other men for advice. He's a guy that would rather starve than get survival tips from me.

Just then, Rick trips on a log. His feet tangle and he stumbles, falling face first into the sand.

"Careful Rick," I say, unable to help myself. "Gotta look *past* that color pattern."

My Mom whispers over my shoulder, "That wasn't very nice." She's smiling from ear to ear.

Finally, we spot something *not* found in nature, looming far off in the distance. It's a collection of dome-shaped tents, arranged in a circle.

"A campsite!" Tori cries. She takes off running. Everyone follows.

My breath catches in my throat, because I know what Logan's trying to do. He's trying to take me back to Yosemite, to the valley that I never really left.

Mike stays behind, because he knows what I'm thinking.

"The tents look the same, don't they?" he says, remembering our trip.

He's right. They're the same color, the same size, maybe even the same brand as the tents we used in the forest. "I'm not sleeping in one of those things," I tell him.

"You don't have to ask me twice," he answers.

He slips my hand into his. A few dozen feet in front of us, Cassandra looks over her shoulder, her expression darkening when she sees us. She was silent during our walk, but I noticed her listening to the others with a careful ear. She collects information. She's an observer. It's a quality I'm familiar with, as I own it myself.

"Oi! Kids!" Oliver calls out from the campsite. He waves a hand at Mike and I, beckoning. "You ought to have a look this."

Everyone has gathered around something at the edge of the campsite, where the soil turns to sand and the tents butt up against the beach. When we reach the group, they separate, revealing a motorboat. It's a long, white cylinder with a racing stripe swirling on the side in faded blue paint. It hasn't been well-maintained. Despite its condition, it's large enough to fit the group.

"It's a way off the island," Tori says.

"Francois," Mike turns to Francois, excited, "If we get this thing running, could you lead us to Mahé?"

"Perhaps," Francois nods, scanning the horizon. "If I saw the other islands, I could determine where we are. Mahé is large. It will be hard to miss if we orient ourselves in the correct direction."

I'm about to climb into the boat, but a small voice stops me. "What's that?" Cassandra points to the boat's ignition. It takes me a second to see what she's reaching for. I push past the others, and when I catch a glimpse, my stomach turns.

"Nobody move!" I shout. I bend down, looking at the tiny electronic item connected to the boat's ignition. It's a small, black box. A keyboard sits idly by its side, the two items connected by wires. A screen on the black box's surface displays a single blank line— an input field of some kind, marked by a blinking cursor. Above the input field is a clock. It's a timer, counting down in hours, minutes, and seconds.

A red wire sticks out of the box's top. It's connected to the ignition, slid into the hole where the key would normally go. Beneath the box, a green wire curves beneath the seat. I follow it, tracing it with my eyes to the spot where it ends on the floor of the seat next to the Captain's position.

A pile of C-4 stares back at me.

"Bomb," I barely croak out the word before the panic ensues. Everyone backs up. Mike pulls me away from the boat. Rick tries to step closer— most likely to get a better look and offer his expertise— but Lana grips his arm to keep him in place.

"It's tied into the ignition," I say. "There's a control box with a keyboard attached."

"A letter!" Jason gasps, still clutching his camera, recording every moment. He looks thrilled to be a part of this experience, as if capturing this adventure is his documentary film debut.

An envelope has been taped to the boat's hull, stuck inside a clear plastic envelope to protect it from the elements.

"Anyone up for it?" Oliver asks. Nobody volunteers. "Well then, age before beauty."

Oliver marches toward the boat and rips off the tape in one smooth motion. He pulls out the envelope, opens the letter, and shakes the pages loose.

"It's typed," he says. "A poem? Good Lord..." He clears his throat and begins to read.

"*IF YOU TEST IT, She will blow,*
   The key-code's what you need, you know.
   Find the word that answers this;
   Careful now, for if you mis-
   -take the one that you can't trust,
   The boat will blow, because it must.
   The key-code is a name, it's true:
   Someone helped me hoodwink you.
   This person stands among you— close!
   Find six clues, or else you're toast.
   You have three days, so solve it fast,
   otherwise the boat will blast.
   The key-code is this person's name.
   Thanks for playing, my death-time game."

WHEN OLIVER FINISHES READING, silence settles over the group. Nobody dares say anything, as if the words themselves will cause the boat to explode.

It's Rick who finally speaks up, his face red, swelling with fury.

"I say we blow the boat up ourselves, just to show the psycho he doesn't own us," Rick says, pushing Lana away. She's been leaning on his shoulder for support. Now, she stands alone, a wind-battered palm tree in a tropical storm.

"It's our only way off the island," I answer, shaking my head. "If the boat dies, we die."

"She's right," Francois adds. "Wherever we are, it's surely

one of the remote archipelagos. I have not seen a single ship pass by. Has anyone else?"

No one answers.

Francois continues, "The nature preserves in the Seychelles are left untouched. Visitors are not permitted in order to allow the wildlife to thrive. Researchers might visit to collect samples, but time is not on our side."

"How long before they might find us?" Lana asks, hands trembling.

"Years," Francois answers, simply.

"We won't survive on this island for years," I say, feeling something burn inside of me. "We need that boat."

I step forward, standing in the middle of the group. I'm the only one here who has survived in the wild. Deep in that Yosemite darkness, I discovered my inner animal— the piece of me that does whatever it takes to survive. I hear her howling, now, and I know what I have to do.

"We're going to solve his puzzle, but we're going to do it on our terms," I think out loud. "I want half the group working on finding the key code, and the other half looking at the way the explosives connect to the boat. Maybe we can re-wire it."

"I'll take a look," Lana nods. Her hands have stopped shaking. She's a type-A personality. Having a direction— a strategy— kicks her into gear.

"Good," I say, motioning to Oliver. "Oliver, you must know something about the way engines are constructed because you worked with planes, right?"

"I'm hardly an expert. But I can try," he says humbly. My Mom beams at him.

"Pair up with Lana. The two of you are in charge of the boat. No one goes near it without their permission." I glance at Rick, because he's still got that rebellious look in his eye.

"Maybe I could build us a back-up boat. A raft." Mike says. "In case we don't get the key code in time, or something goes wrong with the..". he pauses, searching for the right way to say what we're all thinking, "...rewiring."

"Yes, that's perfect," I answer, trying not to think about the fact that a failed rewiring might mean pieces of Lana and Oliver spread across the beach. "Mom, Tori, you can help Mike with trying to make a raft. He'll need wood—whatever we can find— and maybe something heavy to break it with."

"The lighter the wood the better. More buoyant," Mike adds. "And we'll need some kind of rope to tie pieces together. We'll have to weave it ourselves, maybe from these leaves." He points to the spiky palms fronds above our heads.

"Good," I say, feeling empowered. "The rest of us will work on the key-code by searching the island for clues.

"Why don't we just type in every name?" Tori asks, tapping her foot on the sand. She's always been impatient. "You know, try our best guesses!"

"Didn't you listen?!" Donald practically shouts back at her. He's a lawyer with no patience for anyone who's not quick on the uptake. He grabs the note from Oliver's hand, reading, "'*If you test it, she will blow.*' If we put in the wrong name, the boat will explode, likely killing one of us with it."

"We have to be sure," I say. "Before we type a name into that box, we have to be sure."

"How long do we have?" Jason asks, gripping his camera tighter. Based on his frantic finger movements on the control panel, he's frantically zooming in on the motorboat.

I lean in, taking a glance at the screen. The countdown clock features square, robotic numbers, and the whole setup looks like it was based off an old computer from the early

90s. "Seventy hours, thirty-two minutes, fifteen— no, fourteen seconds," I say. "A little under three days, just like the poem said."

"Is anyone going to point out the elephant on the beach?" Alicia sighs, clicking together her perfectly manicured nails. When no one answers, she clucks her tongue, reading over Donald's shoulder.

"*The key-code is a name, it's true:*
Someone helped me hoodwink you.
This person stands among you— close!
Find six clues or else you're toast."

She folds the page in half when she's done, scanning our faces like we're stupid children in an elementary school class.

"The key code is the name of someone in this group! Someone who *helped* him kidnap the rest of us!" She pauses, savoring the moment, relishing the feeling of having all eyes on her. "You all get what that means, right?"

We do, but she decides to say it out loud anyway.

"One of us is working with him." Then, for dramatic affect, she adds, "We can't trust anyone."

20

CASSANDRA

That little prick.

Logan told me his plan would have the group spread across the island, looking for clues, making them hate each other. My job was to be a mole, an internal plant making sure things went according to schedule. I was supposed to make sure they stayed on track and followed his clues by encouraging them to play the game. Already, I've made sure they stayed on the course outlined by the arrows, and even stopped Zoe from accidentally blowing up the boat. My job was to supervise, and watch the mess unfold. I was never supposed to be part of the game.

How dare he.

Logan hasn't just put me in danger. He's robbed me of an experience I was looking forward to. I enjoy causing chaos and creating unrest. I'm named after a Greek prophet doomed to speak the truth, but never be believed. This island escapade was to be my revenge: I'd speak lies, and ensure they'd *all* be believed. I would make Mike and Zoe fall out of love with each other. I would make Mike pay attention to me again.

Logan didn't tell me he'd use my name as the key code. This is not what I signed up for.

"It has to be one of us!" Alicia continues, beating the point to death when I wish she'd just leave it alone. "Right?"

Zoe's eyes scan the group, and I swear she looks at me twice. She turns to Alicia, thoughtful.

"Maybe," she says, her voice still scratchy. "Or maybe not. Logan lies. He strategizes. Either way, if someone on this island really *is* working with him, the best thing we can do is stay in groups of three."

She speaks to the entire group now, describing her strategy. "No one should ever be alone with another person. It's a buddy system. You, plus two other people at all times. Agreed?"

Everyone nods, except Rick. "And who nominated *you* as president of the island?" He snarls.

"Hey, watch yourself..." Mike starts to say, but Zoe holds out an arm, pushing him back. She steps toward Rick, her eyes like fire. She's molten lava hardened into human form. The word she says next spills out from some inner depth I didn't know she had, sounding regal, undeniable.

"Me."

It's enough. No one else seems to question the legitimacy of her leadership. Rick backs off, but there's a twitch at the edge of his mouth that says this isn't over yet.

The group sets to work on their respective tasks, and I quietly head toward Mike's team. He's already scavenging for materials, searching the island for pieces to make a raft.

"Could you use another eye?" I ask him. He's silent, refusing to look my way. "You and me used to work pretty well together."

"Go away, Cass."

"There's only two people on this beach with experience building things."

He doesn't answer. His silence infuriates me. Is it so hard to notice a person? So hard to look their way?

"I'll follow you anyway," I add, walking beside him as he searches through fallen palm fronds. "You can't avoid me here, Mike."

He stops, turning toward me, and I'm shocked at the rage that's built up behind his features. It's as if years of anger have distilled into a single moment. "If you follow me, it's at your own risk. My advice is to stay the fuck away."

He turns and disappears into the trees, leaving me behind, as usual. I want to run after him, but do my best to resist.

You're here for the long game, I remind myself. One day, I'll get Mike alone and force him to talk to me. One day, I'll make him see me, make him care.

I assimilate into Zoe's team— the one that's going to try and discover the key code— because it's the only option left.

"Can I join?" I ask. A group has gathered around Zoe. Jason and his permanently-attached camera went to work with Lana and Oliver, even though Lana looked like she'd rather not have him. Zoe's Mom, Tori, and Mike are working on the raft, where I'm obviously not wanted. That leaves Francois, Donald, Alicia, and me to help Zoe find the key code. My past knowledge of Donald and Alicia tells me they'll be about as useful as a couple of seagulls in the hunt for clues. Francois is another story. He wasn't supposed to be here— he wasn't part of Logan's plan. The lackeys Logan hired only picked him up because he was with Mike and Zoe. He's an unintended guest. There's something quiet about him. He's thoughtful, with a deep, soulful kind of mystery.

Zoe scans my figure like she's trying to decide if she can trust me. "I don't know anything about engines or explosives, and I don't think Mike wants me to help with the raft," I tell her. It's true. Mike hasn't looked at me once since I got here. Jerk. "I'd really like to be useful."

There's a long pause that makes me think Zoe will turn me away. Instead, she smiles at me, linking an arm over mine like we're old girlfriends from high school. "Of course," she says, like it was a foregone conclusion that I'd be on her side.

It almost makes me like her for a second. The truth is, it's hard to watch people for so long and *not* grow to care for them. In my pursuit of Mike, I've also watched Zoe. I *know* her. The way she wakes up in the middle of the night and looks at Mike, like she wants to make sure he's breathing. The way she positions herself near windows and doors, as if she'd rather be outside than in any given room. The flowers she plants in the front yard. The herb garden she grows on the porch. Her self-reliance. If she weren't married to Mike, we'd probably be friends.

Unfortunately, she is married to Mike, which makes me want to drag her out to the ocean and hold her head underwater until the bubbles stop. I would never actually do it, of course. But it's fun to think about.

As much as I hate her, I wish I could tell her the truth. I could really use someone to confide in right now, because I've just offered my services riddling out a mystery I've already solved. The fact of the matter is, I'm the only one here who knows what that key-code is. I've been spelling it since kindergarten.

C-A-S-S-A-N-D-R-A.

I bite my tongue to keep from saying it out loud.

Zoe grabs a stick and draws a circle in the sand. "The

poem said there would be clues. We need to search the island."

Donald sniffs, a reluctant manager at a team meeting. "We don't even know what we're looking for."

"Logan isn't subtle," Zoe says. "When we find it, we'll know." She uses the stick to draw more lines in the sand, dividing the circle into three parts. "We'll search two quadrants a day. The poem said we're looking for six clues and, assuming they're evenly spread out, each quadrant should yield at least two."

"That's a big assumption," Francois says. "We'd cover more ground if we split up."

"We'll do our best," Zoe shrugs. There's a tension between them I can't quite place. Zoe doesn't trust him; that much is clear. "Let's get started."

With that, Zoe leads us away from the beach, setting course toward the interior of the island. She navigates away from the direction we came in. She's avoiding ground we've already covered. She's smart.

"Make sure you check the trees as well as the ground," she says to the group. Everyone is combing through leaves and fallen branches, looking for something that stands out. "It could be anywhere."

WE SEARCH for about thirty minutes before I see a clue, hanging from a tree about twenty feet away. It's a big silver box, dangling in the wind, a red X painted on its lid. Impossible to miss, and clearly not germane to the island. I'm desperate to lead the group in another direction. Logan's already lied to me about the key-code on the boat. What if what I *think* is in those boxes isn't there after all? But before

I can lead us in another direction, Donald's already spotted the box.

"There's something up in the tree!" he shouts.

Everyone gathers around. Donald and Francois lift Zoe onto their shoulders, making her just tall enough to grab the box by its strings. She lands on the group with a thud, kneeling down to open it.

My heart tries to leave my chest. This is the moment they find out it's me. Logan's sent me out here to die by angry mob. Zoe opens the box and pulls out the item inside.

It's a necklace. A familiar one, because I stole it myself at the wedding. A gold ring dangles from the chain like a pendant.

I can't help but exhale. It's exactly as Logan planned it. I knew the items I stole would be used in Logan's game, but he refused to tell me in what capacity. Maybe he didn't mean to set me up. Maybe I'm not part of the game after all. Maybe there's a lesson in it I don't understand, and he's mentoring me, grooming me to become a better 'bad guy.' He said he *wanted* Zoe to guess the right answer, but never told me the riddle would involve other members of the group, or that the right answer might be my name. Maybe there's more I don't understand.

"Whose is it?" Alicia asks, her eyes sparkling at the sight of a piece of jewelry.

Zoe holds the ring in the air, reading an inscription on the inside out loud. "'*To Rachel, my forever.*'" She pauses, looking betrayed. "They got married. And they didn't tell me."

"There's a document, too," Francois reaches inside the box, pulling out an official looking piece of paper "It's a plane charter."

Zoe grabs the document, scanning it for what it might mean. Then, her breath catches in her throat.

She takes off the way we came, running toward the campsite like a prize race-horse set looks. My stomach turns.

I'm not sure what the document says, but I knew she would react this way to the ring. So why does it feel so awful?

Suddenly, being the bad guy isn't fun anymore.

21

———

ZOE

"You got married and didn't even *invite* me?" I'm standing in front of my Mom and Oliver, the ring dangling on its chain. It swings from side to side at the edge of my fingers, filling the silence with its momentum, refusing to stop until answers are provided.

"Sweetie," my Mom says, using that same voice she does when I'm sick, or upset. "I was going to tell you when you kids got back from the honeymoon."

Mike's beside me, looking confused. I haven't had a chance to explain what we found.

"Zoe, we wanted you there," Oliver adds, his accent suddenly less charming than it is irritating. "It was quite spontaneous, just the two of us. And we felt so connected in the middle of the Icelandic wilderness. We realized how completely smitten we were."

"And a little intoxicated, to be honest."

My Mom nods. "We were drunk, sweetie. Very, very drunk."

"But the sentiment itself was sober!" Oliver takes my

Mom's hand in his. "We planned to have a bigger wedding when we got home, but your Mom was worried..." Oliver stops short.

"Worried about what?" I push.

"Sweetheart, *I* was worried." my Mom eyes Mike, as if hoping he'll back her on this one. "Sometimes, you look for ways, I suppose, to..."

"Just say it!"

"To run!" She finally says. The words echo, like she's boxed me in the ears. "I'm sorry, but you *do* tend to look for an escape from a relationship! The slightest thing and you start to overthink! I didn't want to give you any reason to postpone the wedding, because you two are so great together. Mike is wonderful."

Mike pretends to tip an invisible hat. "Why, thank you, Ma'am."

I mentally shoot daggers at him.

"What if our wedding had stolen your thunder?" my Mom continues. "Or what if it had gone belly-up rather quickly, and give you two kids cold feet about marriage? We haven't known each other very long. It was quite sponta-neous, but at our age, who wants to waste time?"

"Very true," Oliver adds.

"So you *lied*?" I ask, voice shaking.

My Mom's eyes fill with tears. "Yes," she admits. "But only because I was so afraid of ruining your happiness. Being a parent is so difficult. One day you'll know. I just— I didn't want to give you an excuse to back out of something you've always been afraid of."

"Am I *that* aloof?" I turn to Mike, waiting for him to assure me it isn't true.

"Well," he says, with careful precision. "To be honest, I thought the odds of you walking down the aisle were fifty-

fifty. I had already worked out what I was going to say to you if you changed your mind."

"What were you going to say?"

"Something like, 'Let's wait until next year! Don't worry, I'm fine!'" Mike says, smirking. "Then I would cry, secretly, at night, probably in the wood-shop, with a cigarette and the window open."

"You're ridiculous."

"Ridiculously in love with you."

The temperature in the air seems to shift. I see my own image reflected back at me, from their own eyes. Nobody in this group meant to hurt me. They were only trying to help.

I pass the ring to my Mom, who clasps the chain it's dangling from back around her neck.

"And the plane charter?" I turn back to Oliver. "You knew about it?"

"What charter?" He looks confused. I pass him the document. He scans it, face darkening as he reads.

"That's your company, isn't it? I prompt. "Atlas Private Charters."

Oliver nods. "I recognize the document. I just don't know what it's doing here." He turns to my Mom and passes her the paper for review.

My Mom is a brilliant business woman. When they met, Oliver had just retired from flying. In less than a year, she helped him use his connections in the industry to open a private plane service. He doesn't own the planes— he just serves as a broker, connecting passengers to unused private aircraft at near-wholesale prices. It's already profitable, even though it's a new endeavor.

"Honey," she says, pointing the date on the agreement. "This is the man we met in Iceland, remember?"

"Of course!" Oliver snaps his fingers.

"Who did you meet in Iceland?" My heart pounds, because my body is already guessing at the answer, a familiar sweat gathering in the creases of my palms.

"We were jet-setting around. Remember when I called you from a new city each night? It was the trip where we never stayed longer than a day in any one place."

I remember it well. My Mom would call me with each new destination, and by the end of the trip they all seemed to blend together.

"Iceland was the last stop on our itinerary. It was there we got married, funny enough. We'd had some wonderful food, some strong drinks."

"*Very* strong," Oliver emphasizes.

"And we ran off and got married right then and there."

"Doesn't it take time to file the paperwork?" Mike asks.

"Well, it was a small fireside spiritual ceremony with a group we met at the restaurant. I'm not actually sure it's legally binding," my Mom shrugs as if it's of no consequence whatsoever. "Oliver was going to look into that when we got home. But then we decided to engrave the ring and call it a day. Who cares about a piece of paper anyway?"

"Mom!" I try very hard not to shout. "The man you met?"

"Right!" Oliver interjects, sensing my frustration, my urgency. "He was a bloke who helped with the ceremony. An ex-pat from the US of all places, just like us. Was actually him who told us about the shotgun wedding. Said he knew a group of spiritualists who had left the states for greener pastures abroad. Very connected to nature, these people."

"The charter," I push. If Oliver doesn't get to the point soon, I'm going to lose it. "Get to the charter."

"Well, he was wonderful. Helped arrange the whole thing. Bought us the drinks that encouraged us to go through with it all. Afterwards, well, I paid him back by offering him a one-off."

"A one-off?"

"A freebie. A charter of his choice to wherever he'd like."

"What did he look like? What was his name?"

"He said his name was Josh. Young fellow, about your ages."

Suddenly, I feel sick. The island is all open space, yet it seems as if the sky is closing in on me, falling closer to the Earth. Everything churns.

"Zoe, are you alright?" My Mom asks, putting an arm around my shoulder

"That's Logan's alias," I say, sure of it. "The name on this form is Josh Q. He doesn't even put a full last name. It's how he looked on his dating profile, when we first met."

"Oh my God, Zoe!" My Mom gasps. "It can't be. We would have known. Would have *sensed* it."

"Look at the destination," I point to the charter. "He provided his own pilot. The only thing he used was the plane."

"The destination is here," Oliver confirms, looking at the document. "He had the company fly him to the Seychelles."

"Not just him," I add. "All of you. He used the plane to get you here."

My Mom leans on Oliver, looking sick. "We didn't know. We would never have offered."

"Of course not," I scoff, even though a terrible idea is brewing deep inside my gut. "You guys didn't know."

"I'll look into it, Zoe," Oliver promises. "I'll have the owner of the plane get us more information when we're home. We can use this to catch him. We can turn it over to the FBI. He's just given us the keys to tracking him down."

"Great idea," I say, even though I don't really believe it will work. Logan will have created a corporate umbrella to shield his true identity. The FBI said he was a ghost. There is no Logan. Just a million aliases, all of them masquerading as each other.

Everyone heads for the tents. I follow, my feet heavy, heart pounding. An old narrative resurfaces, whispering in my ear. I try to push it away, but it sits on my shoulder, digging its claws into my clavicle.

I've known Oliver less than a year. My Mom met him right after Mike and I were rescued from Yosemite, battered and bruised. It didn't occur to me at the time, but his arrival came at an unusual crossroads in my Mom's life. She had just watched her only daughter recover from a life-and-death experience unlike any other. She was vulnerable. When the call came in that Mike and I were in the hospital, she drove to Yosemite alone, tackling that eight-hour stretch of black asphalt with nothing but her own two hands gripping the steering wheel the whole way there. How much easier would it have been if she'd had a partner to support her, sitting passenger side on that drive?

And then, like magic, Oliver appeared. At the time, I thought he was a God-send. Someone for her to spend her golden years with. He was a man of the world who could fly them to a new location on a whim. He was educated, but grounded, the perfect mix of safety and adventure wrapped up into one red-faced, kind-eyed Englishman.

Now, a part of me wonders: what if Oliver's arrival wasn't divinely orchestrated? What if *Logan* sent Oliver into my Mom's life? Beneath the charming accent, the refined exterior, Oliver might be hiding another version of himself.

I look back at the motorboat, where the keyboard

strapped to the bomb waits for me. When I type my answer into that blank line—when the blinking cursor turns into a word— will I being typing out Oliver's name?

22

CASSANDRA

I listened to them talking about the plane charter, hiding out of sight. I had to excuse myself from the rest of the group, claiming I was going to the bathroom. It took careful concentration to make sure I didn't create any noise. I found the perfect spot to eavesdrop, hiding behind a rock formation, using my invisibility to my advantage.

Logan chartered the plane from Oliver's company.

It's an interesting turn of events— one I didn't see coming. It makes me wonder what else Logan didn't tell me. For now, I'm relieved the clue has nothing to do with me. Maybe his intention is to lead her down the wrong trail, far away from me.

Later, the group decides on lunch. They've found the icebox Logan left, filled with exactly three days worth of food supplies.

Jason pulls out a package of beef jerky, holding it up to the sun. "This stuff has so much salt," he laments, handing it to Tori. "If I retain water, my face will bloat on camera."

"We wouldn't want *that*," Rick answers, his eyes lingering

a little too long on the perfect, straight edge of Jason's nose. It's jealousy, mixed with a little something else I can't quite place.

"We have to ration this," Zoe says, taking stock of what's in the cooler. "The water, especially. He's left us enough for a few days, but if we can't get the boat started and we're stuck here."

"We're done for," Mike finishes her sentence, nodding. There was a time when he finished my sentences, but he rarely guessed their endings right. He never knew where I was heading, could never get inside my head and really understand me.

The group settles on some bread and peanut butter for tonight's meal, but Zoe makes us all promise we'll try foraging and fishing tomorrow. "I don't want to rely on this," she says, motioning to the supplies. "We need to make it stretch, just in case."

Zoe gets to work creating a fire using Rick's lighter. She arranges dry palm leaves in a circle, making a pyre. The lighter clicks on and the fire roars to life, sending embers toward the sky.

We sit in a circle to eat. Donald and Alicia keep to themselves, but everyone else huddles together, like they're afraid of some unseen danger hiding behind the palm trees.

"Your video," Francois nods at Jason, who's scrolling through the footage on his camera, rewatching it. "Are you making a movie?"

"I'm a YouTuber. An influencer," Jason says, proud of himself and not trying to hide it. "I just crossed the two-hundred thousand subscriber mark."

Tori beams at him like a doting aunt. "I'm a publicist," she adds, gearing up to pitch Jason to the group. "And I knew the second I saw his channel that he's really onto something. The way the fans *respond* to him. It's like they're emotionally in-tune with each other. He calls it 'connecting through the soul,' right, babe?"

"That's right," Jason says seriously. "Viewers have to know you're there for them. Not just as a celebrity figure, but as a friend."

"What's your show about?" Oliver asks. He looks relieved the group has something else to talk about besides the life insurance policy.

"It's multi-faceted, but mostly it's about my life," Jason explains. "I let viewers into the deepest, most personal parts of my existence, and together we share an experience. See, I don't believe in 'privacy.'"

"I'm sorry, what?" Rachel says, frowning. Rachel is from a generation that believed in small Government, partly in pursuit of individual privacy. Now, she's about to find out how happy the "Jasons" of the world are to throw it all away, in exchange for some lousy product placement fees.

"As far as I'm concerned, privacy is an old idea. With the internet, privacy is becoming more and more a thing of the past. Think about it." he leans in, eyes gleaming. "You can't even search for an item you want to buy without that information being recorded and stored on a server somewhere. Facebook and Youtube store your search history and use it to provide advertisements you might be interested in."

"They *do*?" Rachel gasps, looking at Zoe, who nods.

"They do, Mom."

Rachel shakes her head, sighing heavily. Zoe pats her shoulder.

"I'll delete your Facebook for you when we get home."

"Anyway," Jason continues, encouraged by Rachel's reaction, as if her desire for privacy is somehow evidence of its need to be destroyed. "Everything we do is monitored. If you mention out loud you want to buy a sofa, next thing you know, you'll see ads for it on the internet. Why? Because our phones are listening to us, and not just for advertisers. We already know our phone calls and emails are being saved in metadata by the NSA."

"That's true," Lana nods, looking like she's surprised she agrees with Jason about anything at all. "Every call we make is stored somewhere."

"So I took a look around at what I see as the utter destruction of privacy. It's so bad, it's irreversible. And I thought, 'Why fight it?'" Jason shrugs, taking a bite of his bread. "Other people are profiting, so why shouldn't I? That's when I got the idea for the show. My first episode was a live stream of my day, and I took the camera everywhere with me. Into the car. Into the bathroom."

"Into the loo?!" Oliver exclaims. "Who on Earth would want to see that?"

"Well, when your ass looks like his," Rick mutters. Lana slaps his arm.

"It was like *The Truman Show*," Jason continues. "It went totally viral. I realized I was onto something and kicked it up a notch. I shared my every thought. Every crazy, moronic thought that came into my head, I said it on camera." This aspect of his show makes me shudder, because if I said every one of my crazy thoughts aloud, someone would lock me away.

"I started to form this *connection* with my viewers. It's the purest love I've ever found in my life," he says, and I swear I see his eyes watering. "They accept me for all my flaws, and love me anyway. Sure, there's some criticism, but that just makes the love I do get even more meaningful. We live in a post-privacy world, and I truly believe it's our path to unconditional connection. So I'm not hiding any part of myself. Here's me, naked and real."

"Does that mean," Francois asks, looking disturbed, "If you were sick and had to throw up?"

"Yes," Jason nods. "If the show were operating to my ideal specifications, I would take the camera with me."

"What about the two of you." Rachel motions back and forth between Jason and Tori, "Making, you know, *love*."

"We're still working on that," Tori jumps in before Jason can answer. "Jason and I have some disagreements about his philosophy and what sharing *his* life means for his life partner."

"It's a discussion," Jason says. "Right now, I only livestream for eight hours a day, taking the nights off. But my ultimate goal is to be totally observed, twenty-four-seven. Youtube's terms of service have some restrictions about content which makes it impossible to show *every* moment, so I'm looking at a private server. We'd create a site where viewers can go to live-stream me at any point in the day. It would operate independently from any existing network. I just need a big enough base to merit the expense. Whoever I'm with might have to be alright being filmed in every scenario, because at that point, it really becomes a lifestyle. If I'm going to commit to it, I need to commit one-hundred-percent."

It's clear, now, that Jason is a total weirdo. He might be the only person on this island crazier than I am. It annoys me. The weird, not-quite-right persona is my territory, and mine alone.

"We're working on going wide," Tori adds, her inner publicist shining through. "It's been— *tricky*— getting interviews with major platforms lined up. Not everyone takes internet influencers seriously yet."

"But we're changing the world!" Jason cries.

"I know, babe, it's true," she pats his leg like she's calming down a temperamental child. "It's not a matter of 'if,' it's a matter of 'when.' Once outlets figure out how groundbreaking his work is, Jason's show will be everywhere. We just need that major breakthrough, something so topical they can't ignore it."

"Cassandra?" Zoe says my name, and everyone goes quiet. "What do *you* think?

"Me?"

"Yes, *you*," Zoe says, not a hint of anger in her tone. "What do you think about being watched all day long? About not having any privacy?"

Oh God. She's going to tell everyone I've spent the last few years stalking Mike. I glance at Mike, who makes eye contact with me for the first time since we arrived. There's red-hot anger in his irises, but also confusion, and hurt, and a question mark that deserves an answer.

I think for a long time before I say anything. Then, I give them the only response I can muster.

"I worry more about the viewer than the viewed."

"In what way?" Lana asks, curious. All eyes are on me. It's uncomfortable. I'm not used to being around this many people at one time.

Rachel looks at me from across the fire, and even though she isn't my Mom, I wish I could give her a hug. There's sympathy in her face. I'm sure Mike has told her what an awful person I am, but she still looks at me like I'm somebody's daughter.

"Well, um, I guess," I stutter, trying to find the words. "If you're watching someone else, no one's watching you. And like Jason said, to love someone you have to *see* them. You have to understand who they are on some deep, meaningful level. Without, um..."

"Pretense," Jason nods.

"Yes. Without that. So if you're not worth paying attention to, no one can really get to know you. And if no one knows you, they can't 'see' you in that deeper way. And if no one sees you..."

"There's no love," Zoe summarizes the thought.

"Yeah," I say. "There's no love. So I guess that's why— I guess that's why I feel bad for all those people on the other side of the screen, watching Jason. Because, uh..."

There's a long pause as I clear my throat, where a knot is stuck, threatening to make me cry.

"... because no one is watching them."

The words feel heavy in my mouth, and once I say them I'm glad they're outside of me. I've pulled some poison through my veins, a string of words tied in a bow and left on the sand.

Mike crosses his arms, doubtful. But Zoe leans toward me. Her face warps behind the fire, going all red and hazy. Golden light weaves through her dark hair, making it turn caramel, not so far off of from the shade I was born with, the one I'm known for, the only thing that sets me apart from other people.

For a second, I imagine us as twins, two people who share one appearance but different souls, looking at each other in a mirror, trying to decide who is who.

I clear my throat, and the spell is broken. "It's just an idea," I shrug. "Just another way of looking at it."

"I understand," Zoe says, and for now, I believe she does.

23

ZOE

I 'm rinsing my clothes out in the ocean when I see it. It's hard to make out the shape from afar, but it's clearly rectangular, a man-made object. It's about a foot long, a perfect square.

I remove my clothes from the water, then walk toward it, a foreboding sense of dread churning in my ribcage.

It couldn't be.

Sure enough, when I get closer to the object, it reveals itself as a silver box with an "X" painted on top: one of Logan's clues.

But something is very wrong.

It's embedded in the sand, sucked into the Earth by the wet pull of the tides. Its lid is wide open, the interior box completely empty.

Logan would never hide a clue this close to the tides. He's too smart to allow his work to be washed away by the sea. No, someone must have found this box. Found it, and emptied it, leaving the sad, assaulted remains behind. Whoever found the clue most likely tossed the box into the sea, hoping evidence of their interference would be carried away for good. But they didn't account for the tides, the push and pull of the ocean, which forces secrets from below to rise to the surface.

WHEN I TAKE the box back to camp, everyone looks it over.

"Maybe it was already here. Maybe it's unrelated. Could be trash from a passing ship," Donald reasons, crafting a defense like the high-powered lawyer he is.

"No," my Mom shakes her head, "there's one of those red 'X's on the top, see?"

"Who cares?" Rick says, rolling his eyes. "This entire thing is a wild goose chase anyway," he glares at me, unable to hide his disdain. "Led by *her*."

"Watch it," Mike says.

Rick softens. "I'm only pointing out that we should be signaling for help! Thinking of other ways to get off the island."

Mike sighs. "We are. If you can build a boat faster than me with those investment-banker brains of yours, by all means, try." Rick's face flushes, but not from anger. He looks wounded.

"You know that's not what I meant," he says, almost in a whisper. "I just don't get why Zoe's in charge!" He's whining now, like a grade-school child. "It should be all of us! Or maybe someone more qualified, someone with survival experience!"

"My wife survived in impossible conditions, alone, in the backcountry of Yosemite. She *is* the most qualified."

"It's a national park," Rick mutters. "Couldn't have been that bad."

Mike holds up his left hand, the one missing a pinky finger. "Really?" His voices raises, almost to a shout. "If you want to talk about how fucking bad it was, I'm happy to share." He puts his hand down. "Zoe is in charge. That's it."

"The real question is, who would get rid of a clue?" Lana interjects, turning the box over. "All of us want to get off this island, right?"

"It's obvious, isn't it?" Alicia says, twirling a piece of hair in her hand. She clucks her tongue like we're children who aren't cooperating. "Whoever got rid of the clue must be working with him!"

"I truly hate to think," Oliver ponders, pushing his glasses up higher on his nose, "that anyone on this island would have nefarious intentions."

"Oh come *on*," Alicia snarls. "People are selfish."

"Just because you live your life that way doesn't mean the rest of us do," Tori snaps.

"Truly?" Alicia smiles, barring her teeth. "You can honestly say you've never done something you knew was wrong because it got you ahead?"

An expression flashes across Tori's face. It's one I recognize from our childhood. The look she gave when a teacher caught her cheating on a test. It's hard to catch, and disappears as quickly as it arrived. I wouldn't have caught, if I didn't know her so well.

"But not *kidnapping!*" Tori cries.

Alicia sighs. "All I'm saying is that we've been *told* right off the bat— someone on this island is working with him. We can look for these clues and try to find the answer, but at the end of the day, it really comes down to who is trustworthy and who isn't, doesn't it?" She scans the crowd, calculating. "Someone in this group is the odd man out. Someone doesn't *want* us to know the truth. It's time we start looking for him. The clues aren't the only way."

"What do you recommend we do?" Jason asks, his perfect

hair swaying in the breeze. "Torture everyone until we get an answer?"

"That can be arranged!" Alicia exclaims, her voice a little manic. "My husband is a first-class attorney. I suggest everyone submit to a line of questioning!"

Donald clears his throat, not liking where this is going. "Well, I..."

"And who's to say *he's* not the one who's guilty?" My Mom retorts, motioning to Donald. They've never gotten on well. She knows how awful Donald and Alicia were to Mike in his childhood.

"We could say the same for you!" Alicia shoots back.

"Really? Your brilliant theory is that I put my own daughter's life in danger? That's the path you want to trod? You'd make an excellent investigator!"

"Fine," Alicia caves, "Maybe not *you*, but what about him!" She points at Francois, who looks taken aback. "You're a local, you know the islands! Maybe you told him where to strand us all so we wouldn't be found."

"What would be in it for me?" Francois asks, confused.

"Money, probably!" Alicia is on a rampage. "And you *two*," she turns to Tori and Jason. "I don't think I've ever met you in my life. How do I know you weren't involved?"

"Alicia," Tori sighs. "You've met me three times."

Suddenly, everyone starts talking at once. Rick is shouting at Mike. Tori and Alicia are nose-to-nose, debating where and how often they met. Donald grips Alicia's arm, trying to pull her away, while Francois and Cassandra look on, shoulder-to-shoulder, just as disturbed as I am.

I'd resisted the idea that one of us betrayed the others, but now, as much as I hate to admit it— Alicia's right. We're in danger. Someone here is actively interfering. The only question is... *who*?

24

———

CASSANDRA

It wasn't me who emptied out the box.

If I'd emptied it out, I would have done a better job hiding it. I would have buried it beneath the Earth like I did that medical kit, making sure no signs were left behind.

Who would be stupid enough to throw it into the Ocean? Obviously someone who doesn't know shit about the way tides work. Or maybe, someone desperate. Someone with a secret they didn't want revealed. Throwing it into the sea might have been a crime of passion in a moment of a panic.

Whoever it was, I wonder how they found the box in the first place? Was it luck? Did they happen to stumble onto it? Or did they already *know* where it was?

A terrible question settles in my chest.

Is somebody else here working with Logan?

〜

WHEN THE SUN sinks below the horizon, our party gets ready for nightfall. When I pictured myself stuck on this island, I never imagined it would feel so much like summer camp. We work together to light a fire, and to make sure everyone has sleeping bags. As I pass out blankets from the supply bag left for us, I try to remember the last time I felt like I was part of a group. Like I shared a common purpose with other people. It's been a long time.

"Quite the madman, isn't he?" Oliver says to me, as a I pass him a foil blanket.

"What do you mean?"

"Strands us here but gives us blankets. Odd," he says, shrugging.

I almost slip and tell him what I know about Logan. That he's the kind of person who want others to survive long enough to know they're fucked. It's not the killing that appeals to him: it's the intellectual win. He's the type of madman who wants to see recognition of failure in his opponents eyes. He gets off on other people knowing they've been beat. Especially when that other person challenges an essential piece of the way he sees the world. Logan always needs to be right.

But I don't tell Oliver any of that. Instead, I just shrug and say, "Beats me."

Tori is in charge of the food. She gives everyone a nutrition bar, some powdered eggs, and a bottle of water. We eat separately this time, everyone keeping to themselves. Alicia's words have permeated the camp, soaking into skin, creeping under fingernails. Even as we work together to survive, doubt about who is to be trusted divides us. Sideways glances and guarded looks shoot across the camp. Tori sticks near Jason, the two of them huddled together with their food. Donald and Alicia sit separate at the edge of the beach. They claimed they wanted to take in the water, but I think they just wanted to get as far as possible from the rest of us. Francois has gone to have another look at the motorboat, guided by Lana and Rick. "It's wired in good," Lana told him, sighing.

"I've seen many of these small boats," Francois nodded. "Maybe I can offer some assistance."

Zoe and Mike ate together for awhile, but then Mike went to work on the raft, taking Rachel and Oliver with him. Now, she's alone, sitting in the sand, eating by herself— just like me.

I wonder what he sees in her? What makes her worth noticing, in his eyes?

She catches me staring at her. Our eyes lock. I look away, but not soon enough. She's standing now, walking across the sand. She plops down next to me.

"It's too quiet here, isn't it?" She asks, talking to me like I'm her next-door neighbor and not her nemesis.

"Uh, it's, um..." I hate myself for stuttering. It's odd talking to her in person. I've watched her for so long that it feels a little like meeting a celebrity. My brain keeps running through the ways she's different up close. There's a small wrinkle between her eyebrows I didn't notice from afar. Her lips are chapped. There's signs of dry skin on her forehead. She's still beautiful, but watching her from a distance created a blur effect. It's as if the airbrushing has been removed and now she's human. "Honestly, I'm used to quiet," I say, accidentally telling her the truth.

"Huh," There's not a hint of judgement in her voice. "And you like silence?"

"Sometimes."

"Why do you watch us?" She asks the question so abruptly that I'm not sure how to answer.

"Excuse me?"

"I want to know. Why do you watch Mike and I?" It feels rude that she's being so forthright with her questioning, but then again, I'm the one invading their privacy, so I've little right to complain.

"I'm—" the words tangle in my throat. "I'm *not* watching you."

"Yes, you are. You have been. For a long time."

"It's not watching so much," Tears start to well in my eyes, but I absolutely refuse to cry. "It's just kind of... *buzzing.*"

"Buzzing?" She repeats after me, genuinely curious.

"Yes," I say. "I'm just buzzing around you."

"Huh," Zoe ponders. "So you're a bee, then?"

My hands are sweating. I've never told anyone about the game I play— how I figure out what kind of insects people are. She's gotten to the point so quickly— uncovered the things inside my head that I hide. The dark pieces I don't share with anyone.

"Yeah," I tell her, nodding. "I think of myself that way. As a bee."

There's a long silence as she takes this in.

"Are you going to sting us?" She asks, very serious.

"No," I say.

It's the last lie I'll tell today. We eat the rest of our meal in silence. But I keep thinking about the things we say to each other, and how our lies run deep. I look out at the ocean, wondering at the depth of the water, picturing every lie I've ever told sunk right down to its sandy floor, like treasure from a shipwreck that I caused all on my own.

25

ZOE

It's the middle of the night, and I'm alone. The sky looks enormous, a blanket for a giant. I wonder who else is looking up at that sky. On a piece of rock separated from the rest of the world, night becomes something that connects you to the mainland. Everyone is looking at the same stars.

I dig my feet into the sand. A wind whips its way through the tops of the palm trees, making them sing. I snuck away from camp while everyone else was sleeping to get some space, to think.

I used to think gaps existed between people— distances that can't be crossed, oceans of misunderstanding, like the space between the edge of an island and the mainland. But now I see that we're all connected, if you only dig deep enough. Every island rests on a tectonic plate, every tectonic plate touches another. What happens on one edge of the Earth affects another, and we can never, ever untangle the many ways in which we're all connected.

Now, as I look up at the infinite, milky sky that blankets our planet, I'm reminded of that truth. The darkness is broken by stars, all of them made from the same elements, the same gas, the same fragments of the biggest explosion the universe has ever known.

Someone in this group is lying to me.

"You're thinking," Mike says, his voice making me smile. I don't turn around, because I already know it's him. He sits next to me. Even when I feel like being alone, Mike is someone I'm happy to be around.

"He's trying to tell me something," I say, not daring to use Logan's name.

"What?"

"Not sure yet. But there's a point to it all. The game. Our wedding party being here. The clues. There's something he wants me to realize. Something that will make him feel like he's won."

"Maybe it's just chaos he wants," Mike says, picking up a seashell and turning it over in his hand. It's broken in some parts, its outer edges curling forward like a spiral.

"No. It's more than that," I answer, trying to find the words to explain what I can feel deep down to the soles of my feet. "He isn't chaos. Logan is a predator stalking his prey. He's— the opposite of whatever happiness is. Whatever love is. Whatever trust is."

"You talk about him like he's more of an idea than a person."

"Maybe for me he is," I say, lying flat on my back, staring up at the stars again, hoping that if I stare hard enough they'll rearrange themselves into the answer I'm looking for.

Mike rolls over, laying on top of me, strong arms holding him up.

"I don't understand it," he says, "but I believe you."

Of course Mike doesn't understand. Mike sees the best in people, where Logan and I see the worst. Sometimes I wonder who I'd be without Mike, and the answer isn't pretty. Mike makes me believe in love. In safety. In a home you can rely on. The term "other half," has never meant more to me. He is my equal, built in reverse, as if God gave him all the personality traits he didn't put in me and vice versa. Together, we are balanced.

"Thank you for being you" I whisper, running my hand over his chin, where a beard is already growing.

He kisses me, and I get lost in the moment. No man has ever kissed me like Mike. In the arms of past connections, I've felt like an object, an item, a body. With Mike, I'm a person with a soul, seen in her entirety, flaws and all. I don't know how he does it. It's his own kind of magic.

"Let's not go back to camp," he whispers.

We make love on the beach, the waves crashing behind us.

26

CASSANDRA

They're having sex on the beach. I'm watching them.

Mike didn't know I followed him out there. Everyone else was asleep, quiet inside their tents. Mike and Zoe never claimed theirs, leaving it empty instead. They spent hours by the campfire, waiting until the embers died down. When the fire finally died, they laid down together, Mike's arm over Zoe. I peaked out at them through the entrance to my tent, hiding inside, observing. When Mike's breathing leveled, Zoe moved his arm out from around her waist, the sand muffling her noises. She snuck out toward the water, disappearing into the humid, velvet night.

It didn't take long for Mike to wake up. When he did, he looked off in the direction she'd gone, almost like he could sense her. Almost like she could go anywhere in the world and he'd still feel her heartbeat.

Now, they're making love on the sand. It's totally inappropriate. Wild. Out of left field. Like something I would do.

I watch Mike kiss her, and wonder— for the thousandth time— why he never kissed me like that.

To stop myself from thinking about it too much, I play my favorite game while I watch them make love. I try to figure out what kind of insect each of them would be if they were born again as a bug. It seems only fair, now that Zoe knows mine.

It's easy to guess Mike's insect. Mike is a termite. In his furniture business he works with wood, crafting it into beautiful shapes. He also consumes when he should give. He did it to me— chiseling away at the parts of me I relied on to stay steady, to stay sane. He was greedy, and selfish, and I was the house he ate. Maybe he's different now, with Zoe. It's hard to say for sure.

I used to study interior design. My love for designing spaces was what led me to Mike. Hours were spent debating the merits of carpets, some flat, some plush. I knew the difference between baroque and impressionist. Red wasn't just red, then, but a hundred different shades of subtle distinction; cranberry, brick, rust, oxblood. Patterns were my specialty. I could mix spots and stripes as if they weren't two opposing animals, but pieces of the same beast, always intended to live as one.

It was my own secret world, a place only I could see. I'd walk into a room and know exactly *why* it looked the way it did, making sense out of the landscape with an ease— a lightness— I'd never known before. It was as if I was wearing special glasses with a prismatic effect, turning the ordinary into the extraordinary. A chair wasn't just a chair, but a statement, living history, influenced by a thousand chairs that came before it. Books on a shelf weren't there to be read, but to be organized in one of a dozen ways: by color, by size, horizontally, vertically. Interior design revealed the structure of daily life to me, and for the first time, the world started to make sense. That was my favorite thing about it.

Design turned chaos into structure. Even the most seemingly haphazard, carefree arrangement brought with it a feeling of intention, of personality.

It gave me purpose. I'd found my calling.

Then Mike happened.

The first time I met him, he was in the wood-working shop of our design school, sawdust clouding the air, the smell of freshly cut pine burning my nose. The workshop wasn't elegant, but still, the ever-present hands of interior design had arranged it in a utilitarian way. The table saws were separated by exactly three feet each— just enough room for someone carrying a two-by-four to navigate the aisles. A concrete floor hinted at a modern aesthetic. Welded, iron light fixtures hung down in spirals, Edison bulbs searing, burning, like eyes in their centers. A slat in the roof had been removed, creating a skylight, clear plastic letting in just enough sun, breaking its rays into soft, golden strands.

Mike was standing under that skylight when I saw him. It was hard to make him out at first, because so many particles of sawdust clouded the air around him. He wore thick, leather gloves, headphones covering his ears, ripped jeans and a white t-shirt.

You know that saying, "time stood still?"

This wasn't that. Time kept right on moving, the wheels of her bus shredding asphalt, leaving tire tracks in her wake. But there was still something infinite about the moment. Maybe it was the way everyone else in the workshop seemed to disappear, caught up in a strange vignette that made Mike the focal point. Even that slat in the roof seemed to widen, letting in more rays of sun like golden knives, splitting a space in the air, spotlighting Mike with a ferociousness that made me gasp.

I wasn't in love with him. Not at first sight.

I was just curious. Something in me prickled when I saw him, some dark piece of me that wanted to know more. A voice in my chest whispered, *"Be careful, he might not be for you."* But I ignored it, because I was twenty, and he had nice arms, and I could sense— even across the room— that the worst parts of Mike might feed the worst parts of me.

"What are you making?" I didn't remember walking across the room, but apparently I had done it, because now I was standing right in front of him, running my hands over a carved table leg. I knew it was a table leg by the joints. Obviously he was making a table. Any idiot could see that. But even then, with nothing at stake, with nothing to lose, I already sensed that I couldn't be myself with him. I played stupid.

"A table," he smiled as if it was a secret. "See here," he pointed at the top of the leg. "You can tell by the joints."

"Good sense of movement," I said, nodding at the way the tips of the legs spiraled into flared ends.

"I hope so," he answered. His voice sounded humble, but a twitch at the corner of his mouth betrayed him: Mike knew he was talented. Probably the best in class. He was young, and cocky, but there was still a deep insecurity hiding in his eyes; like he knew he was great at making furniture, but he wondered if he was good enough to *love*, and needed someone to tell him so. "It's going to be a Queen Anne," he paused, scanning my face. He opened a sketchbook, pointing to a rough drawing and a swatch of stain. "Traditional is cherry, but I'm going darker, more mahogany. I'm putting iron fasteners on the chairs, adding a bit of an edge. Queen Annes are whimsical, but I thought I could juxtapose that with rougher finishes."

He paused to let me take it all in.

"What do you think?"

"I like it," I told him, even though I thought juxtaposition in general was a little crass. Leave well enough alone and stop trying to reinvent the wheel.

He talked for another hour about the table, and I don't even think he realized I was flirting with him until I asked for his number.

That was when I discovered what it was— the thing that drew me to him, the darkness I needed to explore. I could sense, even from a distance, that the worst parts of Mike might feed the worst parts of me, and now I knew how. Not consciously of course. I wouldn't decode all of this on a conscious level until many years later. In the moment, all I knew was that I wanted him, because he would enable me to self-destruct in the way I'd been craving. Mike's flaws would allow me to explore my own flaws, and I'd be blameless in the whole thing, obscured by a cloak of "love."

Some things you can tell about a person without even needing to know them very long, and already, after just a handful of minutes, here's what I knew about Mike:

Mike loved his work more than anything.

He loved it more than cities. More than oceans. More than planets. And he would certainly love it more than me.

If I'm being honest, Mike wasn't interested in me when we first met. In the same way his presence made the rest of the workshop fade into a vignette, Mike's work made me look like any other girl to him— pale in comparison to table legs and chairs with iron bolts. I never felt like Mike saw what was "special" about me, and I was right, but it wasn't because I *wasn't* special. It was just that he was too busy building furniture to notice anyone at all. A Victoria's Secret model could have walked in the room, and he would only have looked twice if she was carrying a power-tool.

If I could time-travel, I would tell myself to wait for someone else. I'd take college-aged me by the ponytail— the stupid one I used to wear, with the giant scrunchie holding it in place— and set her down with a cup of coffee before giving it to her straight. *Find someone who's obsessed with you, I'd tell her. Find a man who loves you so much he'd take a bullet for you. Don't settle for anyone else.*

Whether we like it or not, relationships live and die on the love of the man. It's just the way the world is structured. A marriage can survive a woman who's only "kind of" in love with her husband, but it won't survive a man who "sort of" loves his wife. That's the key, I've realized, to female happiness in a partnership. Find a man that loves you so much he'd do anything for you. Biologically, this is imperative. We may not live in caves anymore, but one day you'll be pregnant, and tired, and the clock will read "2 a.m.," but you won't be sleeping, because you'll be thinking about vanilla ice-cream from the 24/7 McDonad's down the road. Marry the guy who goes and gets you that ice-cream, even though he's tired, and not sleeping, and worked hard that day, too. Don't marry the guy who rolls over and goes back to sleep. Marry the one who loves you so much, it makes him selfless. Marry the one who will go to war for you, whether it's pregnancy cravings or something more serious. Cleopatra made Antony launch a thousand ships. *Wait for him*, I'd tell younger me. *Wait for the man who launches a thousand ships.*

Sometimes I wonder if that voice inside me— the one that whispered Mike might not be mine— was actually just future me, begging her past self not to make a terrible mistake.

After that moment in the workshop, I *made* our relationship happen. I sought Mike out. I reminded him about our dates. Sure, he cared, he grew attached to me, but the driving engine in our connection was *me*, initiating the plans, watering the plant of our relationship. I want to believe I did this because I loved him, but if we're being honest, that love only grew because of that first dark attraction, the piece of me that wanted the worst of him.

I didn't make our relationship happen because I loved Mike. I made our relationship happen because I was scared shitless of the new, beautiful path I had found for myself. I was afraid interior design wasn't a real career. I was terrified that the glasses I wore would come off at any moment, and I'd lose the ability to make sense out of chaos. What if brick, and oxblood, and cranberry turned back into red? What if my uniqueness— the fact that I'd always been just a little bit "off" as my Dad liked to say— made me fail at the only thing I'd ever been good at? I'd found my path, but it was a scary one to tread, and I wasn't sure I was up to the task.

So I attached myself to Mike, and trusted him to live it for me— for both of us.

He never saw my talent. He never noticed that he wasn't the only one in the room with a bright and promising future. He never acknowledged what I gave up for him, by moving with him to a new city even when we both were aware I wouldn't handle it well.

Even that wouldn't have mattered, if he had just paid some attention to me.

If he had just noticed me.

I don't design any more. Not really, anyway. Occasionally, I'll sit down with a pad of paper and a box of colored pencils, sketching out a room that mirrors how I feel. Cayan and cerulean for the days I can't make sense of things. Pale yellow walls and modern furniture for the sun room I wish I had, the one I would've owned with Mike, in the house we might have gotten, where we would've lived unhappily for decades to come.

Most times, I end up closing the pad and hiding it under my bed. Design requires a person to sit in silence, with no one else around.

I don't like to be alone with myself for too long. But Mike — he doesn't like to be alone either.

They roll over on the sand, and Mike runs his hands through Zoe's hair, pulling on it just a little. I should look away, but instead I lean in closer. I focus on Zoe instead of Mike, wondering what kind of insect she would be if she were a bug instead of a human.

I think about it for awhile, then settle on a cicada. They're a private little bug. Certain species of cicada live underground and only emerge every ten years or so, when they find something worth climbing out of their holes for. From what I've seen, that's Zoe. She's guarded, and she won't let her walls down until someone really special makes her do it. When she does open up, she sings, just like those cicadas on warm summer nights, showing pieces of herself you never knew existed.

Mike and Zoe fade into the darkness, and suddenly the fact that they're together makes me angry. They have no idea I'm up here. They won't bother to check, either. Neither one of them thinks about me at all. Neither one of them notices me, buzzing around them, always waiting, always hoping.

I know what kind of bugs they are.

And in this moment, I wish I could squash them both.

27

ZOE

The next morning, we wake up to the sound of shouting in the distance. Mike and I fell asleep on the beach, our clothes layered on top of us like blankets. In any ordinary circumstances, I'd be afraid of being caught in such an arrangement, but I'm pretty sure we're going to die here anyway. It's funny what you stop caring about when your life is in danger.

The shouts grow louder, and now it's clear: something bad is happening back at the tents.

We get dressed in a hurry and run toward the campsite, fearing the worst. Mike doesn't even bother putting on his pants, making a run for it in nothing but his boxers. When we get there, the fire's died down, but the group is gathered in a circle around the charred pyre.

"Everyone okay?" Mike asks, out of breath.

"We found another one," Tori says, pointing to the center of the circle, where a silver box sits, unopened. Just like the last clue, a red "X" is painted on its lid.

"Did you open it?" I ask. Everyone shakes their heads.

I crouch down, my knees sinking into the sand. The box clinks when I open it, reminding me of wind chimes in the summer. I peel the lid away and set it aside, reaching into the box and pulling out its contents.

"It's a wallet," Oliver sighs, relieved. The last box didn't do him any favors. I can understand his concerns about this one.

"Open it up," Alicia urges, prim and bossy even when we're stranded in the middle of nowhere.

I unfold the wallet. It's a slim, light-weight model made from cheap vinyl, with rubber bands where there should be credit card holders. There's no stamp on the outside advertising a certain brand, no designer label. It's peeling on the edges, begging to be replaced. Whoever owns it isn't rich.

The interior pocket doesn't house any cash, proving my theory. There's no credit cards or ATM cards to speak of either, but the rubber bands intended to hold cards in place are loose and saggy, as if they once were used. Someone must have removed whatever cards used to call the wallet home.

I turn the wallet over and a crumpled collection of papers falls out. They were jammed in the section intended for cash, stuffed into the bottom as an after-thought.

"Notes?" Donald asks, leaning over my shoulder.

"Receipts," I lay them flat on a nearby rock, smoothing out the wrinkles. The ink is faded, but I can still make out certain pieces.

"They're all from the last few days," I say, straining to read the faded type. "This one's from an electronics store in Burbank. Hard Drives. Batteries."

I set it aside, moving onto the next receipt. "This one is from a shoe store. One pair, from the men's department," I add, not sure what it all means yet.

"This one is so wrinkled, I can't quite..." I strain, trying to make out the words on the third receipt, but they're faded into oblivion. I pass it to Mike, who holds it up to the sun, squinting.

"Wow," Mike says, his eyebrows raising in surprise.

"What is it?" Lana asks.

"It's from a steakhouse," he shrugs. "Someone spent seventy dollars at a steakhouse."

"Sounds good to me," Donald sighs, wistful, rubbing his ample belly.

"What's weird is they only ordered one entree. A steak. A side of mashed potatoes. A very expensive glass of wine. A piece of cake for dessert." Mike pauses, thinking. "Who goes to a steakhouse alone?"

"Me," Jason steps forward, reaching out for the receipt. "Let me see it."

Mike passes the receipt to Jason, who looks it over.

"The wallet is mine. These receipts are mine."

"Why didn't you say something sooner?" Tori gasps, horrified at her partner's silence.

Jason shrugs. "As you've so often pointed out, I don't pay much attention to my fashion choices. It's a plain black wallet. I didn't know it was mine until Mike mentioned the steakhouse."

"You went to a stake house alone?" Tori's eyes widen, and she grabs the receipt out of his hand. "This is dated the day before the wedding!" She stares at him, betrayed. "You told me you were going to a candlelight yoga class!"

"I needed a break, okay?" Jason says, exasperated. "You *know* how hard it is being in front of the camera all the time. I just wanted to reconnect with my higher purpose!"

"By eating a defenseless animal?"

"It was *one* time," Jason shouts.

They're about to get into a full-blown couple's fight, but I step between them, raising a hand.

"Why?" I ask, looking at Jason.

"Why what?"

"Why is your wallet in the box?"

"I have no idea," he says, looking just as confused as the rest of us.

"These receipts are supposed to tell us something useful. What do they mean?"

"I don't know!" Jason shakes his head, exasperated. "How the fuck should I know what some maniac wants you to think about my *trash*? They're receipts from one day. I got shoes, picked up some equipment I needed, and yes..." he looks at Tori, annoyed, "Had a steak. So sue me."

"There must be something he wants us to know!" I'm pacing now, frustrated at my own inability to understand the message. "Logan doesn't do anything without a purpose. It's all pre-planned, all pre-arranged. There must be *something* we're missing."

Jason steps forward, and— for a second— the carefree, bohemian mask he wears slips away. What's left behind is the face of a man who isn't an artist but an entertainer. The sort of person who can take the truth and reflect it back to you in a way that suits him best.

"Maybe what he wants," Jason says, eyes cold, "Is to distract you with some bullshit that means nothing at all."

He grabs the wallet from my hands, marching across the sand toward the beach. Tori runs after him, her much shorter legs taking twice as long to keep up with his stride.

"Jason!" She shouts.

He doesn't turn around.

"What do you think it means?" Mike asks, worried. "The wallet. The receipts? What are we missing."

I could try to make sense of it, to look for meaning, but instead, I go with the truth. "Honestly," I tell him. "I have no idea."

28

CASSANDRA

Receipts?

When Logan added Jason's wallet to the list of items I needed to steal from the wedding, I figured he wanted it to use his credit cards.

What a waste of my talents, sending me out to grab some crappy, meaningless pieces of paper. Asshole. If he wanted to put Zoe on the wrong trail, he could have come up with something else.

Jason stays by the water all morning, battling it out with Tori. In the meantime, everyone goes about their business, trying to give the pair some privacy. We can't hear much of their argument back at camp, except for some garbled words like "liar" and "useless." Tori's need to get to the bottom of Jason's solo dinner tells me she's worried he wasn't alone when he ordered that steak. Idiot. Why waste time pining after a guy who can only be in love with himself? At least by chasing Mike, I'm desperately craving someone who can love. He just doesn't love *me*.

Later, Tori and Jason make their way back toward camp, looking weathered, but holding hands.

Our group gathers for lunch in awkward silence, munching on the packaged, preservative-laden nutrition bars Logan left on the island. When Logan and I chose the food we'd leave for everyone, I though it sounded like a fun adventure to live on the bare necessities. But now that I'm here, I would kill for a bag of spicy hot Cheetos. I silently curse myself for not sneaking a bag into the bottom of the cooler when I had a chance.

"Nice, in't?" Oliver says, completely out of nowhere. His words shatter the uncomfortable silence we've all settled into. He nods toward the ocean. "Wonder what it would've been like, to be out there a few hundred years ago?"

Rachel rolls her eyes. "You wouldn't be able to fly planes!"

Oliver nods. "True, but I'd have found something else to captain."

"A pirate ship, perhaps," Francois exchanges a smile with Mike. It's the most he's said in hours. He's quiet, like me. I wonder if he ever worries about whether people notice him.

"I like the sound of it!" Oliver laughs, brandishing a fake sword. "Captain No-Pants, the fiercest pirate on the sea."

"Ah, no my friend," Francois shakes his head. "*La Buse* was the fiercest pirate on the sea. They say he buried his treasure in the Seychelles. It waits to be found."

"Bollocks!" Oliver shouts. Rachel slaps his arm.

"Oliver!"

"I'm sorry, but those stories are all rubbish. They're quite the wild goose chase. Meant to keep us all running around."

Francois' face hardens. I recognize that expression. It's the one a person makes when he's spent his whole life being looked at like he's crazy. I can relate.

"Francois is an archaeologist," Zoe says. "He's one of the only ones in the world who specializes on the Seychelles."

"If you're a serious archaeologist, why are you wasting time on hunting treasure? Shouldn't you be looking for like, serious historical stuff?" Tori asks, always happy to seize an opportunity to be contrarian.

"This is serious," Francois replies, curt. "If I can't personally locate these items and ensure their safe return to a museum here in the Seychelles, they will undoubtedly be found by another party and shipped abroad, to some concrete, foreign monstrosity." He pauses, as if deciding whether it's worth proving himself to this group of idiots. "Do you still have it?" Francois asks Mike.

Mike reaches into the pocket of his jeans, fishing out a piece of paper. He passes it to Francois, who holds it up in front of Oliver. Symbols mark its surface— triangles, squares, and circles arranged in lines.

"What is it?" Donald asks, leaning in.

"Proof that this story is based on science. *This* story is true."

"I've seen those before," Alicia says, voice soft. Everyone stops eating.

"In a book?" Francois asks, deeply curious.

"No., Alicia stutters, like she wishes she could backtrack. "I saw them here. When we were looking for clues."

Francois stands. His shoulders don't move at all, and I'm pretty sure he's stopped breathing. His voice comes out like fire and ice.

"Where?"

"Over there," Alicia points North, toward the part of the beach where the passage narrows. Ghost-like, legs shaking, Francois walks toward the sea. When he realizes no one is following him, he stops and looks over his shoulder. The waves crash in the distance, their roaring call filling his silence.

He waits. One by one, everyone in our party rises. Alicia is the last to stand.

"I could have been mistaken," she murmurs, voice timid, but Francois won't let her take back what she's said.

"Show me." This man is as obsessive about ancient treasure as I am about Mike. It makes me curious about him. Maybe if I can get inside Francois' head and understand what makes him tick, I could figure out the workings of my own brain.

Alicia heads for the beach at Francois' prompting. Our entire party follows, single file, trudging behind them. Somehow, I find myself in line behind Mike. The back of the t-shirt he's wearing has a tiny hole in it, and I remember it's one had when we were together. It's an old college shirt, the kind men never throw away.

Mike turns and looks at me. His eyes darken when he catches me staring. He speeds up to walk next to Rachel, ruining the symmetry of our perfect straight line. A knife stabs through my heart, but I ignore it. I've wanted so long to get some time with him, and now that I have it, I don't know what to say. He wouldn't listen, anyway. This is exactly why I need Logan to deliver him to me— so I can tie him to that chair and make him see our relationship through my eyes. He would make this so much easier on both of us if he'd just notice me.

After a long, silent stroll, Alicia stops in place. She points at a rock formation where the beach becomes the ocean.

"Here, I think," she says, straining to recall. "Or maybe, that one, over there? I'm not sure," she turns to Donald as if this is all far too overwhelming for one person to handle. She really is an obnoxious human. She can't handle the smallest imposition without becoming a victim. It's a good thing Donald is rich. Alicia probably needs help with everything she does, whether it's getting dressed or eating dinner.

Francois examines the rock formation, climbing over the uneven terrain, laser-focused on what he's looking for. Zoe goes to help him, along with Lana, and it's not long before half our group is scattered over the rocks, weaving in and out as they search.

"Now I can't tell. What if I'm wrong?" Alicia's lower lip trembles, like a child crying over a broken toy.

"Mike! This is too much to ask of her," Donald tugs at his hair. He gets deeply involved in Alicia's dramas. Together, they are actors in a play, letting banal, ordinary discomforts become a soap opera. Mike is usually cast as the villain. His greatest crime is existing.

"What am I supposed to do about it?" Mike answers.

Alicia gasps. Donald's mouth drops open. I stifle a laugh. Mike looks at me, and for a second— just a second— we make eye contact. There's a recognition of a shared past, because Mike and I both know what an earth-shattering event this is. Mike never stands up to his relatives. Never.

As quickly as it came, the moment leaves. Mike looks away, leaving me empty again. He turns to his aunt and uncle.

"What—" Donald starts to say something, but Mike cuts him off.

"Life is hard. Get over it," he says, simply. Alicia looks like he's slapped her. Mike leaves them to join the search, scanning the rocks with the rest of the group.

Hours go by, and I'm starting to wonder if maybe Alicia made the whole thing up for attention when a shout echoes from further down the beach.

Rick waves a hand in the air. Francois runs toward him, and the entire group gathers around a jagged, icicle-shaped rock. It's porous and uneven, but on the back of its edge is a small section that's been spared from the attacking salt water. It's smoother than the other rocks.

"Look at this," Rick motions to Francois, who leans in closer.

A series of symbols have been carved into the smooth portion of the rock's backside. They've faded over the years, barely perceptible now, the depth of the carvings growing shallower by the day. They're whispers of their former selves, but they're there, and they're real.

Francois holds up the paper he showed us at the campsite, comparing it to the symbols.

It's a perfect match.

"*La Buse,*" he whispers, and suddenly my predicament just got a whole lot more interesting.

I'm just not just trapped on an island with a group of people who don't know I betrayed them. I'm trapped on an island with *treasure.*

29

ZOE

"It's been hours. He's obsessed," I say to Mike, who's using a rock to break a piece of wood into pieces. Sweat gathers on his forehead.

"Well, you can't blame the man. His family's been on about it for generations. Do you remember when he said that's why Oxford let him go?"

"No," I answer, genuinely unsure. "When did he say that?"

"On the way back to his place. You were walking ahead. He was embarrassed. Turns out he's a bit of a joke in the archeological community."

I glance over at Francois, who's crouched beside Cassandra. The two of them are in hushed conversation, analyzing the facsimile of the paper with La Buse's symbols on it.

"Cassandra is helping him."

"Does that surprise you? She *needs* something to obsess over. Let's just be glad it's not us. Maybe it'll last a whole hour and I'll get some peace."

"How can Francois worry about finding treasure? Does he understand it won't matter if we're dead?" His obsession with the treasure irritates me because of its impracticality. It's an affront to the natural order of human priorities, which dictates that survival comes first, and objects come last. "Let's say he *does* find it. We'll be stuck on this island, starving to death, surrounded by a bunch of gold and silver. We'll have nothing to eat. No shelter. No water. No escape. But hey, we'll have *gold!*"

"Zoe," Mike puts down he rock he's holding, flexing his arm. He looks worn out. "Not to play devil's advocate here, but I'm trying to build a raft from four materials, and you're hunting clues left behind by maniac game-master. Are we really in a position to judge?"

"He's distracting Cassandra. This means I have to look for clues alone."

"My aunt and uncle will go with you."

"Like I said, I'll be alone."

Mike smiles. "Do you want to take Tori? Or your Mom?"

On a log at the end of the campsite, my Mom and Tori are hard at work, weaving palm leaves into rope. "No. They're fine. Your raft might be the best chance we have at getting off this rock." The raft Mike's building is only about two feet long so far. It's a scrap of a thing, uneven and splintered. I won't say it outlaid, but so far, it's unimpressive.

"That's bad news," he says, grimacing.

"You can build anything."

"With tools." He crosses his arms, looking at the pile of wood in front of him as if willing it into a different form. "This is..." he pauses. "I'm trying. I won't quit until I'm dead. But even if I can get something together that will withstand the water, I don't know."

"What?"

"I don't know if it will fit everyone."

"It has to fit everyone."

"It might not," he runs a hand though his hair. "If that happens, one person has to go. The rest of us might have to stay." He pauses. "I think it should be you."

"That's not an option."

"It may be our *only* option."

The idea of going out to sea on a raft— looking over my shoulder at Mike and everyone I love still stranded on a beach— is something I can't stomach. Whatever happens, we can't let it come to that. We have to find the name of the person working with Logan and type into that boat.

The possibilities arrange themselves in a neat little line inside my head. Mike would never betray me, and neither would my Mom. Tori has been my best friend for twenty years. She can be shallow, and so hungry for love that she'll put her own interests aside in a desperate attempt to gain a man's affection. But I know she would never do anything to hurt me. That leaves Oliver, who came into our family a mere year ago. He's lovely and charming on the outside, but I haven't known him long enough to feel confident in his intentions. And when you factor in the life insurance policy, and the fact that he met my Mom right after Mike and I were lost in Yosemite, there's a reason to ask questions. Donald and Alicia are potential suspects as well, but only because they're selfish. Then again, being selfish doesn't make them criminals. Cassandra is another legacy from Mike's past, but we thought she was to blame for Yosemite and were proven wrong. It's unlikely she's involved. Rick's behavior at the wedding certainly shows he's angry at Mike, and doesn't approve of our wedding. But would that really cause him to work with Logan? Lana doesn't know us very well, which makes her seem innocent. The same could be said for Jason. What reason would either have to hurt us?

In fact, I can't think of *anything* that would motivate

someone in our group to work with Logan. And even if someone here *is* working with Logan, why strand themselves on this island? What's the end-game? Are they planning to die with us? Or to reveal themselves at the proper moment?

I can't shake the nagging feeling that the answer is right in front of me, and I'm overlooking it. My only move is to look for another silver box— to play the game.

MY FEET DIG into the sand as I walk toward the campsite. Donald and Alicia are huddled on a log, splitting a bottle of water. They're whispering about something, talking in hushed voices.

"Too late, now," Donald says, the words coming out in a rushed cascade. "It would only serve to distract from—"

The moment he sees me, Donald shuts up. Whatever they're talking about, they don't want to share. Their position on my list of subjects changes.

"Did I interrupt?"

Donald doesn't say anything. Alicia comes to his rescue, an expert at girl-on-girl manipulation.

"We were just talking about the boys' tennis game," she lies like a pro. "And how worried they must be that we're not home."

"Ready to search?" I ask.

Alicia flips her hair. The ends are sticking together. It's the first time I've seen her look less than perfect. It's nice.

"How far are we walking today?" Her bottom lip sticks out, pouty and truculent.

"As fas as we need too. Until we find a silver box."

"Are we going to die on this island?" Her voice shakes,

and she looks at Donald for reassurance. He puts an arm around her.

"I don't know," I say, not really caring. "Better look hard."

I turn and walk into the trees. Leaves crunch behind me, letting me know that they've followed me.

The three of us search for hours, trying to cover the ground we missed yesterday. To Alicia's credit, she genuinely does look hard. She's motivated this time around, like she's suddenly realized that solving Logan's puzzle is our only way to get off this rock.

Finally, I notice the edge of a silver box, poking around a split in a tree where two branches go in opposite directions. Alicia helps me pull it down, and Donald opens up the top.

"What am I looking at?" He says, removing something familiar, something I've seen before.

It's a long, pink sash. The sash my bridesmaids wore.

My heart pounds, and I know what will be on the inside. Still, I need to see it.

"Flip it over," I tell Donald. He shrugs, flipping the sash one-hundred-and-eighty degrees. Inside, the number "20" has been hand-stitched in a dark, red thread.

"Twenty?" Alicia asks, confused.

"It's how long Tori and I have known each other." I remove the sash from Donald's fat fingers, handling it like an explosive.

"The texture feels different," I say, folding it in half. "There's something inside."

White thread stitches the sash's lining to its border. It's a thread that looks foreign to the overall design, like it was added later to mend a tear. It screams as I pull it apart, a terrible ripping sound emanating from the fabric.

A hole forms between the front and the back of the sash.

Inside, a piece of paper lies, waiting. It's a single page, unassuming, folded into a square. Whatever it says won't be good for me. It won't help me. If Logan hid this piece of paper inside the sash, it's only because he knew it would weaken me.

I pull it out, and begin to read.

30

CASSANDRA

I'm in another world. Francois has captivated me. Not with his body. Not with his mind. But with his story.

"Tell me again," I ask him. We're climbing over the rock formation, looking for more symbols, hunting for treasure.

Francois laughs. He's told me the story of La Buse three times now. He's beginning to notice that I'm not quite right, that I have this need to buzz around things. But I'm the only person on this island interested in helping him with his search, so he's stuck with me. He doesn't seem to mind.

"It will be long to repeat," he says. There's a smile in his eyes. He's teasing me, making me prove that I want to hear it again.

"Just the ending, then," I urge.

"If we must," he sighs, even though we both know he loves telling the story as much as I love hearing it. "We are at the point in the story where La Buse had betrayed his men. He was about to be executed..."

"Preparing to die!" I hold out an invisible sword like a pirate.

Francois faces me, also conjuring a fake-sword from midair. "Yes," he says. "Preparing to die!" Francois pretends to lunge at me. I dodge the blow. He turns, and we continue searching. "But La Buse was not to go quietly," Francois says. "He threw a document with symbols etched on its face into the crowd and shouted—"

"I killed the rabbit!"

"*No,*" Francois shakes his head. "*J'ai posé un lapin.* I put a rabbit to him. Which means—"

"He broke a date."

"Yes. Or, more accurately, he did not keep his promises."

"What an asshole!"

"Absolutely," Francois says. "Look over there, keep searching, yes?" He poses it as a question, but Francois is quite singular in his focus. It's more of a demand, a hunger, a thirst, a need. This is a feeling I can relate to.

Francois, if he were a bug, would be a moth, patient and steady, but not particularly concerned with anything except the flame he circles. It's too bad. How strange, would it feel, if someone like Francois could turn that obsession toward me?

But he won't. I thought I caught him looking at me in *that* way more than once, but as I watch him scan the rocks for symbols, I realize I was mistaken. Someone as smart, as clever, as him would never bother to notice me. This man will never love anything as much as he does this treasure. He could never notice someone like me— someone so invisible— when the promise of priceless artifacts lies so close. He hasn't even asked me why I'm helping him.

If Francois *were* to ask me why I'm helping him, maybe I'd tell him the truth. It helps that he's attractive, a fun, fitting distraction. But that's not the reason I'm here. It's also not about money, or riches. Francois has made it clear he intends to keep the artifacts in a museum, here on the Seychelles, where he says they belong. It's not even about the fact that I'm a bee— the kind of person who needs something to circle, to suck pollen from.

No, I'm looking for the treasure because Mike won't notice me. Even here, on an island, where we're trapped together, he refuses to look my way. He won't invest in my every move, won't deign to give me the attention I so freely offer him.

"J'ai un posé lapin."

La Buse is not the only guilty party, here. I know another man who didn't keep a date. Finding the treasure is a chance to get back at him. I imagine the ghost of La Buse watching me pull his precious treasure from the ground. I picture him — helpless, seething— as I take those priceless objects as my own. Rubies. Diamonds. Necklaces that touch the ground. The crew he betrayed cheers, because they were stood up, just like me. They were stood up by a man who didn't keep his promises.

Suddenly, his figure morphs into Mike, ghost-like and tortured. He watches me— dripping in gems, coated in gold — admiration in his eyes.

Maybe, if I find the treasure of La Buse, Mike will realize I'm not crazy. Maybe he'll see what makes me special. The way I notice things others don't. My eye for detail, for shapes, for patterns. In college, I always hoped Mike would acknowledge my brilliance. I showed him my designs, my sketches— but all he ever cared about was his own work. *His* tables. *His* chairs. Maybe if I find the treasure, Mike will see me for what I am.

Maybe, if I find the treasure, he'll notice me.

If I find the treasure, I'll buzz around it in circles, spiraling into its golden glow, letting it make me larger. Its light will engorge my yellow tummy, tripling my size, making me into a remarkable creature unlike any other. The treasure will feed me.

Mike will look at me— dripping in gems, coated in gold — and see my value. He'll notice me. He'll realize my obsessive nature isn't a weakness, but as an asset. "She did it," he'll say. "She found the treasure because of her oddness. No one could have done it but her. My girl."

For once, he'll see why bees matter.

Don't make it about Mike, I say to myself.

But I can't help it.

31

———

ZOE

"**I**s it true?"

Tori stands in front of a pile of palm fronds. They've been shucked clean, the driest leaves discarded into a cemetery of crunchy bodies. The green, stronger pieces are set aside, waiting to be woven into rope for Mike's raft. The team in charge of building the raft— Mike, Tori, and my Mom— have created an assembly line. It's impressive. If I weren't so angry, I'd tell them so.

"Zoe—"

Tori looks up from the paper and the sash. She's holding both in one hand, her arm stretched out in front of her like she's touching radioactive waste.

"It was an opportunity to get Jason some publicity!"

"And that justifies selling us out?"

"Selling *who* out?" Mike appears behind me, collecting the makeshift rope. I grab the piece of paper from Tori— who looks relieved to be rid of it— and pass it to Mike. He reads.

"An email?"

"An email from Tori," I tell him, seething. "To a paparazzi who claimed to be from the *Sun Times*."

"Is that the one you read in the bathtub sometimes?" Mike asks. I ignore him.

"She sold our guest list!"

"Not sold!" Tori cries, eyes watering. "It's just *such* a great story," she throws her hands up in the air. "'Couple, stalked in Yosemite, finally finds their happy ending!' And the fact that you had a celebrity attendee meant the world needed to know."

"We had a celebrity at our wedding?" Mike asks, looking to me to verify. He's genuinely sorry to have missed this mysterious celebrity presence at our wedding.

"She means *Jason*."

"Oh. Does he count?"

Tori gasps, offended. Mike doesn't mean anything by it. He doesn't know anything about online influencers. Mike is a luddite in every sense of the word. He doesn't even have an instagram for his furniture business.

"She reached out to me *because* she heard Jason might be attending," Tori says. "She thought it was a great angle. A celebrity influencer who deals with meta questions of privacy attending the wedding of two people who have had their privacy violated unwillingly in major way, in front of the entire world? It's a cool take."

"That's," Mike pauses, searching. "An interesting way of looking at it."

"Exactly!" Tori says, mistaking the concerned furrow between Mike's eyes for approval. "I've been working so hard to get major outlets to understand why what Jason does is so important. And this was a major breakthrough."

"You *knew* we were trying to keep our wedding quiet," I say to Tori, shaking the email in her face. "Our *lives* were in danger in Yosemite. It wasn't a PR stunt. It was a real, terrible thing that happened to us. We *told* you we were worried about Logan waiting, somewhere, for a chance to try again."

"I figured he'd never try again with so much attention on it. You said the FBI was hunting him down!"

"You cared more about making sure Jason gets famous than protecting our safety!"

"It was just the guest list!" Tori shouts. "This reporter wouldn't cover it without a who's-who! And it didn't matter anyway because she never showed up, did she?"

"You don't get it."

Tori's eyes widen, searching for what she's missing,

"She didn't show up because she wasn't real."

"I—"

"Logan made a fake identity and reached out to you because he *knew* you'd be desperate to get Jason covered in the media. He wanted the guest list so he'd know who the most important people in our lives are."

Tori shakes her head. "That can't be true."

"Look around, Tori. Everyone here was either in our wedding party, or seated at the friends and family table. Did you research this woman? Make a call? Verify her identity before you gave away our personal information?"

Tori's silence says everything.

"That's what I thought." The words slide out of my mouth like poison. They take on a life of their own, out of my control, hot, sticky lava. "It's your fault we're all here."

"Zoe, I'm—" Tori's crying now, still holding the sash with the number twenty sewn inside. "I'm so sorry. I've been trying to live more freely, be less concerned about privacy. You know, because of Jason and his—"

"Bullshit?" Mike says.

"—ideology," Tori counters. "I never meant to hurt you."

I crumple the email into a ball, throwing it at Tori's feet. She can say what she wants, but now, I know whose name will answer Logan's riddle.

When I go to type a name into the boat, I'll only need four letters.

T-O-R-I.

32

CASSANDRA

Francois and I are still searching by the rocks when I notice it: a silver box. It's smaller than the others. This one is about a half a foot long, and only a few inches tall.

For a moment, I think it's treasure and imagine myself parading in front of Mike, covered in silver and gold, dripping in gemstones. But then I remember Logan's game, and the clues, and I know exactly what's in the box. Sure enough, I open the box and find a familiar object inside.

The gun. I stole it myself. I liked it when I saw it at the wedding— liked the way holding it made me feel. It was different from any other gun I'd ever seen. After only a couple days on the island, that feels like a lifetime ago. I knew Logan had instructed the kidnappers he hired to leave it somewhere on the island, but wasn't sure where. Now that we've reunited, it feels like fate. Maybe the gun was always meant to be mine.

I *should* share my discovery with the others. But the gun is so pretty. So powerful.

Francois is on the other side of the rocks.

"Cassandra?" He calls, a nervous edge to his voice. Could it be that he's worried about me? Unlikely. He's probably worried I've found the treasure and run off with it.

He shouts my name again, trying to figure out where I've gone off to. The seconds tick by— time is running out. If I don't hide the box now, Francois will see it and tell the others I've found another clue.

The gun looks up at me, innocent, pleading. It wants to be useful. It wants to help me. There's no way I'm getting off this island on my own. I'm convinced Logan won't come back for me— another man who won't keep his promises. That leaves me to rely on the group. Zoe's going to figure out I'm the one who helped Logan put her here, and when she does, she'll leave me behind to die. That's a best case scenario. The worst case scenario is that the others stone me to death.

A gun could come in handy.

Without thinking too much about it, I slip the box into my pocket. My pants are baggy; the loose, comfortable kind with wide, masculine pockets meant to hold things rather than be fashionable. The gun my pants down, making them hang lower around my waist. It's comforting, feeling the heft of the gun in my pockets.

Maybe diamonds aren't a girl's best friend after all.

Francois appears over the edge of the rock. He clutches his chest when he sees me. "I thought, perhaps, you had washed out to sea!" He exclaims, totally unaware that I've found another clue. I push the box aside, out of view.

Later, Francois and I sit on the rocks together, taking a break from the search. We're back where we started, seated near the symbols Alicia found. Francois runs a finger over them, stopping at each tail.

"And you're sure they don't say anything? Not in other language even?"

"I believe they are a map," he shakes his head. "They match no known alphabet."

He traces the edges, rehashing a conversation we've had a dozen times.

"I believe they are directional symbols. A compass. The points of the tails tell you which way to go."

"But they contradict each other," I say. "This one says straight. That one says toward the mountains."

"We walked in order, yes? Perhaps it's a matter of how far."

I stand, exasperated. "How can you be like this?" I'm practically shouting at him.

"Like what? Intoxicating? Wonderful to be around?"

"So— *calm*!" The word comes out like a curse. "Doesn't it frustrate you? Not getting what you want?" I motion at the island, its infinite possibilities exposed in full relief. "This place is *mocking* us!"

Francois laughs. His reaction makes me even angrier.

"Stop that!" I shout. "It's not funny! We've looked all day and haven't found a thing. I know you're as obsessed with this as I am."

"More," he agrees.

"Then how can you just *sit* here? Aren't you angry?"

Francois shakes his head. "Life is just life. Nature is just nature."

"But it's not giving you what you want!" My voice climbs and suddenly this isn't about the treasure anymore, but Mike, and the fact that he's with Zoe, and the way he ignores me. Why won't he give me what I want and look at me, at least once?

I just want him to see me.

"If I had everything I wanted, I would not have to try," Francois says. "Then what would be the point of this life, no?"

"You're not even supposed to be here," I say, frustrated at his refusal to react. "You don't know anyone on this island! You should be furious that you're here."

"Yes, but look where it brought me."

"To the treasure," I answer.

"And to more, perhaps" he says, not caring to explain further.

His quiet, calm exterior— the one that used to appeal to me—suddenly infuriates me. I want to push him against the rocks and beat him. I wish I could take all my rage— all my anger at Mike— and send it careening into Francois like a laser. Instead, I pick up a handful of sand, forming it into a ball. My arm pulls back, releasing the ball at the perfect point. It sails through the air slamming against the rocks where the symbols lay, falling apart into thousands of tiny shards.

"Do you feel better?" he says. Then, we're both laughing. Laughing at the treasure. At our predicament. At life. My rage melts away. Francois has diffused it, somehow, just by being himself. I sit beside him, looking out at the sea.

"You are so angry, at not getting what you want."

"Yes," I say.

"It is not about the island."

"No," I want to explain, but it's impossible to tell him the story without making him hate me. "I'm just looking for— closure."

"Perhaps whoever you seek answers from will never give them to you. But you will have spent your whole life wanting."

"You've spent decades seeking a treasure that might not

even exist," I say, shaking my head. "What would you know about it?"

"That's where you are wrong," Francois says, quietly. "You think I am obsessed with the finding the treasure. With wealth. But no. I am captivated by protecting it from harm."

"You want to put it in a museum."

"Yes," he says. "Even if I spend my life trying and fail, it will have been for a good cause. Can you say the same?"

"I don't know." I pause, wondering how Francois contains his emotions, where he puts them. "Why are you spending time with me?"

"You don't find you own company interesting enough to warrant attention?" He shakes his head, embarrassed for me.

"Why?" I ask again.

He shrugs. "Your soul is like mine in the ways that matter, and different in the ways that don't. It interests me."

We leave it at that. The gun sits heavy in my pocket, and suddenly I feel guilty for lying to Francois, like I owe him some piece of myself I'm not ready to give away, yet.

33

ZOE

Sand kicks up behind me as I rush toward the little boat. It's parked on the beach, just out of the tide's reach. Lana, Jason, and Oliver are sitting against its metal side, taking a break from examining the engine. They're too relaxed. They've forgotten what's inside. A single faulty wire. An incorrect word entered on the keypad. It would take so little to make the boat blow. But this is what happens when you work around danger for an extended period of time: you get desensitized.

On a grander scale, this is what has happened to me. *I am desensitized.* I've been stalked in Yosemite. I've been tortured. I've been betrayed. And now, it's happening again. And I can't take anymore. I want off this island.

Right. Now.

"Zoe," Lana says, surprised. "We've been looking at the way the cords tie into the engine— "

"No luck yet," Oliver adds. "But we're working on an idea— "

"It doesn't matter." I push them aside, leaning over the

metal frame. I take off my shoes, stepping into the boat barefoot, my weight making it lean. The others gasp.

"What are you doing?" Lana cries out, horrified.

"I know who's been working with Logan," I say, simply.

"Who?" Jason asks, taking a step back.

My hand shakes as I slip into the driver's seat, leaning over the keyboard and the tiny black box that sits passenger side. They're shiny. Inviting. Daring me to touch them.

Just then, Mike arrives, my Mom and Tori right behind him.

"Zoe," my Mom croaks, "Get out of that boat right now!"

I don't listen to her. Instead, I pick up the keyboard, settling it into my lap.

"Zoe!" Mike shouts. I've never heard him sound this way. It's a mix of fear and anger. Mike never gets angry, at least not at me.

"I know who did it," I say simply, staring at the keyboard. It's hypnotizing. The little black squares. Pieces of plastic that can say everything. An odd calm washes over me. If I'm right, we'll get to leave the island. If I'm wrong, and the boat blows, I'll still get to leave the island, just in a different way.

"Stand back," I say. Jason moves away, taking Tori with him. His camera is still attached to his hand, and he's raised it in the air, screen extended, filming me. Tori notices and tries to pull his arm down, but he doesn't budge. Behind them, Donald and Alicia stand in stunned silence. Alicia hides behind Donald, pushing him forward ever so slightly. Everyone else stays in place.

"Let's talk it out," Lana says, touching my arm. I move away. She's too gentle. Too kind. Her softness hurts. "Aren't you afraid you might be wrong?"

She has a point. But I'm not afraid. Whatever piece of

me used to feel fear has been replaced by something else. Something numb. Something finished.

"Get her out of the boat!" My Mom is slapping Mike's arm, frantic.

"Zoe, *get out!*" Mike takes off his shoes and piles them next to mine, preparing to get in with me. I don't have much time.

I type in the first letter.

T-

Sobbing fills the air. It's Tori, crying. "It wasn't me! Zoe, I promise, it wasn't! Please!"

O-

Mike is in the boat now, and he's going to try and pull me out. Time is of the essence.

R-

Only one letter left. Something in me asks me to wait, to be patient, to hold off until we find the rest of the clues. But I've *been* waiting. Since that week in Yosemite, I've been waiting to leave the forest. Waiting to feel normal again. Waiting to become something like the person I used to be.

I'm done waiting.

I-

The final letter makes a clicking noise when I hit they key. My finger hovers above the "return" button, the final step.

It's all that separates me from freedom.

34

CASSANDRA

The crazy bitch is going to blow herself up.

Francois and I make our way across the beach just in time to see Zoe climbing into the boat. "Has she found the word?" Francois asks, hopeful. I shake my head, pointing behind the boat. Tori is shouting, waving her arms. Her face is contorted in a round, sorrowful scream. She's red with guilt. "I don't think so," I tell him, because now, I know:

Zoe must have found the sash.

I don't know what Logan paired it with, but I understand enough now to guess how the game works. She thinks Tori is the one who worked with Logan. She thinks her best friend betrayed her.

The situation makes me pause for a moment, because it's not *all* bad. At least, not all bad for me. If Zoe dies, no one else on this island will solve the mystery. It was tailor-made for her. Logan said as much. They'll never know who's to blame.

I silently curse myself for following his lead. Why didn't I ask more questions? If I had, I would have realized he was planning to use my name as the answer to his riddle, driving Zoe crazy in the interim.

Mike climbs into the boat, trying not to let it sway beneath his feet. It moves side-to-side. The two of them are creating a huge disturbance, making it rock on the sand. The inertia alone might make the bomb blow. A wrong answer isn't even necessary.

What would my life be like, if Mike and Zoe died in this moment?

I've buzzed around them for so long that I can't imagine a world without them. I picture their house, put up to market. A "For Sale" sign in the front yard. Their furniture sold, piece by piece. A tragic write-up in the LA Times about the young couple who escaped death once, only to meet it again. I'd sit underneath their window— the one outside the kitchen— listening, waiting. But a new family would live there. Their stories wouldn't interest me. I would miss Zoe's laugh. The way Mike sighs when he's bored. The purpose they gave me.

Would I be happier, if they didn't exist?

You can't buzz around another person if they're not alive anymore. Maybe their deaths would free me. I wouldn't even have to work at it. No effort would be required on my end. It would be like I was never sick in the first place.

Mike puts his arm around Zoe's chest. He's going to try and lift her out of the boat. But her finger is already over the "return" button. He won't move her in time. She's beat him. She's faster.

For a moment, I remember sitting by the fire, seeing my own reflection in Zoe's eyes. The way her hair looked like mine. The strange, familiar feeling that we'd known each other long before Mike entered the world. It's hard to put my finger on what the feeling meant, except that we benefit from some shared past. Not *because* of Mike, but outside of him. A primal, familiar sisterhood— one that exists because we do.

If Zoe were gone— if she were dead— Mike might notice me more often.

But then I remember what Francois said, and I think about how I've spent so much of my life waiting for Mike to look my way again. I wonder if that's a good cause.

The little silver box is smooth against my hand as I step forward, removing it from my pocket.

"Stop!" my voice rings across the sand with an authority it's never possessed before. Zoe freezes. The box catches the sunlight, reflecting a glare off its edges.

Francois stares at me, clearly wondering where I found the box and why I didn't tell him.

"You need to see this," I call out to Zoe, the words burning my throat. "It will change your mind."

There's a long silence. Zoe takes me in, scanning my form, wondering if she can trust me. She knows she can't. But that same connection we felt by the fire overrides her doubts. She won't leave this Earth without hearing me out. She'll make sure I'm seen, that my opinion is considered important. She won't render me voiceless.

She climbs out of the boat. Her legs stomp across the sand. She grabs the box from my hand and disappears into a tent, without saying a word.

The rest of our party approaches, some of them still shaking, still rattled. Rachel hugs me, then darts into the tent to check on Zoe. Mike stands in front of me.

He holds out a hand. I take it.

He locks eyes with me, and there's new colors in his irises. Shades of brown and grey that weren't there before. Not when we dated. It shocks me to see any piece of him has changed. I've been watching him so closely. How could I have missed it?

"Thank you," he says.

"You're welcome."

He disappears into the tent. It's the most he's acknowledged me in years. It strikes me how strange it is, that the one time Mike noticed me, I wasn't even trying to get his attention.

Still by my side, Francois looks at me like he wants to say something. He opens his mouth, then shuts it again.

"I can't talk about it," I tell him. Francoise nods, taking me in like he does those symbols from La Buse's letters, wondering if I'm hiding a secret message, or if— maybe— I don't mean anything at all.

35

ZOE

"A pink gun?" My Mom turns the gun over in her hands, keeping her finger away from the trigger. Mike moves away a little when she turns it over, its barrel pointing toward him for a moment. "How odd? Oliver, have you ever seen such a thing?"

Oliver enters the tent. Its green, plastic entrance closes behind him, blocking out the sunlight. "Not one that looks like that, I suppose. It's quite feminine, isn't it?" My Mom passes him the gun. He opens up the barrel with an expert hand. "Three bullets inside," he clucks his tongue. "It's elementary gun safety. You always ought to store the amunition separately."

"Been around guns much?" Mike asks.

"Used go duck hunting as a boy," Oliver sighs, his glasses fogging up at the memory. "Didn't particularly enjoy the sport. Was never a good shot. And the one instance my bullet did meet its target, well," he blushes. "I'm not the brutal sort, I'm afraid."

"He cried," my Mom says, smiling. "His brothers never took hunting him again."

"Which was quite alright with me."

"Is there a number on the gun?" My voice comes out as a whisper. The arrival of this new clue has made me embarrassed at my outburst on the boat. I could have killed us all. What's wrong with me?

"A number?" Oliver asks. "There's a serial number. You can always find it here, on the side." He flips the gun over, pointing to the grip area beneath the trigger. He pulls his glasses off and peers beneath their curved edges, trying to make out the faint lines engraved in the metal. "You'll have to look, son," he gives up, passing the gun to Mike. "Younger eyes."

Mike holds the gun up to the light, a sliver of sunshine pouring in through a slit in the tent's entrance. "323-475-11—"

"—23." I finish for him.

"Yes," he nods. "How did you know?"

I hold up a piece of paper from the inside of the box. It was tucked underneath the gun, marked by the symbol of the state of California.

"It's a permit," I tell him. "A license to carry."

"Strange," Oliver says. "Why would he want us to have the permit? It's not as if we need one out here."

"He wanted us to have it so we would know who it belongs to," I answer.

"Why would that matter?"

"Because I've seen this gun before."

My Mom gasps. "You have?"

Mike stares at me, recognition in his eyes. "I didn't realize it at first. Zoe, the guy who attacked me at Francois' apartment. I was so busy fending him off I didn't look closely at his partner. The one by the door?"

"Yes."

"The one that went after you."

"We were attacked," I tell my Mom and Oliver, skipping over the worst parts to avoid frightening them. "Two men came to an apartment we were in. They brought us to the island, and must have been working for Logan. They were armed. It was messy. It all happened so fast. But I remember, one of the men—"

"—he was holding a pink gun," Mike finishes my sentence. "Their faces were covered. The first guy who entered had an ordinary handgun, but the second was carrying one that looked just like that." Mike nods at the gun, still in Oliver's hands. Oliver sets it down between us all, as if it might burn him. "It *was* really strange. These two burly guys in full out camo gear, and one of them chooses a pink weapon?"

"Is there a name on that permit?" My Mom nods at the paper.

"There is," I say, hands shaking.

"Is he someone on this island?" Oliver says, almost bouncing up and down like he's about to win a gameshow prize.

"Yes," I pass them the permit. "But it's not a *he.*"

"You mean—"

"The gun belongs to a woman."

LANA GASPS when she sees the gun. She runs toward it, reaching out to grab it like she's greeting an old friend. "Where did you find it?" She asks, holding out a hand, waiting for me to pass it to her. I don't.

"Take a guess."

"No. Not—" She stutters as she pieces it together. "Not in one of those boxes?"

"The permit was in there too," my Mom says.

"With your name on it," Mike adds.

"Why would Logan plant my gun on this island?" Lana takes a step back, sitting down on a nearby log, hand on her stomach. She balances on the edge of her seat. "What's the point in giving us a weapon? How does that benefit him?"

Nobody says anything. Donald and Alicia are standing off to the side, looking concerned. Alicia whispers something in his ear, frantic and hushed. Undoubtedly she's convincing him that the introduction of a gun makes this situation even more dangerous, and is prompting him to do something about it "at once." Sure enough, Donald clears his throat.

"As an attorney, I'd like to suggest we implement some possession laws," Donald paces, turning the island into a miniature courtroom. "An object such as this presents a grave risk to all inhabitants of this— *minuscule island community.*"

"I'd hardly call it a community," Tori mutters. "More like purgatory."

"We should nominate one individual to oversee the use, implementation, and protection of said weapon," Donald continues. "My status as a protector of justice makes me the obvious candidate. Given that I am the only one on this island with a legal background, I'd like to nominate myself. Anyone second this?"

"I do!" Alicia raises her hand.

"Your vote doesn't count because you're married to him," Tori spits. "You're practically the same person."

Alicia is about to offer a retort, but Donald touches her arm, signaling that she should stand down. "Whatever the case, we need *someone* trustworthy to make sure the weapon is used appropriately. As the only person here with a knowledge of the legal applications of such an item, I'm the obvious— if not *only*— choice."

"Donald?" I ask, earnest.

"Yes," he smiles at me.

"Shut up."

Alicia gasps. I turn back to Lana, determined to get to the bottom of this. "When was the last time you saw this gun?"

"I keep it in my glove compartment," Lana answers. "My car window was broken during the wedding. There was a rock nearby. I didn't think anything of it, because I keep the glove compartment locked. But when I got home, something just felt *off*. I got into bed, and tossed and turned. Finally, I went back out to the car, unlocked the glove compartment, and realized the gun was gone."

"You didn't say anything!" Rick cries. He's sitting next to Mike on a nearby rock. It bothers me. He should be with Lana, comforting her. "Why didn't you tell me?"

"Why do you think you deserve to know?" She asks him, fire in her eyes. Rick backs off.

"You took separate cars to the wedding?" I ask, confused.

"What?"

"You took separate cars. You're married. Why wouldn't you drive together?"

There's a long silence. Rick digs his fingers into the sand, sorting through its tiny grains like he's looking for gold. He glance over at Mike, seeking support, but finds none. "Well, technically..." Rick begins.

"We're separated," Lana answers, unapologetic. "We thought some time apart might help create intimacy."

"How could time apart *ever* create intimacy?" Tori exclaims, clapping a hand over her mouth as if she didn't mean to say anything aloud. "I'm sorry, that was really rude of me. I didn't mean—"

"No, no, that's quite alright, Tori," Lana's tone is patient and steady, like she's talking to a three-year-old. "I happen to share the same concern. It seems— to many *smart* people— that time apart would only *increase* distance in an already distant marriage. It seems— again, to many *smart* people— that if one were actually trying work on one's marriage, one would *not* go rent an apartment on the west-side, while leaving his spouse behind in the valley."

"Time apart can be good!" Rick shouts, turning red. "It can give a man the chance to find himself!"

"And how's that working out for you?" Lana stands, her long, beautiful hair catching the sun, becoming a waterfall of fiery locks. "Have you," she makes quotations in the air, "'found yourself' yet?! Because we're all waiting, Rick! Waiting for you! To find this precious, invaluable side that you seem to be missing. You have all the money in the world, a wife, who *loves* you, but by all means, please, *find* whatever it is you're looking for! And, by the way, did it ever occur to you that I might want to find *myself*? Or is that just not quite as important."

"It's different!" Rick shouts. "You're not—"

"Not what? As important as *you* are? Well excuse me, I didn't realize I married a member of the royal family!"

"Can we—" I motion to the gun, trying not to be rude. "Lana, I need to ask you—"

"Sure, Zoe," she nods at me. "It's fine."

"No, actually, it's not—" Rick tries to intervene, but Lana waves him away. Still, he tries again, "You can't ask my wife questions in a hostile manner!" He shouts at me, spit flying.

"The only hostile one, here," Lana tells him. "Is you."

Rick steps back like she's hit him.

"Go ahead, Zoe." She leans back, intertwining her fingers.

"You said the gun was stolen?" I ask.

"Yes."

"Why didn't you tell us?"

"Honestly," Lana sighs. "It was your wedding night! I didn't want to you bother you with a simple matter of theft. I assumed it was random— someone breaking into cars, checking the glove box, and stealing what was valuable. I never dreamed they were after *my* gun, specifically."

"But when we got to the island, you *still* didn't say anything."

"I never imagined the events were related," she answers. Everything in her eyes makes me think she's telling the truth. "I was so shocked to wake up here, so confused and disoriented. The night of your wedding felt like it happened years ago. The gun just wasn't on my mind." She picks up a nearby leaf, breaking it into pieces absent-mindedly. The shards crumble, slipping through her fingers. "I was more concerned about finding my cell phone. I just kept thinking 'if only my phone were in my pocket. If only they'd missed it.'"

"Why did you get a gun in the first place?"

"That's enough—" Rick says, but Lana makes the *Shh* sign. He sits down again.

"Our house was broken into a couple months before we separated," she looks at Rick when she says it. He turns his head away, staring into the palm trees like he's trying to forget. "Whoever it was went through Rick's office. His computer was broken. Files scattered everywhere. They let my dog out."

"No!" Tori cries.

"It's okay," Lana says, shaking a little. "A neighbor found

him and returned him a few hours later. Still, I was—*affected*. I'd never had anything like that happen before. When we separated, I felt even less safe. I was on my own now, because my husband was 'finding himself.'" She says the last part directly to Rick. His face turns beet red. "So I decided to get a gun."

"But that could have been related!" I say, a gut instinct telling me I'm onto something. "When the break-in happened at the house you shared, did they take anything?"

"Nothing," Rick says quickly. "Probably some druggies looking for money."

"That doesn't make any sense," I shake my head. "Lana, didn't you think it was strange? *Two* bad things happening in such a short period of time?"

For the first time, Lana breaks down. She puts her head in her hands, big, wet tears spilling onto the sand. "I can't explain it," she says between sobs. "My marriage was falling apart. My focus was on Rick, on us." She wipes her nose on the bottom of her shirt. "It's like..." She pauses, choosing her words. "It's like when one bad thing happens, it's surprising. But when the next bad thing happens, you're a little *less* surprised. And then when the third bad thing happens, you kind of shrug and think, 'makes sense.'"

Our party quiets.

"When it rains, it pours," Oliver adds, his voice throaty and warm.

"Yes," Lana nods. "When it rains, it pours."

"This was one of the guns our attackers used to bring us to the island," I say, holding up the deadly pink object. Lana inhales sharply. The color drains from her face.

Over my shoulder, Francois nods. He recognizes it too. "I knew it as soon as I saw it," he says.

"Zoe, you have to know, I would never, ever, have helped

the man who put us here." I must look like I'm not sure she's innocent, because she thinks to add, "What would be in it for me? What would I stand to gain stranding myself with all of you?"

She's right, of course. She has nothing to gain. None of us do.

So why is it that I can't shake the feeling that someone in my party is lying to me? I take in our group, rolling through my list of suspects. Donald and Aleisha stand side by side, as aloof and self-interested as ever. Francois— whose apartment was the place where this roller coaster began—stands in front of Cassandra like a shield. Cassandra— the only person on this island with a history of stalking and dangerous behavior— watches over his shoulder. She's been so quiet. So observant. Next to her, Tori leans on into Jason, his arm around her waist. In his other hand is, of course, his camera, miraculously still operating on battery power even though he never shuts the thing off.

I think about Francois' story— the one of a pirate named La Buse who didn't trust his men. That fatal trait became his downfall. I wonder if it will be what ruins, me, too.

36

———

CASSANDRA

After dinner, Francois and I return to the rocks to search for more symbols. They're becoming our own little oasis, an island on an island. We separate to cover more ground, and eventually I lose sight of him, which is fine with me. I always feel safe, here, because I have a purpose.

The uneven boulders spread out from the cliffs in a trickle, making their way into the water. When the tides pull back, pools of water are left behind like little snow globes, rife with life. Sea urchins breathe in and out, soft beneath their spines. When I need a break from looking for treasure, I sit beside the tide-pools wishing I could shrink myself down and hide beneath their smooth, glassy skin. Now, I'm crouched by the miniature oceans, dipping my hand in and out, letting my fingers graze leftover seaweed. The water-plants are slimy. I pop their pods, liking the way they squish between my fingers.

I've given away the gun. My pocket feels empty without its weight. That gun was my security blanket, my plan B, my way off this island. Now, when the group discovers the truth, I'll have nothing to defend myself against their wrath.

Why did it I give away?

Was it another attempt to destroy myself? It didn't feel like an act of self-loathing. If anything it felt like self-protection— like losing Zoe might mean losing a slice of myself. The look in her eyes when she climbed into that boat said she didn't care if she lived or died. But I cared. It was as if the death of Zoe would have meant the death of a piece of me.

It's impossible to buzz around another person and not fall in love with them. It has to do with the act of noticing— with seeing all the details. When you circle someone long enough, you begin to notice all their beautiful pieces. The way she takes her coffee. The way he makes the bed. The life force of the observed bleeds into the environment around them, and the viewer is a part of that experience. Watching someone means they become a piece of you. Part of that person crawls under your skin, trapped there, waiting. It's like pollen from a flower, ingested by a bee. The flower has pollen. The bee has pollen. They are connected by golden dust.

When I started watching Mike, I hated Zoe. She was the person who took my place. She was the other woman. The better me. I spent long nights imagining ways to get rid of her— ways to make her disappear. My daydreams weren't actively violent. Just happy accidents. For example, I used to imagine luring her onto a boat and then *accidentally* letting it float out to sea. See? Nothing violent. Just a gentle, peaceful departure. A casual missing person's case. I didn't want her in pain. I just wanted her out of the way.

For a long time, I tried to not even look at her. When Mike had her over at his house, I would hold up one hand

and cover her shape with my fingers, from a distance, so it looked like Mike was alone. But, as their relationship became more serious, watching Mike meant watching Zoe. It was the watching that made her grow on me. Her pollen got under my skin. It was the little things at first. The way she stopped to say hello to every dog on the street. Her insistence that every room should have at least one houseplant in it. Her failure to then *water* said houseplants, dooming them to a slow, terrible death. Then it was the big things. The way she held Mike when he found out his mentor— an older man from Berkeley who taught him everything he knew— had passed away. The way she brought life into their house. Her smile. Her tears. It all came together into one beautiful picture of a radiant, messy person. A person I couldn't help but love just a little.

Maybe Jason's not wrong about privacy. Maybe, if we got rid of it and existed as our fully-exposed, most private selves, everyone would love each other.

I stand, wiping sand off my legs, determined to shift my attention. The treasure will make me whole. The treasure will make Mike notice me. I'll be impossible to look away from, which is all I've ever wanted.

HOURS PASS BY, but I don't stop my search. The sun beats down on my forehead, hot and angry, punishing me with each step I take.

I follow the rocks further down the shore. Francois and I had limited our search to the original area Alicia indicated, mainly because we thought La Buse wouldn't have had time to explore too far across the island. But something about that theory didn't sit right with me. Francois said the symbols are navigational. A swirl with a longer tail. A

Pyramid with a tall point. A line with a graduated edge. They were asymmetrical in design, heavier one side. Francois compared them to the symbols on the paper his family passed down to him— a copy of La Buse's own handwriting — and they're an exact copy. We've tried to follow them in order on the rocks, but could never determine how far we're supposed to go.

Maybe they really are just leading us nowhere at all.

I try to remember the exact angle of the heavier edges. I adjust my course slightly, heading inland, away from the beach, re-creating the angle. After walking only a hundred yards further, I find something remarkable.

The palm trees thin, revealing a smooth, stone clearing. It's close to the sea, but further inland than the beach, set at a higher elevation in one of the island's coastal dips. But that's not what makes this spot special. No, it's the dozens of holes in the rock that make me stop in my tracks. Some are wide, some narrow. They cut through the rock, plunging toward the sea below.

It's a honeycomb.

I lean over one of the holes. The sound of the ocean crashing below echoes in my ears. This clearing must hang over a massive series of caves, allowing the tides to rush in when the moon calls.

Just then— *swoosh*. A jet of water shoots upward from one of the holes, spraying salty sea foam into the air. These holes are geysers, the sea caves underneath ending so abruptly that the water has nowhere to go but up. Over thousands of years the water chipped away at the rock, until it finally created these holes and claimed dry land.

A shape in the middle of the honeycomb calls to me, and I approach like any loyal bee would. It sits exactly in the center of the network of geysers, its uneven shape neatly carved by man. It's a symbol: a circle with a million tails reaching outward.

It looks exactly like the symbols on La Buse's paper.

Its shape reminds me of one of the geysers, spraying trails of water everywhere. I know what it means. I picture La Buse, carving it into the rock, smiling at me. His teeth shine, spit forming at the edge of his mouth. He hid the treasure in one of these holes because he knew it would be dangerous to retrieve. It's here, somewhere. Calling me, right beneath my feet.

37

ZOE

We found his body by the tide pools. The water was pushing him toward land, like it had intended to keep him but changed its mind. It was Tori who saw him first. She screamed, a high-pitched, nasal sound that reminded me of the games we played as children. How we'd shout and run around the playground, chasing imaginary butterflies no one else could see. For a moment the sound took me back to that other place— that better time. But then I saw his flopping, empty corpse abandoned on the sand, and reality hit.

Now, our group is assembled in a cloud upon the sand, trying to figure out what to do, what to say.

Rick.

He looks colder in death than he did in life, but there's still something arrogant in his pointed nose, his high cheekbones.

My Mom leans into Oliver, covering her face with her hands. She is a nurse. She has seen death. But not like this. Not so unforgiving. Not so hollow. Tori's entire form shakes.

She looks to Jason for comfort, but finds none. He keeps his camera glued to his hand, filming every second, panning over the group for reactions. Alicia turns on her heel and walks away from the scene, as if she's angry with the beach for presenting her with something so disturbing, so distracting. Donald follows her, their silence deafening.

Mike stands over Rick, broken, shattered. "The last thing I said to him," he whispers, face red. "It wasn't— we never cleared things up."

I take his hand into mine, and he holds it tight.

Behind us, Lana stands, frozen, unsure what to do.

"How?" She says, asking no one in particular.

Oliver leans over the body. "It looks like a gunshot wound. To the head. Rachel, do you think you can handle it?"

My Mom nods, uncovering her face, snapping into nurse mode. She crouches down, takes a long, careful look at his head. By his left temple is a gaping, open hole. "It's symmetrical, uniform. Couldn't be anything else."

"I heard the shot," Tori corroborates. "I was down by the water, just rinsing off when I heard it. At first I thought it was a firework, but I didn't see sparks."

"What did you do with the gun?" I ask Lana. She's still a statue, unmoving, in shock.

"I put it in the cooler with the food," she says, monotone. "Oliver saw me leave it there, didn't you?"

"Yes," he adds. "I was nabbing water."

"Did Rick know it was there?"

"He was with me when I left it," she nods.

"Who else knew it was there?"

My Mom raises her hand. So does Tori. She smacks Jason in the ribs, and his hand goes up too. "We knew. We saw Lana leave it there," she adds, pausing for a moment.

"Francois and Cassandra were with us. They were about to leave to look for that stupid treasure, and they came to get water when Oliver was opening the cooler."

"It isn't *stupid,*" Cassandra sneers. She and Francois have just joined us, their cheeks flushed with excitement. Francois puts a hand on her shoulder, as if silently signaling that this isn't the time.

"We knew the gun was there," Francois adds. "But we've been at the other end of the island all day. We had nothing to do with it."

"You don't think—" Mike's voice trembles as he poses the next question, "He did it to himself?"

Everyone looks at Lana. Suddenly, she crumples into the sand like a marionette, the full gravity of what has happened hitting her. "How could you do this to me?" She crawls toward Rick's lifeless form. "After everything you put me through!"

Oliver leans down, moving Rick's body over. There's no sign of the gun.

"We should look for it," I say, a terrible feeling burning in my gut. "To be sure."

We spread out across the beach, searching for the gun. An hour passes, but nobody finds it.

"Couldn't very well have shot himself without it, could he?" Oliver muses when we gather again by Rick's body, which we've moved further up the sand, away from the pull of the tides.

"Maybe he lost it to the sea?" My Mom asks, the narrow squint in her eyes saying she clearly doubts her own hypothesis.

"It would have washed up with him," Mike runs a hand through his hair.

"How could this have happened?" Lana sinks into the sand, crying over Rick's form.

Behind her, Cassandra's figure looms, casting a shadow across the beach that mirrors her tiny form. "You don't think he..." Cassandra stops mid-sentence, as if she's surprised anyone is listening to her.

"Killed himself?" Oliver asks.

Cassandra nods.

"I don't think he killed himself," the tiny voice comes from over my shoulder. It's Cassandra. Nobody answers. She fills the silence herself. "I mean, he didn't seem—" she pauses, "He didn't seem suicidal to me. And I know what that looks like." She makes eye contact with me on that last part.

"I don't think he killed himself either."

Our party is quiet. If Rick didn't do this to himself, it means someone else did. And there's only so many people left on this island.

LATER, we have a funeral for Rick. Mike digs the grave himself. It's a sandy process, slow and awful, but necessary. We stand around the new lump in the Earth, our small coalition far from the reception Rick would expect. Donald says some words that don't mean anything. Big, empty words for a man he didn't know.

When Donald is done, Mike stands. "Rick was not perfect," he says. "But he was my friend. He was my brother, and I'll miss him." He positions a rock at the head of the makeshift grave.

Later, when it's all over, I spend a long time looking at the horizon, trying hard to remember where we've buried him so we can come back after we've left the island. The thought makes my heart pound, because we might not ever leave. We might die here, too, alone, with no one left to bury us the way we buried Rick.

Maybe Rick was lucky, to die first.

38

CASSANDRA

When I saw Rick's body, I just kept thinking about what Logan said to me the night before I came here: "You've got to play to win."

Is there someone else on this island, playing Logan's game? What would winning look like for that person? And do they know I'm working with him, too?

I find myself scanning the trees, waiting for some unknown shape to emerge. Every shadow becomes a hostile form. Every sound a warning call. The thought that someone else on this island knows I'm working with Logan and is secretly watching me is equal parts frightening, and comforting. For all I know, Logan himself is hiding on this island, looking for opportunities to create mayhem, to destroy.

Maybe he hired someone to pick us off one by one.

The idea seems far-fetched. He would never hire an outside person to murder one of the group. To do so would mean breaking the rules of his own game— the game he invited me to play. The game I didn't know I would participate in. Whoever killed Rick is someone in our party. Someone who doesn't want us to win.

One thing is for sure: if someone else on this island really is working with Logan, that person is much more dangerous than I am.

That person is a killer.

FOR THE REST of the day, Mike works on his raft. Everyone in our group leaves him alone— even Zoe. It's sad, watching him try to invest himself in something. He's looking for a distraction, something to take his mind off the sight of Rick's body and the loss of his friend. Hours pass by. I monitor him from up on the bank, keeping out of sight.

Finally, I decide to approach him. I know what the problem is— why his raft isn't working. I've been watching him try to figure out the pieces, but he can't get past what he's used to doing. That's always been a problem for Mike. He's not as creative as I am. He can't step outside the box he's accustomed to working in.

"I have an idea," I say. He doesn't answer. "You need a better way to hold it together," I pick up one of the braided palm leaves he's using, and it almost breaks beneath my fingers. "There's untapped resources on this island that we haven't even touched— "

He turns, his face red, hot rage burning underneath. He doesn't need to say anything.

The look in his eyes is enough to make walk away.

39

———

ZOE

Sunset drips across the island in a violent cascade. Reds and oranges splatter against the sky like drops of blood— hot, thick, newly spilt. Its uneven pattern strikes me as a warning. It's as if the sky is aware of Rick's death, and is taking the opportunity to mock us. "Another day," the sunset seems to say. "Another day gone, and still, two boxes missing."

Mike's raft isn't working. We're standing on the beach, testing it together, away from prying eyes. I stand on the sand, heart pounding, feet digging into the Earth. Mike pushes the raft out to sea. For a moment, it seems to float. Then, a wave approaches. It's the small, rolling kind, barely shoulder-height. Mike ushers the raft over the wave's crest, but when it reached the other side, the fragile leaves woven into twine separate. The bite of the salt water, the strength of the wave— it's too much. The raft breaks apart, two days of work scattering into the tides. "I'll try again," Mike says as he returns to the shore, his arms filled with whatever scraps he could salvage. The broken wood looks pathetic in his arms.

"What if it doesn't work?"

"It has to."

"But...”

"I'm doing everything I can!" Mike raises his voice, an action so out of character that it makes me step backward. "I don't have my tools. I'm—" he throws the pieces of wood onto the sand. When they land, he kicks the pile for good measure. "I'm flying blind, okay?"

"Okay," I say, keeping my voice level. He's still reeling from Rick's death. However they left it, they were friends too long for Mike not to feel it. "Just do what you can." I kiss him and pull him toward me, but his body feels stiff and unyielding. He holds me for a second, then gently pushes me away, picking up the scraps he spilled.

"Sorry," he says when he notices the look on my face. "It's not you, I'm just not myself.” He runs a hand through his hair.

"I know," I say. "He was your friend."

Mike looks at the pieces of the raft, a tangled mess. "I'm not used to failing. Not at this."

When he puts his arm down, I take a good look at his hands, and what I see rocks me to my core. Red sores, open and still bleeding, created by trying to break wood into pieces with nothing but two rocks. Dirt coats the wounds, promising infection. Massive splinters— big enough to be visible from afar— have burrowed underneath his nails, resting painfully in the skin underneath. The empty spot on his left hand— the pinky finger he lost to frostbite in Yosemite— is glaringly empty, somehow looming larger than ever.

I take his hands in mine. "Let me see?"

"It's fine," he pulls away, gathers the wood up. "I'm fine.”

He pauses, a pained look in his eyes. "Divide and conquer. Look for the clues. I'll keep trying with these." He holds up the shattered pieces. At the end of the sea, the sunset bleeds into the water, signaling nightfall. "We're running out of time," he nods.

It's the last thing he says to me before he strides across the beach, back to the area he's designated for raft-building. I watch him hover over the pieces, laying them out in a new arrangement. There's a manic, frenzied, rhythm to his movements. A long plank here. A short plank there. He rearranges the pieces again and again, like he's trying to solve a puzzle with no answer.

AN HOUR later and I'm pushing through the trees, going farther afield into the only area of the jungle our party hasn't yet explored. My legs burn with the effort, my body aware that I haven't eaten enough today. But I keep moving, driven by the memory of Mike's hands.

I've left the rest of the group behind, eating dinner. Everyone was gathered around the fire, warming up the food. Everyone except Mike, who was still across the beach, arranging wood into a raft. I told them I was going to the bathroom, using the excuse as a means to slip away. They'll be worried, but I don't care. Other people only slow me down. I'm driven by a different kind of hunger— the primal need to get us off this island. I'm faster alone, and more nimble, more flexible. The search would be done by now, if I'd done it myself. I think about Jason, slowing us down with his camera permanently attached to his hands. Donald and Alicia, constantly stopping to complain or address another manufactured sprained ankle. Cassandra and Francois are no use to me either— we haven't seen them since the discovery of those meaningless little symbols carved on the rocks. They would prefer to look for a mirage than to help me get us off this island. Fine. I don't need them anyway.

The sky is an inky, pearlescent shade of blue, now, and I can see the sun's final rays reaching over the horizon. It won't be long before we're plunged into darkness. If I don't find the remaining clues tonight, we'll be left with only a few hours tomorrow to make things right. We need two more boxes to solve Logan's puzzle. Logan's horrible, twisted puzzle. One is missing, and the clues within may have been destroyed for good, it's true. But the other is still out there, waiting for me to find it.

I push further into the trees and the jungle opens up, sparse, less dense. I take it as a sign of encouragement, that the forest is making room for me. Far off in the distance, something beautiful, something welcome appears. It's a waterfall, a clear blue shower trickling down into a liquid pool. In the velvet twilight, the water looks almost black. The sound of the falls tumbling into the basin echoes across the island, a drumbeat calling me toward it. I arrive, hypnotized, humbled by its majesty.

But then, a chill travels up my spine. I'm swallowed whole by the feeling I've been here before. The way the water carves in the rocks is familiar. The angle of the slope is different— steeper— but still, it evokes a memory of another place.

This waterfall reminds me of Bunnel Cascade in Yosemite. The place where I lept into freezing cold water. The place where I was invited to quit, but continued anyway.

I follow the water's path with my eyes, noticing that

there's something strange bobbing directly beneath the falls. It's a buoy.

He's talking to me, I think. *Only me.*

A familiar red flag bobs up and down on top of the buoy, struggling to stay afloat under the falls.

Memories resurface, and suddenly I'm back in Yosemite. The snow-filled valley comes to life, air so cold it bites the skin. I remember jumping into that icy cascade— the only piece of the valley refusing to freeze, preferring instead to churn, to flow. An image of my own hands flashes in front of me, red fingers stretching long, reaching for that single buoy.

I never left the valley. Not really.

I know what Logan wants me to do.

I JUMP into inky black water fully-clothed, thankful that it's warm. My arms propel me forward, cupped hands pushing back against the encroaching water. My movements make little ripples on the surface of the basin, identifying me as an outsider— as an animal that does not belong, here. I wonder what creatures live at the bottom of the pool, waiting to bite a toe, or a foot. It's enough to make me want to turn back, but I do my best to float horizontally on the surface of the water, putting as much distance between me and the bottom of the basin as possible.

Finally, I reach the perimeter of the waterfall. It makes me gasp. It's more violent than I had expected, a churning, tumultuous cauldron threatening to eat me alive. A hostile spray of white foam blinds me, constant and unyielding. The water where the falls empty is dense with bubbles, and once I submerge myself, I know it will be impossible to tell which way is up. I'll have to rely on that buoy, which seems anchored in place, tethered to some rope that will become my lifeline.

I take a deep breath, acknowledging how clean the air feels as it fills my lungs. It occurs to me that— if this goes wrong— I might have just taken my *last* breath. But before I can panic, I submerge my head, disappearing beneath the water, committing myself to the task ahead.

I swim at an angle toward the falls. It's hard to see in the basin— the water is thick with green amoebas, microscopic plant life making fuzz, clouding the water. Ahead of me, white bubbles cascade upward and downward in a tunnel, marking the point where the falls empty out. It's an underwater tornado. I swim toward it, stopping at its edge.

A bright, red rope stands out inside the jetstream, its color impossible to miss against the foam. I reach out with one hand, grabbing on tight to the rope's fraying strands. I'm inside the current now, and it's pushing me downward at a rapid speed. I've lost control. All I can do is hold my breath and keep my fingers wrapped around that rope. Before I know it, my feet hit the bottom. Rocks dig into their unprotected soles. Something sharp nips at my heel, sending an electric heat up my leg. I pray it was a rock and not an animal.

I explore with my free hand, following the rope down to its end. It's attached to a heavy metal anchor, the kind you would use to keep a boat in place. I scan the earth around it, trying not to disturb the soot and sand. For a second, it occurs to me that Logan may have this as a trap. What if it leads to nothing at all? But then, a rectangular outlines emerges from the depths, its silver lid rusting, begging to be opened.

Another clue.

I grab it, tucking it securely beneath my free arm.

Keeping my other hand attached to the rope, I kick off the bottom of the basin, victorious. I expect to surge upward toward dry land, but nothing happens. My body barely moves.

The downward pressure from the falls— the cascade of water that helped me get to the bottom— is now preventing me from making my way back to the surface.

My heart pounds as I use the rope to pull myself upward, one inch at a time. The current pushes against me, rebelling. My arms struggle to move me upward, fighting upstream against a thousand pounds of pressure. My lungs burn.

How much farther?

It's impossible to tell. The world around me is all white foam, menacing bubbles. The rope is my only guide. The desire to inhale floods my system. I remember how sweet fresh air tasted— the way I've taken every breath before now for granted.

My body begs me to inhale. It's going to take over, no matter how much I try to resist. Any second now, my lungs will expand, expecting delicate air and finding only thick, heavy water.

I look upward, and I think I can make out the sky through the bubbles. I'm close to the surface. It's pitch black above the water, a smattering of stars visible even from within the depths of the basin. Or maybe those aren't stars. Maybe I'm just seeing lights.

The outline of a rock appears above my head, and I know I've made it. I'm only a few feet below the surface, so close to clean air.

I reach upward— and that's when my lungs betray me. They open wide, inhaling. The water burns as it enters my airway, filling spaces, intruding in areas where it doesn't belong.

Those stars are so beautiful.

The lights grow brighter. I'm at the surface now, pushed sideways by the falls, but it's too late. Everything blurs together. My eyes close.

And for once, I don't fight it.

40

CASSANDRA

Francois stands in front of the network of blowholes, examining the symbol carved in the middle. The sound of waves crashing below us beats in a steady rhythm, making me feel like we're trapped inside of a seashell.

"Yes, it's like the others," he says. smiling. "When you followed them here, did you walk in the direction of the heavy edge or the light one?"

"The light one," I confirm.

"We'd been searching backwards," he nods. "The side with the least emphasis serves as the arrow."

"But what about this one? It has so many tails. They're all light. It looks like a geyser."

He runs his fingers over the shape. "It appears to mean, 'search here.' We'll need to check all of them."

"So many?"

"Too many," he nods. The symbol with a thousand curved tails looks up at me from its spot on the rock. "La buse meant for us to check them all. We've arrived at the destination. We just don't know where to begin."

Francois leans over the closest blowhole, taking in the distance to the bottom. It's thirty feet at least. The sides are slippery, treacherous, impossible to climb. "

Perhaps La Buse hoped for us to die on the way," I wonder aloud.

"He would have hidden it in a place protected, to be sure. But he also would have wanted to be able to retrieve it with minimal danger to himself. Still," Francois adds, "if we *knew* which hole hid the treasure, it would be better."

"Just like a cheeseburger would be better than that stuff from the cooler that Zoe tried to feed us for dinner. But here we are."

"Here we are," he agrees. "Still, no matter which hole we climb, we are in danger."

"Yes."

"We risk our lives each time."

"Sure."

Every blowhole we attempt to conquer increases the likelihood that one of us will get caught unawares by a fatal spray, falling to the bottom in a bone-shattering catastrophe.

"It's down there. Somewhere," I say, unable to keep the longing out of my voice.

"I feel it too," he nods. Our eyes lock. There's something refreshing about being around a person who shares my reality. Too often I engage in treasure hunts that no one else understands. They label my behavior as "stalking," probably because they don't get what, exactly, I'm after. For once, I'm hunting a treasure that someone else believes in.

"We could make a rope," I look away, embarrassed. "Out of our clothes."

"Interesting," Francois nods, waiting. "Go on?"

His willingness to hear my idea takes me by surprise. I had tried to relay the concept to Mike so he could use it on his raft, but he didn't give me the chance. Francois' encouragement is earth-shattering.

"You're the expert, though," I say, suddenly nervous to share. "You're an archaeologist. You know how to retrieve artifacts. I don't."

"I want to hear your idea," Francois urges.

"Well, we don't have any rope." For some reason, my cheeks flush.

Pull it together, Cass.

I clear my throat. "It's a design concept of found materials and unused resources. You try to take the things you have and give them new life and utility. So, I was thinking about what we have on the island that's an untapped resource, and I realized our clothes are made from fabric. We could take them off and tie the ends together really tight," I explain. "The fabric is stronger than anything we'll find on the island. Stronger than those stupid palm leaves Mike has everyone weaving together. We could tie them together to make a rope. It might hold one of us long enough to check the bottom of a hole for treasure."

"You have not suggested this to him?" Francois furrows his brow.

"Who?"

"Mike. About the clothes. Your idea could help his raft."

"And have an island full of naked people walking around? No thanks. I don't want to picture that. Not with this crowd."

Francois laughs. His eyes soften, the lines underneath disappearing. "Why not tell him?"

I shrug. Francois doesn't know about my past with Mike. "He doesn't want to talk to me. He wouldn't listen."

"Everyone here knows him and his wife, in some way."

My stomach turns over when Francois calls Zoe Mike's wife. "Yes."

"And you must know them, too?"

Here it is. The uncomfortable moment I've been waiting for. I debate lying. There are ways to skirt around the truth. I could tell Francois that Mike and I used to date— that I'm his ex-girlfriend— and leave it at that. No reason to mention anything else. But then, some familiar feeling bubbles up in my stomach. It's the tight, acidic taste of the desire to self-harm. It's the same poison that made me team up with Logan. It's the piece of myself that hates "me," whoever that is.

I like Francois. I like him very much.

Which is why I'm going to sabotage the fuck out of this.

"I *follow* Mike," I say, emphasizing the middle word. "I follow him everywhere. Zoe too. Mike and I dated for a long time. He broke up with me, and now I won't leave him alone. I feel like he owes me attention, because I gave up so much for him. But no matter what I do, he won't see me. Won't look my way. He refuses to notice me. And I know it's wrong to keep tracking him down, but I do it anyway. What," I lean in, "do you think about that?"

Francois pauses. I expect him to walk away. To shiver and recoil. To push me aside. Instead, he reaches up toward my face and tucks a piece of hair behind my ear like I'm something to be treasured, to be revered. "I think it is very sad," he says, his voice earnest, "that you are so focused on what is beautiful about him."

"Why's that?" I whisper, my eyes tearing up a little even though I beg them not to.

"Because," his hand is on my face now, wiping a heavy teardrop off my cheek. "Worrying so much about his beauty has made you lose sight of your own."

"I'm invisible," I say, cautioning him with what I know is true. "One day you will wake up and realize that, and you'll stop noticing me. I buzz around things, around people. But nobody buzzes around me."

"You are very visible to me," Francois says.

"I will disappoint you," I say, thinking of Mike, still hoping he might look my way one day.

"That's quite alright," Francois nods, smiling. "I am used to waiting around for treasure that I may never hold."

"Why do you like me?"

"You are inventive," he answers too easily, needing no thought at all. "You think in a way others don't. It's charming."

"I'm a mess," I say.

"That's true, too," he answers.

I'm not sure who makes the first move, but suddenly my lips are on his, and we're kissing. For a second, I forget all about La Buse, and about Mike, and about the island. I get lost in the moment, imagining some future without any of those things. Imagining some future where the person I'm buzzing around actually wants *me*, too.

WE'RE WALKING BACK toward camp when I see her. Francois and I have taken a side route on the outskirts of the beach, at the far end of the jungle. It appealed over any other path because of the rocks lining the coast, where no trees dare grow. The velvet night has settled on the island, obscuring visibility— adding trees increases the potential for getting lost.

"What is that?" I ask, noticing some long, lanky limb sticky out from the edge of the basin where the waterfall empties out. In the dark of night, it almost looks like a tree root. But then I notice five fingers, bony and bruised, a huge wedding ring glittering away, even in the shadows.

"Zoe?" Francois rushes forward, turns her over. He puts his face near hers. Watching them makes a pang of jealousy ripples through my body before I realize he's listening for air. "She's not breathing!" He opens her mouth and pounds on her chest, a rhythmic *boom, boom, boom.* The compressions make Zoe's entire body move up and down, like a surfboard bobbing on the sea.

"Look!" I shout. Twenty feet away, a silver box is embedded in the soil at the edge of the basin. "She found it." When Logan planted this box, I told him no one would *ever* be able to extract it, not in a million years. He wouldn't tell me what was inside, but I watched him hide it. He ignored my questions, tying that thick, red rope to a heavy anchor before dropping it off the edge of the falls, waiting for the buoy to resurface. He said Zoe would know what it meant, and how to retrieve it. At the time, it annoyed me— the way he made it sound like him and Zoe had some secret code, some secret language only the two of them would understand. Now, as I look down at her body, I know what it is about her that he hates. I understand the piece of her he wishes to destroy.

Zoe is willing to sacrifice herself for others. She loves others so much that she is willing to dispose of herself, if only to save them. She will leave this island as a hero. As a martyr. Mike will love her even more, and in her absence, no other woman will ever fill the void. Not me. Not anyone. She has outplayed me, once again, without even trying.

I sink down into the earth by her lifeless form, my body shaking.

Fuck you, for being so much better than me, I want to shout.

She is a hero and I am a villain. Being the bad guy isn't

fun anymore. This is my fault. The fact that we're here. The fact that she's dead. All of it weighs so heavy on my shoulders that I feel like I might combust. I swallow, and it erupts out of me in a deep, throaty scream. Francois gasps at the animal noises I'm making. He moves aside, stops the compressions.

Suddenly, I'm hitting Zoe's lifeless form. I strike her face. It's not hard enough. I hit her again. "Wake up!" I hear my own voice like I'm outside of myself. Spit flies from my mouth, landing on Zoe's face. I don't care. I strike her in the chest, hard. "Wake *up,* you obnoxious, infuriating piece of—" I hit her again, this time with both fists, right in the place between her breasts where that flat, strong sternum sits.

Suddenly, Zoe coughs. Water pours out of her mouth.

"A miracle," Francois whispers. He crouches down next to me, turning her head to the side so the water evacuates her airway. I sit back on my hands, out of breath, not caring that my shorts are covered in mud.

Zoe's eyelids flutter open. She looks at me like she's trying to place who I am. Then, recognition lights up her face.

"The box—" she starts to say.

"We've got it," I tell her, waving a hand like it's nothing. "Can't believe you followed that red rope, you stupid, stupid cow."

For a second, Zoe laughs. Then, her eyes darken, shaded by some private, wicked thought she'll never share. Francois helps her stand, putting one arm underneath her armpit to support her. I get the other side. She insists on carrying the box herself.

"I'll take it," she says to Francois, still unsteady on her feet, reaching out with both arms like a toddler asking for a toy. Francois passes her the clue, his face skeptical, doubting very much whether she'll be able to handle the added weight.

Together, the three of us stumble through toward the other side of the island, making our way back toward camp. Francois and Zoe talk the entire time, but I stay quiet, astounded by my own good deed. A question rumbles through my head like a freight train, its roaring sounds the only thing I can hear:

Why do I keep saving this bitch?

41

ZOE

The walk back to camp is a haze. Francois and Cassandra help me across the terrain, holding me up as we move. Our progress is slow. Even so, the environment around me blends into an abstract smear, a doppler affect, the sort of motion blur observed out the window of a speeding train.

Francois talks to me, asks me questions, probably to try and keep me awake.

"Why did you go by yourself?" He exclaims, shaking his head.

"Faster," I shrug, not feeling the need to explain further.

"How did you know it was in the water?" He asks motioning to the box in my arms.

"The buoy," I mutter, looking at Cassandra. "I've seen it before." Cassandra trips on a tree branch. Her clumsiness makes us all stumble, the failing team in a three-legged race.

"Sorry," she mutters, dusting herself off and putting my arm back over her shoulders for support. Her arm shakes over mine, but not because of weakness, or effort. The blush in her cheeks gives her away.

She's nervous.

And I know why.

I won't tell her now. I'll wait until the story comes together. Until my head stops spinning, and I have all the information. I'll wait until the picture crystalizes. Because that's the thing about puzzles.

You need all the pieces to solve them.

WHEN WE GET BACK to camp, I'm struck by the way the tents look like little headstones from a distance. Their rounded, simple outlines make vague bumps on the horizon, semi-circles marking a resting place. How could I have missed it before?

Mike's the first to greet us. He runs toward me, pushing Cassandra and Francois aside. He picks me up, carrying me the rest of the way. "What happened?" He asks, concerned. "You're soaked."

"I found a clue."

"She did something dangerous, didn't she?" He's asking Francois and Cassandra. They nod at the same time, selling me out with no hesitation whatsoever.

When we reach the tents, I lay down inside an empty one, drinking tiny sips of water. My Mom sits next to me, Oliver behind her, glancing nervously over her shoulder. Mike is on my other side, Francois and Cassandra standing by the entrance. "I'm fine," I tell the group, annoyed at the expressions on their faces. "Really."

"Don't exhaust yourself," my Mom chides.

"You do look a touch off color, darling," Oliver adds.

"But of course she does!" I had hoped Francois wouldn't mention that they had to resuscitate me, but of course, he's been talking about it since we arrived. "She was near dead when we found her! Pump after pump, she wouldn't wake up," he says to my Mom, who's holding a hand to my forehead, seeking a fever that isn't there.

"That won't help—" I start to say about her hand on my head.

"Don't you think I know that?" She snaps. "I'm a nurse, damnit!" I move to sit up, but she puts a hand on my shoulder. "Stay put. Don't over exert yourself. You'll put stress on your heart."

"Probably twenty seconds I tried to wake her," Francois carries on with the story of what happened. "And nothing. But then this one..." he grabs Cassandra, ruffling her hair. "She went crazy!"

Mike and my Mom exchange a look.

"What do you mean?" Mike asks, a hard edge to his voice. He turns to Cassandra. "What did you do?"

"Nothing!" She cries. Francois rushes to her defense.

"It was hardly nothing," he says, voice dripping with pride. "She summoned this deep, feline power. She was like a jaguar this one! She shouted at Zoe, no— *growled* at her. She shook her, pulled her hair, slapped her—"

"You *hit* my wife?" Mike steps toward Cassandra, but my Mom holds him back.

Francois waves a hand. "No, no, it was to help her! An attempt to wake her, to bring her back from the brink of death!" Cassandra doesn't say anything. She's pushed against a corner of the tent, making herself as small as possible.

"When it didn't work, she pounded on her chest," Francois continues. "And then... a miracle! She woke up, alive again."

"It was you?" I ask. Everyone stares at me, but I'm not looking at them. I'm laser-focused on Cassandra.

"I don't know," she says. "It could have been Francois. All the things he tried before me might have helped."

"But no! It was not..." Francois starts to correct her. I cut him off.

"I need to know," I say, not breaking eye contact with Cassandra. "Did you save my life?"

There's a long pause in which everyone is waiting for her to confirm or deny.

"Yes," she says. Her eyes are watering. Her hands clench into fists. It's not the reaction of a hero. She looks like she hates herself for saving me.

"You had the option to leave me," I tell her. Francois looks horrified at the idea, but Cassandra's face remains unchanged. It's obvious this thought occurred to her as well.

"Francois had already tried to wake me up. Tried and failed. You could have walked away. No one would have held you responsible."

"That's true," she says.

"But you tried again. You saved my life."

"I guess so."

"Why?" I ask her.

She tucks one foot behind the other, looking like a kid who's been caught outside of time-out. Her hands clench around the tent's tarp-like fabric, holding on to steady herself. There's a tormented, stormy look in her eye. She's fighting some battle inside— it's hard to say whether she's winning or losing.

The words she says next come out boiling hot, a churning, acidic sentiment. Her teeth grit, chewing on a mouthful of emotions— confusion, anger, self-loathing.

"I don't *know*."

I believe her. And it complicates things.

She turns, leaving the tent in a hurry, Francois trailing behind her.

42

CASSANDRA

Francois is behind me, trying to keep up. I'm running through the palm trees, breathing heavy. It's pitch black. The night here is thick and heavy. I tear through it like a knife, searing my way across the island. I'm not sure what I'm rushing toward. I just need to get away from camp, and from Zoe. The look on her face when she'd found out what I'd done made me want to disappear. She was *thankful*, grateful even, that I saved her. The surprise in her eyes— it was like she didn't know I had it in me to help another person.

She knows who I really am.

A monster. A mess. A person with nothing in her own life worth circling, worth buzzing around.

A spiky palm branch smacks me in the face, and suddenly I taste blood. The branch has cut my lip. I don't care. I bite down on the wound, sucking on it a little, encourage the blood to flow.

I deserve it.

"Cassandra!" Francois calls out behind me. It's too dark

to see him, which means he can't he see me either. Perfect. Maybe I can lose him if I run fast enough. "Cassandra, wait!"

I break into a full-out run, wondering which direction I should head. Bees need a direction, otherwise they are lost. Suddenly, it hits me.

What better place for a bee than a honeycomb?

I turn, frantically moving in the direction of the honeycomb, leaving Francois behind me. The moonlight makes everything appear in grey and blacks. It's strange, navigating a world without street-lamps. Every rock looks unfamiliar in the dark. Every tree seems to lean over, threatening.

When I reach the honeycomb, I don't even know I'm there until I step forward and find nothing but air. My foot disappears into a geyser, making my whole body tumble forward. I catch myself with my hands, palms grazing against the sharp, wet rocks.

I carefully remove my leg from the hole, then stand back. A cloud in front of the moon moves aside at the perfect moment, allowing silver light to flood the honeycomb. It's almost as if the moon wants me to find the treasure. The moon wants me to be somebody. The moon wants me to matter.

To be the kind of person who is worth noticing.

My clothes land in a pile by my feet when I strip them off. I'm more comfortable like this— as my true self. I take each piece of clothing— first my shirt, then my pants, then my bra— winding them around themselves into long strips. I tie them together. It's not a long rope— maybe three feet or so— but it'll get me started. I peer into the geyser. It's about fifteen feet to the bottom of this particular hole. I'll have to jump the rest of the way when the rope ends. At the hole's bottom, a pool of sea water has gathered, rushing in and out, rising then receding. I scan the border of the geyser realizing I have nothing to tie the rope to. No nearby tree, no hole in the rock.

"Let me."

I turn. Francois is behind me. He takes off his shirt, revealing muscles I didn't know were there. His pants are next. He ties his clothes to mine, and suddenly the rope is eight feet long.

"How did you know where I'd be?" I ask.

"You are not seeking the treasure because you wish to be wealthy," he says.

"No," I say, shaking my head. "Francois," my voice rattles, and I wish I could hide in one of these holes forever. "I've done something awful."

He doesn't ask what. Instead, he holds me close, letting me cry into his shoulder. Minutes pass, with nothing but silence between us. Then, he tilts my chin up, looking deep into my eyes.

"Whatever you have done, *it* may have been awful. But *you* are not awful."

"I need..." I'm trying to tell him that I need to distract myself, but it's not the kind of thing other people always understand. "I need something to buzz around," I say, stepping backward, wiping my face. He looks disappointed that I've increased the distance between us, but doesn't say anything about it. "I need a distraction." I motion at the rope. He nods, understanding.

"It has to be you," he says, looking into the geyser. "I will not fit. And you are not strong enough to bring me back up."

"Yes," I tell him.

"Why do you want the treasure so badly? You understand we will not sell it. It will stay right here, in the Seychelles."

"It's not about money. I think... finding the treasure

would make something right inside me," I say. "It might make me into a person worth noticing."

"I see," he answers. "You are sure you wish to do this?"

I nod. He grabs one end of our makeshift rope, and I take the other. I lean backward over the hole. Before I disappear over the edge, I look upward at his almond eyes; warm, concerned, so different from Logan's icy irises. It occurs to me that Francois could drop me if he wanted to, sending me tumbling to my death. He could leave me stranded, trapped at the bottom of a geyser. If it were to blow while I was inside, the water might drown me, bashing me against the rocks before forcing my lungs to expand one final, horrible time.

In considering such a scenario, it's not death that scares me. Not really. It's the idea of knowing I was betrayed again. Of being unwanted by yet another person who I would have liked to have buzzed around.

"You won't leave me?" I ask him.

"If there is no way to bring you up," he says, "I will climb down there with you, and we will die together."

It's good enough for me. My bare feet slide against the geyser's wet, slippery walls as I repel backward into its gaping mouth.

WE WORK THROUGH THE NIGHT. The first three holes are terrifying. The process takes time at first. I move slowly, feeling as if each step backward might end in death. When I get to the bottom, I search the caves within, running my fingers through every nook and cranny without the benefit of a light. Cracks run along uneven stone, smelling like seaweed and salt water. Water rushes in from an outlet to the sea, swelling first around my ankles, sometimes reaching as high as my neck. Each time the water level rises, I wonder if the geyser I'm trespassing on will blow. Luckily, it doesn't take much time to tell if a given hole is the one. According to Francois, the treasure is so big that it would be un-missable. The correct hole would need to have a network of vast caverns hidden within, protecting from both the water's intrusion and prying eyes. Most of the geysers are nothing but tubes, ending in a single cave.

Soon, the terror subsides. Francois and I work out a system. We find a rhythm. A method. Having a process helps. We realize that not every hole requires me to touch my feet to the bottom. Sometimes, I get far enough down that I can see into the interior cavern without needing to make contact with the water. More often than not, the geysers are dead-ends. There's no network of caves within— no spaces big enough to hide hundreds of pounds of treasure. In most of the geysers we explore, there's nothing but a long tunnel landing in an abrupt dead-end. Here, the holes reveal themselves as a L-shaped. They're a vertical line meeting a horizontal one, which allows the sea to come and go as it pleases. Still, even the simplest hole is fascinating. My feet touch the soft, tangled limbs of anemones. Tiny crabs run over the rocks, aware of my presence. Seaweed lands in big, tangled blobs when the tide receeds, abandoned by the ocean, left behind to wait for the next swelling of the tide.

Finding my way up is more difficult than climbing down, because Francois has to pull on the rope to help me ascend. We are both tired, both dripping in sweat. Trails of salt linger on our skin, some from the sea, but most from our pores.

The night passes, and the darkness lifts. The sun isn't out yet, but there's a twilight affect in the air, signaling an approaching dawn. It's easier to see, now, and the entire honeycomb sprawls out before us, fully visible for the first time in hours.

"How many have we checked?" I ask Francois, wiping my brow.

"Ten," he answers.

"How many do you think we have left?"

We look out at the honeycomb. It's a mixture of dozens of holes, some big, some small. Even if we eliminate the smallest geysers— which are no wider than my fist— we're left with too many to count.

"Many," he says.

"One more?" I ask, hopeful. "Then we'll stop. We'll rest."

"One more. Ladies choice."

We've been taking turns deciding on which hole to check. Strangely, it's the most difficult part of the process. My heart pounds every time it's my turn to decide, wondering if *this* geyser could be the one that changes my life forever. Each one I choose that doesn't yield results is a massive disappointment, reminding me that I might be holding treasure, now, if I'd only picked correctly.

"It's hard," I scan the honeycomb, wondering if I should justify my choice with intuition or logic. "That one looks like a peace sign," I point toward a geyser in the middle of the honeycomb. "It's funny that it looks like that, isn't it?" I hold up two fingers, making the sign for 'peace.' "With a circle in the center and then the two long pieces. It could have more caves inside."

"It could," Francois agrees.

"But the water comes up so often. I'm not sure I'll be fast enough." Just then, a huge blast of water surges into the air from the geyser in question, proving my point.

"We could time it," Francois says, considering. "But it

would be dangerous. Perhaps we leave the most dangerous for last?"

"Yes," I agree. "How about that one?" I point to a hole that's about twice as wide in circumference as I am. We peer inside. It's a straight shot to the bottom. The descent looks the same as the others, but anything could be waiting at the bottom.

Francois grabs one end of our rope, checking the knots for good measure, like he does every time. Then, he lowers me inside, and I wonder if this will be the moment that changes everything.

43

ZOE

It's morning. I know it before I open my eyes. The crisp, tingling feel of sunshine on my cheek tells me so. Sunlight seeps in through a slit at the tent's entrance, sticky and dripping. If I could, I'd stay in this moment where I'm warm, where I'm safe.

But there's another clue to find.

My body jolts into action, forcing itself upright.

"Today's the last day," I mutter. Mike is beside me, sprawled out on his back, arms wide. His only response is a snore.

I tumble out of the tent, stomach churning, panic bubbling in my throat. Most of our party is still asleep. The only people awake besides me are my Mom and Oliver— they've both always been early risers. They're making coffee by the fire we've kept burning twenty-four-seven, using the flames to heat water in tin mugs.

"You should rest!" my Mom says when she sees me, clucking her tongue.

"We're almost out of time," I nod at the motorboat across the beach. It sits in the same position, mocking me, physical evidence of my failure to beat Logan at his own game. "It'll blow today."

My Mom sighs. "Then it blows."

Mike appears behind me, bedhead making him even more attractive than usual. It isn't fair we were cheated out of our honeymoon. I want to dwell on it— to brood, to bake in the injustice of it all. But there's no time.

"Any left?" Mike motions to the coffee. Oliver passes him a cup.

"Where is it?" I ask. "The clue? What did you guys do with it?"

Oliver and my Mom change a look.

"Sweetie..."

"Where *is* it?"

"You don't have to do this."

"What's that supposed to mean?"

"Your life is more important than that boat," she says, annoyed. "There are other ways off the island. We could wait for rescue. Mike's working on his raft..."

Mike cringes. We both know construction of the raft is not going well.

"Zoe..." my Mom hesitates.

"What?"

"Is this really about survival?"

"Of course it is."

"You're so determined to solve this puzzle," she sighs. "What if there *is* no answer? What if we just forget it and *let* the boat explode."

"Then we'll die here! Is that what you want?"

"Zoe, we *are* on a tropical island," Mike says, trying to light the mood. "If you can forget about the fact they'll find our skeletons eaten by birds, it's practically paradise!"

"Eventually, someone will come along," my Mom continues, ignoring him. "We'll survive in the meantime."

"Where *is* it?!" I'm shouting now, but I can't help it. I'm frustrated. Not because she's wrong, but because there's some truth in what she's saying. By playing Logan's game, I'm allowing him to make the rules. If I would just decline to participate, I could make my own. But there's a piece of me that wants to beat him at his own game. "I want that box!"

"You almost *died*," she yells back, voice cracking. "Twice!" She's crying, now. Oliver wraps an arm around her shoulders.

"I'm really sorry," it comes out a whisper. There's a moment where my Mom waits, like she's deciding if she believes me. Then, she nods.

"If it helps, I'm trying really hard *not* to die," I add. Everyone laughs, except my Mom. Her eyes darken, and I immediately change my expression to a somber, serious one. "I mean it," I say.

She points at a cluster of palm trees about five hundred feet away. "It's over there." Her tone says she still doesn't approve, but I'm already heading for the silver box, desperate to know what's inside.

44

CASSANDRA

We didn't find the treasure.

That final hole was nothing but another dead end, promising at the beginning but empty at the bottom. I wanted to keep looking, but the sky turned blue, and the sun beat down on us so hard that Francois said it wasn't safe to continue. "The heat," he said, and we both knew it was over.

Now, we're back at camp, checking the tents for the rest of our party.

"Where did everyone go?" Francois asks.

The tents are empty. We checked each one, and it made me feel a strange sense of deja vu. Like my life now is just checking empty holes for items that aren't there.

"I don't know," I say, scanning the beach.

"Do you think they got the boat to work?" Francois' eyebrows raise higher on his forehead, and I know he's wondering the same thing I am.

Could they have left us behind?

My heart sinks. Maybe my name really *is* the answer to Logan's puzzle, and Zoe figured out that I'm the one who helped him. What if she typed my name into that blinking, empty cursor, and the motorboat's engine started? I wouldn't blame the rest of the group for leaving me stranded here. But the fact that Francois is forced to bear the burden with me makes me want to divide into little pieces. I imagine everyone climbing into the boat, watching the island get smaller as it pushes out to sea, two empty spots where Francois and I might have sat. He doesn't deserve to die here. Not because of me.

My feet push against the sand as I run toward the edge of the rocks— the overview where you can catch sight of the motorboat. I expect to see an empty spot on the sand, but instead, the motorboat is exactly where we left it, waiting, taunting.

"It's still here!"

Francois releases a sigh of relief over my shoulder. It strikes me that he doesn't know how dangerous our allegiance is. He's attached himself to a sinking ship. Out of every person on this island he could have befriended, he picked the worst one. "Perhaps, in the trees?"

He motions toward the palms on the other side of the camp site. It's as good a guess as any. We head toward them, and when we hear voices, we know we're on the right track.

We push through the palms, stopping in our tracks when we find an odd sort of gathering— a seance in progress. There's something holy about the silence, like I've interrupted a ceremony or a ritual. Our party stands in a cluster, gathered around a silver box. The expressions across the group range from horror, to disbelief— like they've just seen a ghost. Rachel is holding Oliver's hand. Donald and Alicia are coupled up behind them, using Oliver as a shield. Zoe is physically restraining Mike, who's wearing a look I've never seen on him before. It isn't anger. It's heavier than that, more explosive. The look in his eye is righteous, outraged on a principal. He reminds me of one of those preachers who warns of heaven and hell. Indignation drips from his body.

"The timing is awfully odd, though, isn't it?" he spits, waiving a paper in the air. Donald and Alicia cower behind Oliver, who holds a hand up in the air.

"If we were back in London, I'd suggest this conversation be held at a pub," Oliver jokes. Mike doesn't laugh. "But since we aren't, perhaps it's best had bloke to bloke? Between you and Donald, apart from the group?"

Everyone ignores him. Donald sputters a sad defense. "We didn't know!"

Finally, I catch a glimpse of the paper Mike is clutching. It's littered with fancy writing, the kind of script used for official certificates and government documents.

"What is it?" I lean over and ask Tori. She's standing next to Jason, who's smiling as he films the meltdown. Tori looks surprised I'm speaking to her, like she'd forgotten I existed.

"They found it in the box," she nods at the discarded silver box by her feet. "It's a land transfer deed. Donald and Alicia bought a house in the Seychelles, then transferred it to…"

"Logan?"

She nods, curious that I've guessed correctly. "A company, actually. It's an LLC called 'Logan Yosemite enterprises'."

"Yes," Mike adds. He's overheard Tori's explanation. "An LLC that just happens to use Logan's first name, and the place where he tortured us."

"How were we supposed to guess such a thing?" Donald shouts. "Perhaps if you would have *told* us…"

"Of course I told you! You just never listen because you're so concerned with superficial bullshit."

"But how do you *know* it's him?" Lana asks. She hasn't said much since Rick was murdered, preferring instead to sit quietly on her own, away from the group. She's grieving silently, isolating herself, cocooning away with her thoughts. "It could be a coincidence."

"It's not," Zoe responds. "He could have named the company anything. He could have picked something smarter. Something less obvious. Something that wouldn't give him away. But he chose *Logan Yosemite* to let us know it was him. He *wanted* us to be angry at each other," she says the last part like she's realizing something.

"Didn't you think the name was strange?" Mike asks.

"It was presented to us by a travel experience company!" Donald throws his hands up in the air. "It sounded rugged. We assumed they were appealing to the young and adventurous."

"Why would you buy property in the Seychelles just to sell it?" Mike asks Donald, doubt dripping from his words.

Donald's face flushes. "Well, we've…" Alicia gives him a warning looks but he ignores it. "We've had some money troubles lately. We had an opportunity to clear up some debt. It came our way most unexpectedly and we didn't feel we could refuse."

"What was the offer?"

"It was presented via our financial advisor as a legitimate, uh," he clears his throat. "Offshore opportunity. Quite simple really. We would buy the place for one million United States dollars, then sell it back to this particular LLC for twenty percent more, guaranteed."

"Why would they do that? What's in it for the company?"

"Well," Donald sighs. "Our advisor was told they needed

to show a loss, speaking in a tax sense. The idea was that we would buy this little shack of a place, then they would purchase it from us for twenty percent more. We would then return ten percent to them under the table of course, and keep the remaining ten percent. It was win-win!"

"You were laundering money?" Rachel asks, mouth dropping open in horror.

"It was a legitimate investment opportunity! A chance to help a friend of a friend. What kind of maniac denies a twenty percent return?"

"The kind who doesn't want to go to prison for offshore tax evasion," Rachel says, shaking her head. "And the return is ten percent after the criminals take their cut, you absolute moron."

"He's using this place," Mike shouts. "This is his headquarters. Whatever house you bought, he's been squatting in it, planning this entire thing before we even arrived. It's *your* fault we're here."

I have to bite my tongue to stop from revealing the truth. Mike is right. I've seen the house myself. I walked through it, slept in it. It's just across the sea, a short sail away, close enough that the same birds can fly from that island to the rock that we're stuck on. I didn't know its purchase was made possible by his aunt and uncle. But I know it exists, and Logan would never have been able to set up his game without it.

"What about *him*!" Donald rages, pointing a fat finger at Oliver. "He arranged the flight! Had the maniac deliver us to this abandoned rock!"

"He didn't *know*," Rachel sighs.

"Neither did we!"

"Didn't you think it was strange," Rachel continues, "That the house was in the Seychelles?"

"We've done plenty of offshore banking in the past!" Donald answers. "Switzerland. The Seychelles. Belize. The Cayman Islands. Why would this be any different?"

"Because we *told* you our concerns about Logan, about the wedding." Mike adds. Zoe grips his arm to hold him back. "We asked you to be extra cautious. And you went forward with the deal anyway! You *knew* our honeymoon would be in the Seychelles," Mike is pacing now. "You *knew* we were stalked through Yosemite. You *knew* he uses the name Logan! Maybe if you paid closer attention..."

"I think we've given you *more* than enough attention over the years," Alicia interjects.

"That's enough!" Rachel steps forward, about to come to Mike's defense.

"Oh yes, I'm sorry, I forgot!" Mike pretends to laugh. "I was such an imposition to you! So sorry you had to let me move in when I was just a *child* whose parents had *died*."

"I was a child, too!" Alicia's practically screaming now. "Twenty-two and married! I wasn't expecting children for years!"

"Well now you've got them, haven't you?" Mike says, waving the paper in the air. "What purchase put you in enough debt that you had to jump on this deal? Was it the boys' tennis lesson? Did you hire a pro coach? Were you trying to buy their way into a good college? Or was it all... *this*?" he waves a hand at her face, spotlighting what's probably close to ten thousand dollars worth of plastic surgery.

Tori lets out a huge laugh, then slaps a hand over her mouth. Alicia takes a step back, looking profoundly hurt. "Donald," she says quietly. "I would like to go home now."

Donald scans the group like he's hoping someone else will intervene on his behalf. "Darling, so would I, but I don't see *how*."

"I said," she keeps her voice steady at first, then erupts into volcanic rage, "I would like to go home right *now!*" She marches into the trees. Donald rushes after her.

"You know," Francois smiles at me. "I think our best chance at getting off this island might be following her. That woman tends to get exactly what she wants."

LATER, I watch Mike work on the raft again, far up in my hiding place. He's still trying to make the leaves keep the pieces of wood together, even though it's obvious they lack the strength.

It's strange. Something has changed my perception of him. I used to see Mike as an object to be valued, a special person who belonged on a pedestal. But now— watching him desperately fumble with the pieces of the raft— I realize he's flawed. He's good at two things: loving Zoe, and making furniture in a workshop. That's it. He doesn't know anything about the world beyond his bubble. He's not particularly inventive, or adventurous. The idea smacks me in the face, a possibility I'd never considered before:

Is Mike boring?

I've buzzed around him for so long that I never stopped to consider why I cared. Why did it matter if he noticed me? The Mike I loved so long ago was the center of my world, but I was younger then. Less full. Less interesting. I've been asking for attention from someone who doesn't have half my creativity, half my inventiveness. I've been orbiting around him, but in all my buzzing, in all my attempts to be worthy of his attention, I never stopped to ask if he was worthy of mine.

I slip down the bank, letting my feet dig into the sand.

When Mike sees me, he puts up a hand as if to say, "not now." But I don't let that stop me.

"I have an idea," I tell him.

"I don't need your ideas."

"I'm going to give them to you anyway, and not because I'm obsessed with you."

His eyebrows arch in a skeptical expression. "Really?"

"And you're going to listen to me, because I'm twice the designer you are, and if you don't we all might die on this stupid rock."

"You're not twice the designer I am," he says.

"We both know I am. You have an eye for construction, but not found materials." I pick up one of the palm fronds, crumbling it into pieces. "The fact you thought this could withstand salt water shows you have no idea what you're doing. You've only kept working with it because you get stuck on the first idea that comes to you. You have no imagination. You can't reinvent like I can," I glance at his t-shirt. "Take off your shirt."

"What?" Mike looks horrified, like I've asked him to give me a striptease. It makes me laugh.

"Rip it into pieces," I say, simply. "Fabric will withstand the saltwater. It has more give."

His mouth drops open, like he's completely shocked he didn't see it before. Good.

Moron.

I walk away from him, letting my hips sway as I cross the beach, feeling— for the first time— like I'm impossible not to notice.

Try ignoring me now.

45

———

ZOE

"He *wanted* us all to fight, " I tell Mike later. The rest of the group has disbursed. Everyone hides inside their individual tents, as if determined to prove my point.

"Well, it's working," Mike answers.

"We don't *know* that Logan is using the house."

"He had to find somewhere out here on the islands though, didn't he?" Mike says. "And what are the odds that's a company name? It's hard for me to believe he'd stay away from the place he stranded us. Logan likes to be right in the middle of things. Even in Yosemite, he stayed personally involved in the action. He never left the valley."

"That's true."

"My aunt and uncle only care about themselves. I've told them about Yosemite dozens of time. If they had just listened..."

"I know."

"You don't think they did it on purpose, do you?" His voice is tight, restrained. "They needed the money. Maybe they knew it was him."

"They're awful, but not evil," I tell him. His silence says he's not sure if he agrees.

We approach the motorboat like we're heading toward an angry pit-bull. It's an inanimate object that could determine our fate, and being close to it means noticing an electric charge in the air. Lana and Oliver are standing over the motorboat's side, examining the hookups.

"We thought we'd give it one last college try," Oliver says, looking lost. Lana wipes her eyes. They've been swollen and red since Rick died.

"How much time?"

"Five hours."

My brain tries to do the math to turn hours into minutes and minutes into seconds, but it just makes my head hurt. Mike puts a hand around my waist. "I'll keep trying with the raft," he whispers. "Zoe, go think about the clues."

"I don't want to believe it's someone on this island," I say, finally admitting the thing I've been avoiding.

"I know," he nods, somber. "But you're the only one who can solve this. I'm not sure why, but he meant for it to be that way."

"There's something he's trying to tell me."

"Let's find out what it is," Mike says, serious, "so we can get off this island and catch him. We know where he's staying," Mike passes me the deed, folding it into my open hand. "Maybe this time, we don't have to wait for the police. This time, we come for him ourselves."

AFTER COLLECTING the clues from our unwilling party, I gather them in my arms and find a secluded spot on a cliff that overlooks the sea. The air is thinner up here— cleaner, somehow. It sets my head straight. Looking out over the ocean makes me feel like I have an overview of the world. It's the perfect place to think.

I line up the clues in the order they were found, noticing that each one is connected to a member of our party.

The wedding ring and the plane charter.

Jason's wallet and receipts.

Tori's bridesmaid's sash, and the emails.

The pink gun. The gun is still missing, so I draw a picture of a pistol in the sand with a stick as a placeholder.

The property deed.

We've found five clues out of six. I should focus on what's in front of me, but my mind wanders to that missing clue, its empty box left abandoned on the beach. It's hard not to believe that the clue we haven't found is the key to solving the puzzle Logan's left for me.

A name. I just need a name. One person on this island I believe would lie to me.

I work the problem backwards. Instead of thinking about who could be guilty, I try to understand why Logan meant for me to find each item. I slip into his twisted mind, crawling around the spaces there— the dark hallways, dripping with evil.

The wedding ring. It made me feel betrayed, to realize that my Mom was keeping a secret from me.

The plane charter. The discovery of the charter made me doubt Oliver, and his arrival into our lives.

The receipts and the wallet. All I know is they belong to Jason.

The bridesmaid's sash, and the emails within. They made me question my years of friendship with Tori. It was the emails that did it, but the sash added a gut punch. No doubt, including it in the box was Logan's way of reminding me that no matter how long you know someone, you never *really* know them at all.

The pink gun. It incriminates Lana, who— to be fair— I'm not all that close with. We never became friends in the way people sometimes do, forming a one-on-one rapport outside the circumference of the group in which they met. I tried, once, to ask her to coffee, but Rick stopped the process in its tracks. He never liked me, not from day one. I should have seen it sooner. She's always been a question mark, and I don't feel like I know her well enough to reach a conclusion about whether she's capable of criminal activity.

The property deed. Donald and Alicia look guilty of aiding our tormenter when you consider that they knew we were headed for the Seychelles for our honeymoon. But what was in it for them? Would Donald— a celebrated litigator— really put everything on the line to hurt us this way? He has no motivation, besides money. His type of crime is a full-bellied, greedy sort. The kind that takes place in high rises. Insider trading and vague "business opportunities" are his speed— not kidnapping.

In fact, what was in it for anyone here? I still can't put my finger on a motivation for any member of our group. Not one that makes sense, anyway.

Across the beach, a small portion of our crew is gathered around the motorboat, looking at it like it's a car that won't start. Lana points at a wire tied into the ignition— I've seen her play with that wire a thousand times before, always careful— gentle— in case it blows. Oliver watches the clock ticking down, a sorrowful look on his face that says he's already given up. A little further away, Jason films the entire thing. That camera is still strapped to his hand, just like it was from day one, recording every moment. It irritates me that he can think about his show at a time like this. His camera's battery seems eternal, destined to record forever, even when there's nothing to film but our skeletons lying prostrate under the palm trees. I glance at the camera, imagining what it would feel like to smash it into a thousand pieces.

I wish that stupid thing would die.

Suddenly, the answer hits me like a ton of bricks. I return to Jason's wallet, rifling through those receipts one more time. They didn't mean anything to me when we found them because it was still too early in the game. We'd been stranded here barely one day. They were pointless pieces of paper sent to confuse, to cloud the water— not actual clues. Just meaningless distractions. They meant nothing to me then.

Now, they mean everything.

I take off, running across the beach until I find Mike. He's working on the raft. It's much better than before— almost a complete project.

"You tied the pieces together?" I ask. Strips of ripped fabric weave between planks of wood, lashing them tighter than the pond fronds ever could. I notice Mike isn't wearing a shirt, and the bits of red fabric are the same pale red color as the one he had on earlier.

"I used clothes," he smiles at me. "Not my idea. Can't believe I didn't see it. Feeling a bit like an idiot actually. It took a little— *crazy*— to think outside the box."

"I know the answer to Logan's puzzle," I tell him, unable to wait any longer. "I know who helped him."

Mike drops the piece of wood he's holding, and I lean in to tell him my secret, careful to make sure no one else can hear.

46

CASSANDRA

Francois and I are sitting by the water, our legs stretched out over that curving line where the ocean meets the sand.

"Every time the waves come in, we get a new beach," Francois nods, watching as the tide comes up yet again. The remnants of the old line are washed away, replaced by one that's half an inch further inland. "See?" He adds, smiling at me like he's sharing a big secret. "The beach is always new. Just when you think you know it, it changes on you. It will never let you figure how wide it is. Not really." The waves tumble toward us again, leaving white foam behind on my thighs. The little bubbles pop on top of my skin, tinged crimson from the sun.

"They're not going to figure it out, are they?" I point toward the shore, where our party is gathered around the motorboat. The group looks like a team of Doctors debating how to save a particularly difficult patient laying open on the operating table, organs exposed and oozing. It's not going well. "The boat will blow."

"Maybe," he says.

Their failure is a relief. If my name really is the answer to Logan's puzzle, I would rather see the boat burn. No one will know what I've done. No one will see what I am. I'll die with my stinger intact, a bee who never stung. That will be enough for me. I'm only sad Francois won't be rescued. That he won't find his treasure in a way that can be acknowledged by the outside world. That he won't be noticed. If I could stay here forever only so he could go free, it's a deal I would take.

"Even if we find La Buse's treasure, you won't get to tell anyone about it," I say, my chest heavy with the weight of it all. "I'm really sorry."

"That's alright," he says, looking into my eyes. "I have found another treasure."

Suddenly, I'm crying. "You're not listening to me," the words spill in a tumble, stepping over each other on the way out. "I said, I'm *sorry.*" I want him to understand it was me who did this, without having to actually confess. Even at the bitter end, I am a coward. "Don't you get it?" I repeat the words again and again, a broken record skipping a beat. "I'm sorry, I'm sorry, I'm *sorry...*" He doesn't interrupt, but watches me repeat myself without any judgement in his eyes.

When I'm done, Francois takes me in for a moment, perplexed. Then, he says, simply, "You are afraid to be stuck here. You are like the beach." He puts his hand on top of mine, and it makes my fingers burn with shame. He will never guess what I have done, because he only sees the best in me. My storms are— in his eyes— acts of nature, not of character. "My only regret," he says, "is that I will not keep my date with you."

"I didn't know we had one."

"I have not asked you yet, but I had hoped that escaping

this place might mean I could take you to dinner. Now that we have failed, it seems that is impossible."

"I would have said yes," I tell him.

"*J'ai posé un lapin*," he smiles at me, repeating La Buse's last words.

"I put it a rabbit to it," I repeat the translation he taught me.

Francois nods. "We have stood each other up before the date has even been agreed upon. How bad at this we are!"

"Terrible," I agree. He leans in, and I think we might kiss, when a throat clears behind us. It's Tori, smirking like a sorority sister who's walked in on her roommate in the middle of banging some guy.

"I didn't mean to interrupt..."

Then why do you look like you're enjoying it so much?

"But Zoe wants everyone to meet up at the tents."

"Did she say why?" I ask, heart pounding.

"Something to do with the answer to the riddle."

She turns on her heel, hair flipping as she waddles back up the beach. Francois takes my hand and pulls me onto my feet, impressions left in the wet sand where we sat just seconds ago. I follow him up the sandy slope, looking over my shoulder at the wide open sea, wondering what would happen if I ran straight toward it. I picture my head disappearing beneath the waves, chin first, then nose, then eyes, down to the last of my hair, suspended in the water like pieces of seaweed. I would sink to the bottom and stay there, because it's what I deserve.

Please, don't tell them it's me.

47

ZOE

Our party stands around the motorboat, anxious eyes peaking out from sun-drenched faces. In a matter of days, we've transformed. Soft skin has been made rough by the salt in the air. Long hair tangles into medusa waves, strands competing for space. All the men have grown beards, some grey in places. The women are more monotone now, the last contrasting colors of makeup having ben washed away. No one has been spared. Every one of us looks like a wild thing. Every one of us appears dangerous. If I didn't know these people and you asked me if there was a madman in the group, just by looking at them I would say, "More than one."

But that's the point, isn't it?

Alicia grabs Donald's hand like she's lost in the ocean and he is her personal flotation device. Mike stands next to them, a concerned shadow over his face. I know what he's thinking. He's already heard my solution to Logan's puzzle — my best guess as to what the answer might be. He agrees it's a good one. But there's no way we can be sure it's correct, and if it isn't, the boat will blow. Someone has to type in the answer. Someone has to test the boat. He knows I'll want it to be me. Beside him, my Mom rests her head on Oliver's shoulder, chewing her fingernails. It's a habit she gave up years ago— bad hygiene for a nurse. But she's back at it now. No doubt due to the stress. Apart from the rest of them, Jason takes a step back, panning over the group. In his delusional little inner world, he's Tarantino and this island is the next big blockbuster. It's as if he expects a fight to break out and he's afraid of missing an action shot.

I'll have to thank him, one day.

In the distance, three figures emerge, heading towards us from the other end of the beach. The first is Tori, her short legs working double-time to fight their way through dense, uncooperative sand. Behind her is Francois, so ready to leave this island that he almost breaks into a run. His face is hopeful, eyes wide with anticipation. I appreciate his vote of confidence. Next to him, Cassandra drags herself down the beach, miserable. She expects the worst. Her shoulders slump over, defeated, a resigned kind of energy propelling her toward whatever nightmare fate has in store for her.

When the trio arrive, the group is complete, gathered around the motorboat, awaiting answers. Everyone looks at each other. Nobody wants to make it obvious, but small glances betray mistrust. Someone in our group is about to face justice. Cassandra looks at me, her eyes bottomless and pleading. For a moment, I think she might ask something of me. She even opens her mouth to speak, but shuts it again like she's changed her mind. She takes a step back, practically hiding behind Francois.

"I know the answer to Logan's puzzle," I say, trying to sound as certain as possible.

Murmurs echo throughout the group. Donald clears his

throat, never one to let somebody else take the lead in legal matters.

"I'd like to point that whatever Zoe proposes is a hypothesis, not the result of an actual investigation."

"That's true," I agree, nodding. "It's only my opinion. Just a guess."

He continues on, encouraged. "Exactly. Which is why I don't think we should do anything rash."

"If we find out who helped Logan trap us here, I'm kicking that person's ass," Lana says, face flushing after the words escape her mouth. It's as if she meant to think it to herself, not say it aloud.

"I'm only asking for a little professional restraint," Donald says. His words are drowned out as the group deteriorates, everyone talking over each other.

"Restraint is hardly our biggest concern right now, old sport," Oliver mutters.

Before Oliver can finish his sentence, Francois shouts, in a rare moment of outrage, "Why should I exhibit restraint? I had nothing do with any of you! Didn't choose to be here..."

Alicia calls back, "Don't you undermine my husband! He's a legal *genius*."

"There are no laws here, sweetie," Tori sneers at her. "We're trapped on an island, in case you didn't notice. It's anybody's choice as far as I'm concerned. Whoever did it gets what's coming to them."

I try to get their attention but no one pays me any mind. Suddenly, a sharp, high pitched sound cuts through he air. It's Mike, whistling, two fingers in his mouth. Everyone stares at him. "Zoe has something to say," he admonishes. "And no one's doing anything until she's finished. Zoe, take it away."

I take a deep breath, praying my theory is correct.

"It was the receipts," I say. Nobody seems to know what I'm talking about. "One of the first clues we found. Jason's wallet had all these receipts inside and we thought it was just junk."

Tori gasps, gripping Jason's arm with one claw-like hand. He keeps his camera in the air, but his mouth sets into a thin, hard line.

"But that rubbed me the wrong way. Logan doesn't do anything that's pointless. Every move Logan makes has a purpose. It felt out of character for him to include something without meaning."

"He was trying to confuse you," Jason says, his voice confident. But I notice his hand shaking a little.

"No," I add. "*You* confused me by not being honest, but you couldn't get away with it for long."

"Oh my God," Tori gulps, unlatching her hand from Jason's arm. "Baby? You didn't."

He doesn't say anything.

"Jason, what's your camera battery level?"

"What?" He blinks stupidly, like he's never heard of a camera battery.

"We've been on this island three days and it hasn't died. What's the battery level?"

There's a long moment in which Jason doesn't answer. Then, he turns on his heel, attempting to flee the scene, running toward the other side of the island. Before he gets too far, Oliver grabs him in a headlock. Mike rushes forward to help.

"Don't hurt him!" Mike adds, pulling the two apart and restraining Jason's arms. "Let her finish, before we do anything." Mike pushes Jason forward, holding his hands behind his back at an awkward angle. Oliver bends down and picks up Jason's camera. He passes it Lana, the head of a news network and person among us most familiar with cameras. She clicks a couple buttons, then turns the screen around, showing the group an icon of a battery. It's bright green.

"Ninety percent or more," Lana says.

Tori makes a choking sound. "He couldn't have," she says. "Baby, you didn't. Tell them you didn't!"

Jason doesn't answer.

"It was the receipts," I add, pulling them out of my pocket. "These are from a camera store. You knew you needed extra batteries. You also knew you needed them in your pocket the night of the wedding, because you'd be taken in what you were wearing when you got home. They took our cellphones out of our pockets, but *knew* not to touch your batteries because that was the deal you made. You made sure you'd have enough backup power to document the entire thing."

Jason's lower lip trembles. His terse exterior cracks, showing something like regret underneath. "It was supposed to be a show," he says. "A show about privacy. It was experimental."

Tori gasps again, as if she's heard the worst thing anyone's shared all day. "You got a gig and didn't *tell* me?"

"The email said not to tell anyone," Jason says, breathless. "It came anonymously, but they said they were from an online platform with millions of viewers. They liked my show. They said what I'm doing is revolutionary."

"You asshole," Donald raises a fist and rushes toward Jason, but Oliver redirects him before he can strike.

"Professional restraint, remember sport?"

Donald shakes him away. Mike loosens his hold on

Jason. "I felt the same way when Zoe told me," Mike says. "But trust me. Just wait until she's finished. No one does anything until Zoe says she's done."

"What about the steak dinner?" My Mom asks. Her memory has always been excellent, especially when it comes to frivolous expenditures. "There was a receipt that showed he ate at a fancy restaurant."

"Right," I confirm. "You ate a steak dinner the night before the wedding because you *knew* you'd be trapped here with nothing but some powdered food. It was a last meal, wasn't it?"

Jason's collapsed now, looking like a puppet whose strings have been cut. Mike lets him crumple into the sand, putting a hand on his shoulder. "The producers said the show would be like *Survivor*. They promised we'd all get to leave, though!" he adds hurriedly. "They pitched the concept as part survival show, part social experiment."

"And the shoes," I add, remembering the receipt from the shoe store. "You bought sandals because you knew we'd be on an island. You made sure you were wearing them when they knocked you out."

"Why would Logan want Jason to film all of this anyway?" Lana asks, perplexed.

"Because Logan loves to watch the effects of his work," I tell her. "There's no way he would go to all this trouble just to miss out on seeing the chaos he caused. Logan's footage was the prize at the end of all of this. He was going to find a way to get that memory card, and rewatch everything that happened."

"Serial killers keep mementos from their victims," Tori nods knowingly. Alicia casts her a disgusted look, and Tori shrugs. "I saw it on *Oxygen*."

"And you didn't *ask* who they were or where they were from?" My Mom asks Jason, talking to him like he's a worm, unable to believe the stupidity in front of her.

"They were keeping. a low profile because, well... none of you exactly *consented* to be on the show! It's illegal, isn't it?"

"You bet your ass it is!" Donald shouts, spit flying everywhere. "You'll be subject to a class action suit! I'm going to take you for all you're worth, you little rat."

"Hold off on that, Donald," I say. "That suit might be a bit bigger than you think."

I tuck the receipts back into the wallet. "That explains Jason. But it doesn't explain the rest of the clues."

"They were nothing! It's a riddle isn't it, and now it's solved," Alicia says, clutching pearls that aren't there.

"The only difference between Jason and everyone else is that Jason lied," I say. "Jason lied because he thought he was part of a reality show until he saw the bomb attached to the motorboat, and heard Logan's riddle read out-loud. He realized he had been tricked, and didn't want to confess in case we blamed him for it. Isn't that right?"

Jason nods. He glances at Tori, seeking sympathy, but she avoids making eye contact with him.

"If we really look at it, what happened to Jason isn't unique. Tori was tricked into giving away the guest list."

"Which I regret," she says, shame dripping from her words.

"Donald and Alicia, you were tricked into providing Logan with a place to stay on the islands."

"That's supposition!" Donald interjects.

"Mom and Oliver, you were tricked into providing him with a charter plane."

"Also supposition," Oliver sighs, "But looks likely, yes."

"So I can't confidently blame all of this on Jason. Understanding the receipts doesn't tell us why one clue is missing, or how Rick died."

Everyone quiets. I turn toward Lana. "Is there anything you want to tell us?"

She's crying. "Yes."

The group quiets. Francois and Oliver are standing next her. They take a step back, creating a blank space around her as if she's surrounded by a forcefield that electrocutes anyone within range. She reaches into her pocket, pulling out a piece of paper in a plastic bag. She hands it to me.

I open it, reading silently while the group waits. It's a hand-written letter. A lump forms in my throat. I pass the paper to Mike. Mike reads aloud, "I have enclosed the cashier's check you requested. Half will be paid up front, half once you've proven you can stop the proceedings without creating harm or injury to those involved. This cannot be traced back to me or I will come after you. Don't think I don't have the resources to do it."

"He paid someone to stop the wedding," Lana whispers.

"Why would Rick do that?" Mike says, his voice devoid of all emotion.

"You and I are the same," Lana tells Mike, her voice faltering. "We ignored— the looks. The way he missed you when you spent more time with Zoe. He never loved me," she breaks down again. "And I knew it. He always loved one person. Just one person."

Mike's eyes widen in surprise. "I didn't know," he says.

"He hid it well. Rick was always concerned with looking a certain way, being 'the man,' whatever that means," she wipes her nose.

"You were the one who found the letter, weren't you?" I ask Lana. She nods.

"I was taking a break to walk, to clear my head. I found one of those little silver boxes, and when I opened it, this was inside. I panicked. Figured I'd confront him about it later."

"And you did, didn't you?"

"Yes," she sighs. "He was so *angry*. He said I was crazy, but I knew it was true. Our entire marriage I knew he was hiding something. And still wouldn't own up to it! Even then, with the evidence sitting right in front of us."

"So you killed him for it?" Donald shouts, waving a fat finger in the air. "Pre-meditated murder! A man's life means nothing to you!"

Lana shakes her head. "That's the worst part," she's sobbing, her voice pouring out in an uneven rhythm. "I said —" she inhales, gasping for air. "I said— such awful— things. Called him such terrible names." She motions to the sea, where the waves cover the sand in an uneven line. "He ran out there with the gun. Said I'd be sorry. I might have well have done it myself. I was so angry. He let me waste so much time. I ran after him but it was too late. He had already done it."

"Why did you hide the gun?" Alicia asks, her eyes narrowing.

"I knew all of you would think I murdered him!" Lana says, a panicked look in her eyes. "The gun's mine, isn't it? I'd already been accused of one crime I didn't commit. What if you blamed me for his death?"

"Well," Alicia snarls, clicking her nails together. "I guess we'll never know for sure what happened, will we?"

"Zoe, you believe me, don't you?"

I scan Lana's face. She's torn up, there's no doubt about that. But she's also so capable. She's the kind of person who can make a plan and execute it to the letter. She was angry.

She had a motivation to kill Rick. Of course I want to believe her, but there's something about her story that leaves me cold. For now, I have to agree with Alicia:

We'll never know for sure.

48

CASSANDRA

I made sure to stand at the back of the group when Zoe started her speech. Francois is taller than me, so he made an easy shield— a comfortable person to hide behind. My intention was to stay. I thought about it as we walked to the tents, steeling myself for the bitter taste of my comeuppance.

They'll probably stone me to death, I considered as we neared the campsite, white tents coming into focus, growing bigger with every heartbeat. *It will be biblical. Poetic.*

I wasn't afraid of death. I've wished for it many times in the past— tested it, even, to see if it thought of me too. I've experimented with boundaries, flirted with the grim reaper in a passive way. After a couple of whiskeys, I've downed a handful of painkillers, just to see what happened. After the deed was done, I waited for the man with the cloak and scythe to knock on my door, to notice me. "You've been very bad," I imagined him saying. "I know," I would say, and he'd take me away.

It wasn't fear of death that made me run. No, it was the look on Francois' face when Zoe said she knew who the traitor was. He looked horrified, scanning the group to see where the culprit hid. His eyes burned, outraged that someone could do such a thing.

I couldn't let him see me that way.

Now, I'm pushing through the palm trees, making my way to a place I know I can be alone. A place where I can do what needs to be done. I'm alright with dying— I invite it, in fact. But I can't witness Francois' disappointment in me. I can't watch his face fall when he learns that I've wronged him. Mike already hates me. One person I loved already sees me as a monster, something to be despised. If Francois grows to see me that way, too, I won't be able to lie to myself anymore. I'll have to accept that I'm a monster and always will be. A creepy, feral, unloveable thing, mutated and unholy, with no hope for redemption.

If I'm going to die, I at least want to go out on top. If I'm going to leave this Earth, I might as well do it in a moment where I can still believe someone will be sad for the loss. If I'm going to die, it will be on my terms— not theirs.

49

ZOE

"We don't have much time," I say, motioning toward the clock inside the motorboat, counting down the minutes to explosion. "At this point, everyone seems guilty. Jason, with the receipts. Mom and Oliver, with the plane. Donald and Alicia, with the house..."

"Conjecture!" Donald shouts. I ignore him.

"Tori, with the guest list."

"What about me?" Francois asks, raising a hand as if he's disappointed to be left out.

"You were here accidentally," I tell him. "They only brought you because you were with us when Logan's men meant to take us."

"Unfortunate," he nods. "And in other ways, not so much," he looks over his shoulder like he's expecting someone to be there, but there's only thin air.

"Where's Cassandra?" He asks. Everyone looks around. The group steps aside. She's nowhere to be found. She's disappeared, almost like she was never here in the first place.

"Oh no," An awful thought strikes me, but I can't address it now. I have to get this boat started before the timer runs out.

"What?" Mike asks, concerned.

"We need to hurry," I tell him, turning back to Francois. "Francois, even though it was an accident you ended up here, it was because of you that I figured out the answer."

"Me?"

"Yes. You and the way you talk about La Buse. The story you told about how he didn't trust his men— how he betrayed his crew— stuck with me. And it got me thinking. Here's what I know about Logan," I address the group again. "His fascination with me stems from the fact that I used to be a little— *aloof.*"

"That's an understatement," Mike mutters.

"It was difficult for me to trust others. That changed when I met Mike. And that's what Logan hates about our relationship. It's created an obsession. In Yosemite, he asked me to become more like him. To become a person who believes others are fundamentally selfish. Who cannot see the best in people."

"So, what's the answer?" Alicia sighs. She's bored of this game and wants off the island as soon as possible. I couldn't agree more.

"It's not about the truth," I say, pacing. "It's about what Logan would want me to believe. It's not about the *right* answer. It's about the answer he wants me to give." I pull out the riddle, re-reading one more time, "*Someone helped me hoodwink you.*" I pause for effect. "The real answer is 'no one,' isn't it? Because everyone here was tricked in some way. You didn't mean to hoodwink me. You were deceived, too. We were all deceived."

"But is that the answer Logan would want?" Oliver asks, doubtful.

"No," I say, shaking my head. "Logan would want me to believe the opposite. Logan would want me to give up trusting others for good."

I step toward the boat, reaching for the keyboard. "Zoe..." Mike says, hesitant, but it's too late. I've already got the keyboard in my hands. All he can do is stand next to me and hope I'm right. He cringes as I type, putting his arm around, prepared to die if I'm wrong. The rest of the group backs up.

The letters light up the screen:

E-V-E-R-Y-O-N- E.

There's a long pause after I hit enter. For a moment, I think I'm wrong. But then, a clicking noise comes from the ignition. It's the unmistakable roar of an engine rattling inside the hull, sending vibrations through the boat's frame.

"We're going home," Donald sighs. The groups cheers.

"There's something we have to do first," I say. Donald starts to object, but I hold up a hand before he can get too far. "Trust."

For the first time in his life, Donald shuts his mouth.

Without another word, I step toward Francois and whisper my concerns in his ear. He inhales when I tell him what I believe Cassandra is going to do, looking nauseous.

"The ocean will be faster," I tell him, nodding at the boat.

He shakes his head. "You check the water, in case she's already done it. I'll go by foot. I have a guess where," he says, motioning into the distance. "Head toward the sun. There's a flat area near the bluffs. That way." Without another word, he takes off, running as fast as he can.

"Can you drive this thing?" I ask Oliver, pointing at the motorboat.

"There's nothing I can't drive," he smiles. We push the boat out to sea with Mike's help, the three of us jumping in when the water reaches our knees. We zoom toward the other end of the island, leaving our stunned party standing on the beach, getting smaller and smaller behind us.

50

———

CASSANDRA

My foot slips on the sharp prong of a fallen palm leaf, a rigid thorn digging into my heel. Blood drips onto the Earth. I don't bother to remove it. It won't mean anything, soon enough.

Finally, the destination I've been seeking is in reach. It's a sheer cliff overlooking the sea. I noticed the bluffs when Francois and I were searching for treasure, on a day that feels like a lifetime ago. The sense that decades have passed doesn't surprise me. Time moves more slowly when you know an ending is approaching, and I've sensed from the moment Zoe read Logan's riddle that my journey would close this way.

My lungs burn as I force my way to the top of the bluffs, arriving at the cliff's climax— its highest edge. I stand on the perimeter, so close to the edge that my big toes curl over the rock, touching nothing but thin air. Hundreds of feet down, waves crash against the island, beating her again and again. Despite the sea's assault, the island never gives up. She refuses to quit. She is stronger than I am.

My arms open wide, lungs expanding as I breathe in the

salt air. I haven't heard an explosion, which means the boat didn't blow. They must have solved the puzzle. By now, Francois knows the truth about me. I have limited time to take action, to run away in the only direction I can. My stomach churns as I inch forward, resting on the precipice so that nothing but my heels are touching dry land. White foam sprays toward the sky, its scent calling me toward the blue pit below. I keep my weight shifted back— the smallest movement forward will send me crashing into the rocks, ricocheting off their jagged edges into the angry sea below. I'm not ready to go quite yet. I'm still getting used to the idea. Still testing it out. Childishly, I wonder if it will hurt. I lie to myself and say it won't.

It's as easy as flying.

I'm about to jump when I decide to take one, last look at this beautiful island. This is the place where I was allowed to meet myself again. This is the dot in the middle of an ocean where I got to start over, to try to be a new Cassandra. This is the place where I had a second chance. Seeing it for the last time makes it more vibrant, more real, almost as if the island is trying to entice me to stay. The ocean turns darker, obsidian blue folding over crisp, white foam. The sun seems to sink in the sky, like it's planning to catch me. To my left is the cluster of palm trees I walked through to get here, looking taller than normal. Down below, on my right, I notice a flat landing dotted by holes. Suddenly, salt-water sprays into the air in a long, determined stream. It's the collection of blowholes. The honeycomb. The spot where Francois and I looked for treasure.

How fitting.

I didn't realize the blowholes could be seen from up here. If I'd known, I would have suggested to Francois that we climb higher in order to get an overview. From up here, you can see the shape of every hole, the trajectory of every geyser. It's a shame Francois and I never found the treasure. It would have fixed everything. I could have shared my mistakes with the group, explained why I did what I did, buoyed all the while by an accomplishment unlike any other. I would be Cassandra the fuck-up. I'd be Cassandra the fuck-up who has also discovered priceless historical treasures. People are more forgiving of your flaws when you can provide evidence of tangible achievement to offset your mistakes. Maybe I could have purchased their forgiveness. Mike would have finally understood that there's value in what I do, in the way I am. There's a usefulness in buzzing around things, and in being a bee.

J'ai posé un lapin, I think to myself dryly. It's a date we'll never keep. I'm about to put a rabbit on it.

I lift one foot off the cliff when something catches the corner of my eye. It's a blowhole that stands out from all the others. It's the one I thought looked like the hand signal for "peace." From up here, it takes on a different shape: a round face, blossoming into two tall ovals that look like ears.

J'ai posé un lapin.

La Buse's last words weren't an apology.

They were a clue.

I know where the treasure is.

51

ZOE

The motorboat careens through the water, sending a thick spray into the air. Oliver is at the helm, smiling from ear to ear. He was a born to be a captain, no matter what the transportation device.

"Can you go any faster?" I shout over the engine.

He shakes his head. "Can't risk flooding the engine. We don't know how long this boat has been sitting unused. The insides aren't reliable, and if we push them too hard, we might end up with a dead boat. I still want off this island."

Beside me, Mike grips the railing, frustrated that we're risking anything for Cassandra. "Cass is a free spirit. She's always been this way. She's probably just wandered off somewhere. We could have waited for her back at the beach."

"No." Now that we're alone, I can tell him the whole truth. "She's going to do something awful."

"What do you mean?"

"She's going to hurt herself."

"Why would she do that?" His brow furrows, suddenly concerned.

"She thinks it was her name that made the boat start."

"How do you know?" Mike exclaims, looking seasick, but not from the choppy waters.

"No time," I point toward the far end of the island, where the coastline butts up against the sea. From the ocean, it's easy to tell that this is the island's highest point, its likely apex. "Can you get us toward those cliffs over there?" I shout at Oliver. The boat veers to the right, heading inland toward the bluffs.

"On it!" Oliver calls back, unable to keep from smiling despite our desperate situation. He hums beneath his breath. It takes me a moment to place the song, but then I recognize the familiar tones of Queen's *Bohemian Rhapsody*. Oliver is in his element, and he's loving every second of it.

"Zoe, we're putting ourselves at risk for her! What if the boat runs out of gas?"

A strange calm washes over me. Something's been bothering me from the moment Mike told me about Cassandra. I've avoided mentioning it because I know he beats himself up for the smallest mistakes, and I didn't want to add to the burdens he carries. But now, we've committed to spending the rest of our lives together, and nothing should remain unsaid. Two potential marriages unfold before me. In the first, hard conversations are swept under the rug. It's peaceful, but strained, until one day, it falls apart entirely. The second is rocky. Fights are had. Emotional shots are fired. But nothing goes unsaid. We agree to disagree. It's honest, and allows for resolution of our biggest differences, our darkest shadows.

I choose the second.

"How did you break up with her?"

"What?" Mike asks, sea spray sending droplets of salt water into his eyes.

"Cassandra. You told me yourself you were young, immature. You made her move from her hometown when you knew she wasn't ready."

"And I've regretted it every day since." His voices rises, defensive.

"I know," I confirm, gentle. "But how did you break up with her?"

He's quiet for a moment. Then, his head sinks into his hands. I let him work it out. Then, he emerges, looks me straight in the eye.

"I had her parents come down from Northern California. They were able to get a court-ordered guardianship. I waited until they talked her into leaving."

"Didn't she try to talk you instead?"

"I was already out of the apartment, staying at a friend's place. Her parents told her I'd reached out to them, that I thought she needed help and our relationship wasn't working." He pauses, looking out over the sea. "I drove by around the time I thought they'd be leaving. They got her in the car. She looked so hollow." His voice catches in his throat. "When I got back to the apartment, I cleaned everything out. What they didn't pack, I shipped to her. What was mine, I took with me. And that was it. It was over."

"But *you* never talked to her," I say.

"Every time I tried to break up with her, she came unhinged."

"What about after? When she was getting help?"

"No," he says.

"So she didn't get any closure," I point out.

"We weren't married," he says, rattled. "We were dating. It was a relationship that obviously wasn't working. What more closure could she need?"

"She changed her whole life for you. She *moved* to be

with you. She gave up everything that kept her sane because she didn't think you'd stay with her otherwise."

"She's stalked me!"

"I'm not disagreeing. What she did was wrong. Abusive. I'm just trying to understand what's going on in her head. That's all."

There's a long moment where the only sound is the roar of the engine, and the splash of the sea against the boat's angular bow. It slices through the air like a knife, promising a million chances to carve a new path forward.

"Are you saying I'm a bad guy?" Mike asks, his eyes wide with fear. He looks like he expects me to abandon him, to leap off the boat and throw my wedding ring over my shoulder in a dramatic goodbye.

"No," I answer, pulling closer to him, leaning my head on his chest. "I think you're a human being. My favorite one, actually."

He wraps his arms around me. I can hear his heartbeat, and it's like listening to the roar of the ocean inside a seashell. We stay that way for a long time, wondering what we'll find when the boat reaches the bluffs.

52

———

CASSANDRA

It takes me a long time to shuffle down to the flat patch of earth where the geysers sit. At first, I considered trying to free-climb down the cliff to the level rock below, but the risk of failure is too great. My plans have changed dramatically. I can't afford to die, now: I am the keeper of one of the world's biggest secrets now.

Instead, I go back the way I came, heading in a loop toward the palm trees, making my way to geysers using the path most familiar to me. When I get there, someone else has beaten me.

Francois.

"You ran," he says. It's too hard to tell what he knows. If he's angry, his eyes betray no rage. It occurs to me he might be hiding it. Maybe the others sent him to bring me to justice, to haul me back to camp so I could answer for my crimes. "Cassandra, we need to go back," he starts to say. I cut him off, putting a hand over his mouth.

"Before you tell me how much you hate me," I whisper, barely able to make eye contact with him. "I need you to check one more geyser with me."

His eyes widen.

"It's important. After that you can do what you want with me. But at least let me have this."

He doesn't answer.

"It's not about the treasure," I tell him, suddenly desperate to explain. "The truth is, I've done some terrible things, Francois. They've added up and added up, until eventually I felt like I could never undo them. Like a person can only do so much bad before *becoming* bad. Does that make sense?" Beneath my hand, Francois nods. "And I had decided to just keep being bad, to maybe even be a little bit *worse*, because I thought it was my only option, the only way to feel powerful. But the way you look at me... you've made me feel like I'm a not a *bad* person who does bad things. I'm a *good* person who does bad things. Which is really only one step away from a good person who does *good* things," I'm babbling again, but his eyes say he follows. "Finding the treasure and making sure it stays on the islands would be a good thing."

Francois' eyes crinkle in the corner, and I know he's smiling. I take my hand away.

"Let's find it," I say, the thrill of the words taking my breath away. "You are a moth and I am a bee. This is what we live for."

"Ladies first," Francois says, motioning to the geysers. This time, I don't have any trouble deciding where to begin.

"That one," I say, pointing at the hole I saw from up high. Its outline is stretched from this perspective, but the effect is the same.

It looks exactly like a rabbit.

"J'ai posé un lapin," I whisper, holding my hands in front of his eyes in a square like an old-fashioned film director. He peers through my fingers, the geyser in question coming into view. "What does it look like to you?"

He's silent for a second, and then his mouth drops open, shocked and delighted.

"A rabbit," he smiles.

THIS GEYSER IS DARKER than the others I've explored, thanks to an odd kink in the tubing, a place where the rocks bulge out from the sides, almost meeting in the middle. I pause my descent when I reach it, afraid to go further. But then I think about La Buse, and the treasure, and the idea of it leaving the Seychelles forever for some foreign country. I imagine how disappointed Francois would be. My mind's eye floods with images of goblets and coins on display in an air-conditioned museum, granite walls reflecting cold, fluorescent light over the precious gems. Plexiglass windows keeping them caged. Visitors milling in and out of the hallways, glancing twice with interest, but not with love. Snot-nosed children with dirty hands, clinging to beleaguered parents who drag them through the hallways— none of them aware of what this treasure would have meant to the islands. None of them knowing that the Seychelles would have benefited from its presence. None of them affected by the fact that, a million miles away, a man named Francois would be left in pieces.

"Are you alright?" Francois calls out from up above. His face appears at the top of the geyser, filled with concern.

"Fine," I say, even though I'm not sure it's true. "Just at a tricky part."

I let one foot touch the rock that juts out from the geyser's side, testing it with my weight. It doesn't budge. My other foot lands, and the rock holds steady. Carefully, as gently as I can, I squeeze myself in the small space where the geyser continues heading downward. My stomach flattens, pulling into my spine. I cringe as my chest grazes the rock, sharp edges cutting against my skin. I barely make it through the hole, and when I look back at it, it's so thin I wonder how I'll be able to get back up.

It's darker inside the hole now that I'm past the rocks. They block out the sun, leaving nothing but a ring of light above my head. My breath tickles the back of my throat, every inhale bringing a stale, musty scent with it. I feel like I'm intruding on sacred land. Like I'm at a cemetery and I've dug up the dead.

My feet touch the ground, and I know at once this is where the treasure is hidden. The other holes were covered constantly by an ankle-height surge of sea water. As the tides came in, the water would rise or recede, but never disappear completely. But here, the exit to the ocean slopes downward. When the water recedes, it leaves entirely, allowing the hole to be devoid of its intrusion entirely, at least for a while. If I'm right, it means La Buse would have the opportunity to hide his loot while the hole was empty. If he moved quickly, maybe he would have avoided the sea entirely. How long he had to do his work is difficult to say. The sand beneath my feet is wet, still, and I calculate that the water must not leave for long. The musty smell, the seaweed clinging to its slimy walls. All of it tells me this hole will fill again, soon.

But not before I find the treasure.

I search along the walls, looking for the perfect place. For a horrible moment, I wonder if La Buse might have buried it beneath my feet. If that's the case, years of sediment will have doubled his efforts— the treasure will have sunk so deep that finding it would require excavation by crane.

Then, my hand reaches out for wall and finds nothing but thin air. I follow it, arriving at a sea cave. It's a vast room bigger than my entire apartment, carved by years of assaulting sea water. Cracks in the rocks above let in small pinpricks of light, but there's no access point, no way to reach it except for the hole I've just descended. A dripping sound echoes throughout the cave, tiny drops of water plinking onto the ground from the stalactites above.

It would be beautiful on its own, empty and miraculous, a secret chamber the Earth has made for when she wants to be alone. But it's beautiful this way, too. Not empty, but filled with treasure. Huge chests have been propped up on the highest rock formations, most likely in an attempt to spare them from encroaching water. They're tied together with a net, lashed to the wall so they won't accidentally move. The wood on the exterior has rotted away in some places, letting piles of precious items peek out into the world, held in place by nothing but that net. Strings of pearls and rubies. Gold chains. Coins cut in uneven ovals. Statues carved from solid marble. In the far corner, a golden cross more than twice my height leans against the wall, too heavy to be moved, even by the sea.

I stare at the honey, wondering at what I've found. I think about all the buzzing that brought me here. My love for interior design, which taught me to look at details. Francois' wisdom and expertise, and his willingness to let me circle him without judgement. Mike's rejection, which left me without a hive. My sense that I'm always seeking without purpose— an idea proven wrong by what's in front of me.

The discovery of this treasure means Francois can protect it. Maybe he's right and I'm not a bad person. I'm a good person, who's done both good and bad things. This is a good thing.

I guess bees are useful after all.

I can't wait to tell Francois. That's what I'm thinking, anyway, when a strangely familiar sound echoes through the cave. It's one I've heard in the bathtub at night, when I turn the faucet up to its fastest speed. It's the sound of water filling a small space, taking up room, expanding in a container and pushing out all the air.

The ocean.

I slide toward the entrance to the cave, but it's too late. Water pushes me backward, rapidly filling the cave, waves crashing against walls, hungry to reach that cathedral ceiling. I'm flattened against a wall, quickly losing all direction of up and down. To my right, I notice the edge of the net that keeps the treasure in place. It's all I can do to grab on and pray.

The cave is almost full, now. I followed the net toward the top of the ceiling. I'm eye-level with a stalactite, marveling at how strange it feels to be so close to something I was staring up at just minutes ago.

I raise my lips above the water and take one final, shuddering breath before the cave fills entirely. I'm floating now, suspended in the water, wondering how long I can hold my breath.

Not very long, the quiver in my lungs seems to say. The burning in my chest makes me realize that I need to do something soon to avoid certain death.

It's ironic, isn't it?

Just an hour ago, I was ready to die. Now, I've never been more desperate to stay alive.

The water settles, satisfied now that it's filled the space it targeted— a quiet, peaceful place, dark and restful, the simplest of exits. It's a wet, cold tomb.

One that's about to be mine.

53

ZOE

When we reach the bluffs, there's no sign of Cassandra. I scan the water with anxious eyes, thinking terrible thoughts, wondering how long it takes a body to sink to the bottom of the sea.

"Look," Oliver points upward. My gaze follows his hand, stopping when I see a figure at the top of the cliffs. It's Francois, waving his arms, wearing nothing but his boxers.

"Is he okay?" Mike asks, bewildered.

"His arms!" I shout. As Francois steps closer to the edge of the cliffs, the sun reflects off something shiny coating his biceps, wrapped in his hands, strapped across his chest. It's pieces of treasure— long strands of pearls, golden necklaces — all of it sparkling under the hot, island sun.

"They found it," Oliver says, aghast. Then, he whispers, his accent adding to the effect, making him sound like an old maritime sailor. "The treasure of *La Buse*!"

Mike stares at me, a betrayed look on his face. "You said it wasn't real!"

"Does it help if I admit I was wrong?"

He shakes his head. "We had the chance to find buried

treasure and we missed it." He's disappointed, like a kid who found out his favorite arcade is closing.

Back on the bluffs, Francois hollers into the open air, whooping and throwing a fist upward, finally vindicated. In a matter of hours, he's gone from obsessive, disgraced archeologist to bona fide treasure hunter.

Suddenly, a second figure appears behind him. It's Cassandra, also in nothing but her underwear, grinning from ear to ear. She's draped in jewelry, doing a strange walk across the rocks, almost like she's a model strutting down a runway. I resist the urge to cover Mike's eyes.

"I can't believe the treasure is real," I mutter, chills running down my spine.

There's nothing for us to do but bring the boat around in a circle, a captive audience watching Francois and Cassandra prance across the bluffs, the two of them engaging in a naked victory dance before the wide open sea. They clasp hands and turn in circles, whooping and hollering the entire time.

"Should we ask them to come down?" Mike says, still frozen in place by the miracle unfolding in front of us.

"No," I smile, looking at Cassandra. Something has changed inside of her, like she's finally found herself. She's wide out in the open. She's not hiding anymore. She stares down at us like she's daring us to question her value. She's a woman on top of the world, in every single way.

"Just let them dance."

An hour later and we head toward the beach to pick up the rest of our group. Cassandra and Francois are huddled together in the back of the boat, still coated in precious gems. They made us watch while they removed as many artifacts as possible from the geyser, but they couldn't get it all with just the two of them. Francois said the treasure is so vast that they'll need a team to help them remove heavier items from the cave below. They're planning to hire help when we make it back to the big island. They're whispering between themselves now, no doubt making plans about how to proceed.

"Aren't you worried someone else might find it?" I asked Francois after he brought up the last of the treasure they could carry.

"It waited for me this long," he smiled, unconcerned. "It can wait a day more."

On our way back to the beach, Francois tells us the harrowing story about how they discovered the treasure's whereabouts. Our tiny ship cuts through the water, salt and sea spray adding a dramatic background to the tale he weaves.

"She was brilliant," he says, clutching Cassandra's hand in his. "She'd been down in the hole maybe fifteen minutes when I heard it... a great gush of water heading in from the sea! Terrifying."

"It wasn't that scary," Cassandra shrugs like it's nothing.

"For me, it certainly was!" Francois exclaims. "I was preparing to jump in after her when a great blast of water shot from the hole!" He holds his arms wide, painting the picture of a geyser exploding. "The water burst into the air. It must have been traveling at sixty miles an hour. A stupider person would have been dashed to death against the rocks."

"But not me," Cassandra smirks. She's clearly enjoying Francois' retelling.

"Of course not you! The clever girl clung to the net, didn't you?"

"When the water settled I swam down," she adds. I notice her stealing a glance at Mike, gauging his reaction. "I figured the ocean water had to have come in from somewhere, and when I found the exit, I kicked as hard as I could."

"Right to the surface!"

"It felt like my lungs were exploding.”

"On fire!"

"But then I saw the light overhead, and I made it to the surface, holding...”

“Holding a single strand of pearls!" Francois answers for her. The two of them share a smile.

Oliver— still at the helm— calls out over his shoulder, "Congrats to you both! A job well done. None of us believed it, did we?"

"He's right," I tell him. “We didn't."

"What do *you* think?" Cassandra asks. She's talking only to Mike, now, looking him dead in the eye.

"Me?" He says, skeptical, wondering what her true motivation in asking might be.

"I want to know what you think," she says, her voice suddenly hard and tight in all the wrong places. "Bet you didn't expect this from me. Probably surprised someone as *weak* as me could do it."

"Enough," Mike answers, looking away from her, trying not to escalate the situation.

"But you *do* think I'm unstable. Not worthy of talking to. A person who hardly warrants a call. Or a real conversation," Cassandra is standing now, trying to keep her balance against the rocking of the boat. Francois flushes with surprise, disturbed by the sudden change in her cadence. "I'm just the trash you throw out, isn't that right?" She shakes the necklace she's holding in his face.

Mike doesn't say anything.

"Well?" Cassandra pushes him again. "I asked you a question. What do you think of me now?"

Finally, Mike looks at her. There's an expression of disgust at the corners of his mouth. He resents being forced to interact with a person who has wronged him, a person who has stalked him, a person who has denied him his animal right to freedom. But there's also a warmth in his eyes— a heavy, sad regret that hints at a shared pain. A dozen lost futures swim in his irises— once they could have shared, but never will.

"I think you're Cass, and you've always seen what I can't."

His words seem to change her, physically shifting the tenor of the electromagnetic field around her body. She takes a step back. Mike hasn't said more than a syllable to Cassandra during the duration of our trip, but this small sentence takes root deep inside her, filling her up from feet to crown. She drinks the moment in with a shiver. Then, she answers, regal and stoic, as if she's been waiting her entire life for justice and has only just received it.

"Thank you."

Her hand grips the side of the boat, her face turned toward the horizon. She reaches her other arm toward the sun, looking like she wishes she could catch it, but clasping nothing but air. Her hand closes into an empty fist, clasping some invisible sentiment none of the rest of us can see. Then, she strides across the boat, landing next to Francois. She kisses him hard, burrowing into his shoulder, not saying a word for the rest of the trip. Her silence is medicinal, a heavy salve on a wound she's stitching back together from the inside out.

Suddenly, I'm sure of it: Cassandra won't be bothering us anymore.

WHEN WE MAKE it to the beach, our party is still scattered near the water, waiting for our return. My Mom is the first to see us. She's standing with her feet in the ocean, watching the sun get lower in the sky, a constant lookout who refuses to abandon her post. When she spots our boat, she waves her arms high in the air, signaling for the others to join her.

Tori and Jason are the first reach her, their hands intertwined. Jason's camera is nowhere to be found, and I wonder if Tori made him put it away, for once. Beside them, Donald and Alicia arrive with their arms crossed— I can tell they're furious, even from a distance. My brain fills in the hard lines of their mouths, the nostrils flared with rage. The last to join is Lana, her crimson hair like a smoke signal, impossible to miss. It's strange, seeing all of them looking so small and afraid on a large, unconquerable rock. That was us, mere hours ago, and now we're masters of the universe, with pounds of treasure and a working motorboat to prove it.

Oliver pulls the boat in as close as he can, then drops anchor. He leaps into the water, calling out toward the island, "My Rachel!" He has a flair for the dramatic when it comes to my Mom. When they met, he told her he would never take a flight without her by side, because now he had someone who would miss him if the plane crashed. A ridiculous promise— and one that he's kept.

Oliver rushes toward the beach, and Francois follows, jumping into the water with a few artifacts still in hand. He can't wait to show the group that he was right, all along.

Mike gets ready to jump off the boat, holding out a hand to me as he stands by the railing.

"Ready?"

I glance over my shoulder at Cassandra. Her earlier power is gone. She's standing at bow, looking like she might be sick even though the boat isn't moving anymore.

"Go without me," I tell him. "I'll follow you."

He listens. When he's out of sight, I stand next to Cassandra. Her long, stringy hair hangs like a curtain over her face, greasy roots transitioning into dry ends.

"It was my name that started the boat, wasn't it?" she asks, her voice thin and cracking.

"In a way," I tell her.

She looks at me, hopeful, eyes wide. "What do you mean?"

"The answer was 'everyone.' Everyone helped Logan."

"How can that be?" Her hands shake, and she looks like she wants to vomit. Words pour out of her like poison, dripping all over the deck. "I did so many things. I'm guilty."

"I know," I say.

She almost seems relieved— happy, to confess. "I thought you might," she answers. "What gave me away?"

"It was by the waterfall, when you saved my life." Her eyes scan my face, searching for a memory that will tell her where she revealed herself. "You said I was dumb for following the red rope that was attached to the buoy," I explain. "But the rope wasn't visible from the edge of the basin. You would have had to have seen it yourself, long before the buoy was placed in the water."

"Why didn't you turn me in right away?"

"It didn't make sense," I say, shaking my head. "Logan wouldn't have gone to these lengths just to make me hate you. No offense, but I had plenty of reasons to hate you before now." My honesty makes Cassandra laugh. "Everything Logan does is meant to undermine the best of me. He tries to make me believe I can't trust other people. I think..."

I pause, hating to say the words aloud. "I think his goal is to make me more like him." The thought makes me want to take a shower.

"Are you going to tell them?"

I pause, considering. Cassandra is the only member of our party who *knew* she was working with Logan, it's true. But she's also the most disturbed. She's the loneliest, and the strangest, and the one with the most to gain from a chance at starting over.

"I don't see what the point would be," I acknowledge. She exhales, relieved.

"I feel bad I helped him," she says. Then, she turns to me, something rough and begrudging in her eyes. "I'm sorry," she mutters.

"It was wrong," I agree. "But I appreciate the apology." Then, acting on a hunch, I ask, "What did he promise you?"

"Something I probably don't need anymore." She looks out at Mike, who's talking with the group, laughing as Tori refuses to let go of a pearl necklace Francois has allowed her to hold.

"Are you sure?" I ask, a warning in my voice. "Bees need something to buzz around."

Her eyebrows raise, like she's surprised I remember.

"Are you going to buzz around him?" I ask, nodding at Francois, who has finally managed to pry the necklace out of Tori's unwilling hands. "I hope you've asked him whether he wants the attention. That's important. Some might say essential."

Cassandra shakes her head. There's a deep concern in her eyes, like she's tried on a shirt that doesn't fit right. She shrugs her shoulders, pushing her bodyweight from side to side, trying to find a new sense of balance within herself. It's an unsteady rhythm, painful to watch.

"I don't want to buzz around Francois. I think I love him, though," she adds, like it's a curious footnote. "I just don't want to buzz around him."

"Huh," I say, feeling like we might have had a breakthrough, but afraid to say anything else in case I scare it away. "Then what will you buzz around?"

There's a long silence, and she never fills it.

54

CASSANDRA

We create quite the stir when we arrive on the big island of Mahe. At first glance, our vessel looks like any ordinary motorboat, packed with tourists after a long-day of sight-seeing. But when we pull up to the wooden dock, the shocked faces of onlookers reflect our strangeness back to us. In a matter of days, we've become mottled, horrifying castaways. We're dirty and hungry, some of us burned in all the wrong places from too much sun exposure, all of us insatiable. Next to the serene pastel buildings and the clean, stone walkways, we're a mar on the island's beautiful face. And then, of course, there's the raft we're hauling.

After Zoe and Mike came to get Francois and I by the geyser, we returned to the beach to buck up the rest of the group and make a break for it. But it became clear immediately that we wouldn't be able to bring back the giant chests of treasure we collected while still making room for the others. Even on the ride back, the motorboat groaned under the weight of the treasure. Adding Donald's round belly to the load wouldn't do the boat any favors.

"Something's got to give," I whispered to Zoe as the group debated next steps. "It's obvious what needs to be done."

"We leave the treasure here and come back for it later?"

"I was thinking we leave Donald and Alicia here and come back for *them* later," I reply. Zoe laughs, stifling it into a snort. "But your way is good, too."

The idea of leaving behind the treasure was too painful for Francois, who feared that Logan might come back and get in it our absence, especially if it lay naked and exposed at the edge of the beach. "The larger pieces we were unable to excavate from the cave, those he would not be able to move on his own. He would need a team, just as we do," Francois reasoned. "But the chests. We should take them."

"Quite a strain on the boat, though, isn't it?" Oliver scratched his chin, trying to work out a solution. "Would be a shame to overtax it."

"Then I will stay with the artifacts, and you can send someone back for me," Francois said, defiant.

"No!" I must have said it too loud, because the others stepped back, surprised by my outburst. I was thinking of Logan, and how brutal I know him to be, and what he would do if he found Francois all alone on the island, guarding one of the greatest treasures the world has ever seen. "You can't stay alone. You *can't*."

It was Mike who suggested his raft. I felt a little sorry for him when he mentioned it. The rest of the group looked at him with hazy eyes, a vague sense of recognition dawning slower than he might have liked. In the chaos of the weekend—between the clues, and the fear of the boat exploding, and the hunt for an ancient treasure— everyone forgot what he was building. His sad little project fell by the wayside, written off as a lost cause.

"It works now," he said, trying to convince. "It does. After Cass suggested using our clothes." He glanced at me for a moment. "I tested a piece of it. If you give me an hour, I can fix the rest. I know I can."

"Another hour?" Alicia shouted, horrified by the idea.

"Please," Mike said. "Let me try. We can't leave a man behind, and Francois won't go without the treasure. Let me do this." There was a pleading tone to his voice, and I couldn't help but wonder if this experience had rendered Mike somewhat useless. Zoe solved the puzzle. Francois and I found our treasure. Oliver drove the boat. What did Mike have to contribute, besides this sad raft that he hadn't managed to make work?

"I am *leaving* this island in one hour, with or without you," Alicia snarled.

Mike set off to finish the rest of the raft, Alicia and Tori weaving strips of fabric together as fast as possible, the rest of the group volunteering t-shirts and shorts where they could. He worked with a fervor. And to his credit, he delivered on his promise.

Now, we've arrived at Mahe, and we're stepping onto inhabited land for the first time in days. It's odd seeing other people around. I've been looking at the same handful of faces for so many days that I've begun to feel our tiny party represents the last people on Earth. But Mahé proves me wrong. Sailors peek their heads out from other boats lashed to the dock. Tourists point, their cameras clicking from thick leather bands that lace around their necks.

When my feet touch the dock, I look over my shoulder at the motorboat, hauling the saddest, most uneven little raft I've ever seen. Pieces of wood cling to each other, holding on for fear dear life, their frayed edges sending splinters into the water. Multi-colored strips of fabric weave between the planks, threatening to break apart at any moment. It's like something a child built— a pathetic, imaginary attempt at an actual vessel. It belongs in a suburban backyard somewhere, right underneath a tree house, sitting beside a fake rocket-ship made from cardboard boxes. In ordinary circumstances, we would never test it on the water. It's already half-sinking, having barely survived the journey across the ocean to make it here. It's as if the raft knew it had only one purpose in life, and now that the task has been accomplished, it's ready to be set free.

Mike is looking at the raft with warm, grateful eyes. "I knew it could do it," he says with a sigh. He glances at me. "I don't think I ever thanked you for your idea."

"You're welcome," I tell him.

A crowd has gathered, everyone pointing and muttering at our strange haul. The word spreads, and more people pour out from restaurants on the dock, a thousand insects curious to see what intruder has stepped on their anthill. Waiters wipe their hands on aprons. A tour group pauses to get in on the action. At the front of the dock, a child holding an ice-cream cone pulls on his Mother's skirt. We are a spectacle.

Francois is at the back of the boat, reeling the raft in as fast as he can. Oliver helps him unload the chests into the motorboat, where they're undoubtedly much safer. As he moves the final chest into the boat, it topples over, sending a cascade of galleons into the sea. Francois shoots him a murderous stare. "Be careful with that. It's history."

Suddenly, a plank of wood breaks of from the center of the raft— an important piece of its construction that helped hold two halves together. It breaks apart, each side taking on water, turning vertically just like the Titanic before sinking under the water in one final, mournful cry.

"Then again," Francois says to Oliver, suddenly grateful, "I'm glad we moved the artifacts to safety before that horrible deathtrap sunk entirely."

Mike's face falls. Zoe takes his hand in hers. "It did what it was supposed to do. You built a *great* raft," she tells him, and it seems to brighten him a bit.

Disgusting. I would have been honest with him and said it was only adequate. But maybe that's why Mike and I would never have worked anyway. It would bore me, to have to reassure him all the time. To tell him he's wonderful even if I don't see it. If I'm being perfectly honest, that's what I'd like a partner to do for *me*. I think, maybe, that's why I buzzed around him. Because I wanted him to reassure me. To tell me that I mattered.

It never occurred to me I could give that feeling to myself.

It's a new line of thinking, a new philosophy I'm discovering. It hums in the back of my brain through the rest of the day, a recurring thought that won't leave me alone. Even when they send the ambulances to take us to the hospital— someone must have called them, maybe one of the onlookers— this thought is there, preoccupying my attention.

I am buzzing around something new.

"You'll feel a slight prick," a nurse says to me while we ride in the back of the ambulance. Apparently I am dehydrated. It comes as no surprise, what with the constant sun and the way we rationed our water. I'm not even sure I've *had* a single gulp of water all weekend. I was too focused on other things, too distracted by that which is outside of myself. She hooks me to an I.V., but I barely notice the needle as it slides under my skin.

I am buzzing around something new.

We get to the hospital and our entire group is divided for treatment. They send all of us to different rooms to be examined. The mutters between the nurses and doctors lead me to believe that some of us are in worse shape than others, but that we're generally going to be alright.

At one point, they let Francois into my room. He's asked to see me. He talks to me about a lot of things, and they're all touching and wonderful. He tells me about the treasure, and his plans for it, and how all those little pieces of history will get to stay on the island now, safe and sound. He has such a nice face, and such warm hands. I think I could be with him for a long time. I'm entirely sure, now, that I love him.

Still, I wonder what the new thing is I'm buzzing around. I need to name it, need to identify it.

Maybe I'm buzzing around Francois?

But I know it's not true. I love Francois, but I'm not obsessed with him. There's a different color about the feeling. My love for Francois is peaceful and quiet, a steadying hand so different from obsession. I just want him to be happy, even if it means being without me. If he told me tomorrow he'd live a better life alone and that I should go on my merry way, I would be sad, but I would let him go.

The hospital gets dark. It must be nighttime now. They've rubbed some salve on the top of my head and my shoulders. The nurse said something about a third degree sunburn. It sounded unimportant— or less important, at least, than what I'm fixing in my mind.

I'm alone in my room— still thinking— when I get a surprise visitor. It's Mike. His hands are bandaged, wrapped in a gauze that's the same shade as his skin. He steals a chair from the hallway outside— a light, plastic one, the kind that's never comfortable. He positions it at the end of my bed, and suddenly I'm annoyed at him for bothering me. Whatever he has to say *can't* be more important than what I'm working out in my head.

I am buzzing around something new.

How strange. Days ago I would have died from pleasure if Mike had wanted to talk to me. Now, I wish he would leave.

Just get on with it already.

"Zoe thought the way I broke up with you was wrong," he says.

"It was," I tell him.

"But everything that came after— the stalking me, not letting me go. What you did was wrong, too."

"That's true."

He looks surprised I agree. Idiot. He doesn't know me at all. I knew what I was doing wrong. I just did it anyway because I couldn't help myself.

"Obviously you want something," he throws his hands up in the air. "So what is it? What *is* it, Cass?"

"Logan promised me I could get you in a room if I helped him. He promised me he'd keep you in one place, so I could talk to you."

Mike looks disgusted. His jaw sets firm, his mouth flattening out in a harsh line. "Alright, fine."

"Fine?"

"You've got me. Here I am, delivered to you in a small room, totally at your disposal. I won't leave until you send me away. What is it you want to say?"

The walls seem to expand and contract, as I realize I've finally gotten everything I wanted. Mike is here, and he's promised to listen to me. He's promised to hear me out. He's *noticing* me.

"Even if it takes hours?" I ask.

Mike rolls his eyes, irritated. "However long you need."

Everything I've wanted to tell him comes rushing back in a flood. I've imagined this conversation a thousand times before. I've spent weeks rehearsing what I would say. The monologue fills the pages of a dozen journals shoved under my bed. In my daydreams, I make him see things from my perspective. I issue a speech so moving, so undeniable that he finally understands how he hurt me.

"I changed my entire life for you," imaginary me says in my fantasy. "I left everything even though I knew it was bad for me, because I trusted you to take care of me. And you couldn't even do me the service of breaking up with me to my face."

Imaginary Mike takes responsibility. He apologizes. The Mike of my daydreams tells me that I'm valuable. He says that, for all my flaws, I didn't deserve to be treated that way. He confesses to his crimes, drenched in regret. He admits that the way he broke up with me was inhumane, especially after how much I sacrificed for him. He acknowledges that he humiliated me by making my *parents* do his dirty work. At first, it's a fight. We go back and forth, nit-picking the gritty details of who did what, who was right and who was wrong. But then it becomes a reconciliation— he owns his behavior, because I showed him the way.

But does that mean anything?

My chest tightens, and the walls close in again, and suddenly I'm too aware of my surroundings— the scratchy blanket the nurses laid over me, the tiny hospital room in this place I'm not from, this place I don't belong.

All at once, I understand. The pieces of my life click together like a puzzle— one I've never been able to solve.

I can wrench an apology from Mike if I really want one. I can make him see things my way, get him to admit that he hurt me. I can beg, and plead, and stalk, and cry, all to receive what I'm absolutely entitled to. But if I have to force it out of him, does it *mean* anything? If I have to blaze across the Earth like a hurricane to extract an apology, is it really an apology at all? If someone has wronged you, and they don't take accountability all on their own, why *make* them do it? By forcing him down a path he's not ready to tread, I'm only depriving him of the opportunity to apologize on his own terms. Maybe he will give me an apology one day. Or maybe he won't. Maybe he'll notice me. Or maybe he won't. But if I have to become a force of nature to make him look my way, was it worth it? And in the meantime, while I'm waiting for him to look my way:

What am I doing for myself?

Obsessing over Mike. Feeling wronged by Mike. Wanting Mike to give me the love I deserve. All of it distracted me from what I should have been doing for me. Buzzing around Mike kept me from noticing the pieces of my own life I allowed to fall into disarray. It gave me something else to focus on, so I didn't have to spend time orbiting around myself, admitting my own worthiness. Instead of looking for things I needed from Mike, I should have started a search for them elsewhere. Instead of raging against a change I couldn't control, I should have loved myself enough to go find what I needed from people who were capable of giving it to me.

Everything is clear. I know exactly what I need to do.

"Where's Zoe?" I ask.

Mike bristles. "You're not going to drag her into this."

"Oh my gosh, get over yourself," I sigh, casually ripping the I.V. out of my arm. Mike gasps when the blood rushes from my veins. What a baby. "It's not like that. I just need to tell her something. She'll want to hear it, trust me."

"She's in the waiting room," he says, standing to follow me as I walk down the hall in my bare-feet, not caring that my hospital gown is wide open in the back.

The hallway takes a sharp right before emptying out into the waiting room, which is nothing but a reception desk and a small collection of chairs. Zoe's in one of them, her shocked eyes widening when she sees me entering the lobby, a very confused Mike trailing behind me.

"You asked me earlier what I want to buzz around," I tell her.

She inhales, hopeful. She knows exactly why this is important. She understands things Mike will never understand.

"I did," she nods, cooly.

"Well, I have the answer now." I smile. "I want to buzz around *me*."

I am buzzing around something new.

"I think that's a great idea," she nods, and for the first time, I realize that I'm not just a bee. I'm a Queen Bee, the center of my own hive.

IT TAKES two weeks for Francois to get approval from the Seychelles Government to extract the rest of the artifacts from the cave we found together. He said the process was impossibly fast, that such a deliberation would normally take months. "They shared my sentiment," Francois smiled at me over a shared dinner by the dock, "that the best way to keep the artifacts in the Seychelles was to extract them ourselves."

Later, he takes me to downtown Victoria, where an empty warehouse awaits. Big, double-doors serve as its entrance. An iron lamppost rests beside them, begging to be lit. The exterior walls are stucco, the pastel paint faded over the years to the lightest shade of blue my eyes have ever seen.

Francois pushes the doors open, and we step inside the musty, empty building. It's all one room, as tall as it is wide, the ceilings soaring thirty feet into the air. Particles of dust float on the air, angry at being disturbed. It's an empty, deteriorating gem of a place, waiting to be given new life. It reminds me of the cave at the bottom of that geyser, the place where the treasure waited, for so many years, to be discovered.

"You've decided to design again, yes?" Francois smiles at me. It's true. I've spoken of nothing else for the past several days. In deciding to buzz around myself, I've reclaimed the bits of me I lost. Every room I see has potential. Every space I inhabit can be rearranged. My superpowers have returned, and I intend to use them. I've already started look at design jobs online, hoping to find a place that will let me put my degree to good use. I don't expect to start at the top. But I plan to work my way up there.

"Perhaps, you could start by designing here."

"What do you mean?" I ask, breathless.

"We didn't go through all of this just to allow our treasures to live in a lackluster museum," Francois says, a secret twinkling in his eyes. "Make it a place worthy of them. No one but us understands what it took to retrieve them. Build them a beautiful home."

I stare at the enormous space before me, thinking about

what it took to get here. I pull Francois close to me, feeling, for the first time, that I'm with someone who really sees me.

I had planned to leave the island. To go back to America and start again. But now, I think about my reasons for staying. If I stay on Mahé, it will be for me. I won't stay because it would make Francois happy. I won't stay because I want his approval. I'll stay because all my needs are met, here, and it's a place filled with flowers. It's a place where I can spread pollen into the air, adding new value, making things multiply just by buzzing around myself— just by being a bee.

"What are you thinking?" Francois asks.

"I'm thinking we start with the floors," I say, right before he kisses me.

55

ZOE

As soon as the hospital releases us, Mike and I charter a boat to take us to the island we believe Logan was using as home-base. We researched the address on the property deed from Donald and Alicia, discovering that the little house is a sole residence on a tiny archipelago. When our boat pulls up to the landing point— a strange, rickety dock with no other ships attached— the driver asks if we're sure this is where we want to go.

"We're sure," Mike answers. The driver nods, like it's not his business anyway, and we make our way up the beach, climbing over a rocky barrier that juts up to the dock until we reach the sand.

"It's not well taken care of," Mike nods at the tiny house in front of house. It's a plain, brown color on the outside, surrounded by planter boxes overgrown with weeds.

"If you buy the house, you buy the island," I tell him, shrugging my shoulders. "Maybe it's a good deal in that respect."

This is a small archipelago, the kind of property that's worth everything and nothing all at once. Everything, in the sense it's a private island a person can actually own, theoretically capable of becoming the kind of oasis reserved for movie stars and politicians. Nothing, because there's no services of any kind nearby. Making it live up to its true potential would require an enormous amount of capital, from bringing in plumbing and electric, to refurbishing the landing strip for planes, which is woefully cracked and worn.

"Do you think he's inside?" I ask Mike, even though some piece of me can already sense the answer.

"No," Mike says, confirming what my intuition tells me. "He won't engage in a fair fight. He'll have left the place empty, or rigged it with explosives."

"It's probably a bad idea to do this ourselves," I say.

"Probably," Mike agrees.

We stand shoulder-to-shoulder, accepting the stupidity of our plan, both of us knowing we're going to go ahead with it anyway. We're on international waters, and the FBI couldn't catch Logan in their own backyard. We've both come to realize that whatever battle we fight with him is best won alone.

"Should we get on with it then?" I ask. Mike nods, and we head for the house. When we reach the front door, Mike grabs a heavy rock from a nearby planter box. He hurls it at the doorknob, which breaks clean off. The door slowly squeaks open. We wait, but no charge explodes. No bomb goes off.

"So far, so good," Mike says.

We enter the small dwelling. It's completely empty. We expected as much. There's nothing but wood panels, and the faint electric charge that tells me someone was living here in the recent past. Other than that, the place is deserted.

"We shouldn't be surprised," Mike says, but I'm disappointed all the same. Some piece of me really hoped I'd get the chance to look Logan in the eye and bring him to justice.

"Let's go, Zoe," Mike says, taking my hand and leading me out of the house. My head swims as we head back to the beach. I'm not sure what I expected to happen, but it wasn't this. As we make our way back to the front door, I notice something. It's a plain white envelope taped to the inside of the door, with a single word written across its front in black ink:

Zoe.

Mike sees it too, and I can feel his hand tighten in mine.

"Maybe we shouldn't open it," he says, but I'm already pulling it off the door, leaving behind a broken piece of tape.

LATER, the boat hums across the water as our driver takes us away from the island. I look over my shoulder, memorizing the curves of its shores, trying to create an image I can come back to whenever I need. I'm worried the island might still be hiding secrets. Memorizing its outline will protect me if I find out it's lied.

In my hand sits the envelope, opened, its frayed edges at the top looking like teeth. All that was inside was a postcard. A postcard, with a P.O. Box number on it.

"He wants you to write him," Mike says, looking down at the card like it's a living, breathing thing. He says it like he wants me to deny it. I won't. "You're going to do it," he says, already knowing the answer.

I don't say anything, because I'm not ready to talk about it just yet. A plan is taking shape in my mind— one that, if I'm honest, I've probably been brewing for a long time. Mike won't like it. He won't like what I'll have to do, who I'll have to ask for help.

"I think, maybe, I *will* write him," I answer, still looking out at the horizon.

"Why?"

"Because I have a lot to say."

56

——————

CASSANDRA

A year ago, if you'd told me I'd be having lunch with Mike's wife, I'd have told you to pound sand.

It's uncomfortable, sitting out in the open like this— the two of us wearing ordinary clothes, spending time together not because we're stranded on an island by a madman, but because we chose to be with each other.

"Beautiful, isn't it?" Zoe says, pointing out at the water. When she asked to meet, I chose a place near Francois' apartment, where I'm staying. I wanted to be close to home in case the lunch didn't go well. Zoe and I aren't friends. Not really. But there's something undeniable that we share. There's always been a strange connection between us that's impossible to define. It's what makes this meeting so odd. It's too formal, too planned.

"It is," I agree, sipping on my drink. There's no alcohol in it. I've given that up. If I were going to start again, this would be an opportune moment. For a second, I think about ordering a gin and tonic, but then I remember the museum, and the plans I have to make the place beautiful. My life, very suddenly, has enough good things in it that I'm afraid to risk losing them by hitting the bottle. "You wanted to meet."

"Yes," Zoe says. "Mike and I went to the house Logan was staying at. You've seen it, I gather?"

My stomach churns.

Yes, I want to say, *I saw it when I was helping him. I stayed there and lived there and ate there. Is that what you want to hear?*

"I've seen it," I confirm.

She slides a card across the table. It's a simple postcard, with a P.O. Box Number written on the back.

"He left this for me."

"Why?"

"I was hoping you would know."

"I don't," I say honestly. "If I did, I would tell you."

"That's too bad," she stirs her iced tea like she's punishing it, the straw making circles in her glass. "I didn't want to ask you for a favor, but now I have to."

"There's an argument to be made that I owe you one," I say, intrigued.

"I asked Francois first. Did he tell you?"

I shake my head. It's odd that Francois *wouldn't* tell me, but maybe he wanted to let me make up my own mind. He's like that. Always giving me space, always letting me be.

"No."

"He wouldn't help me. He said I didn't believe him when he talked about the treasure, and that I don't deserve to profit from it." She pauses. "He's absolutely right."

"The same could be said of me," I shrug.

"But you did profit from it, didn't you?"

"A little," I lie.

The truth is, Francois and I would never sell the artifacts for money. His intention was always to keep the treasure in the Seychelles, and even though we could easily sell the artifacts we found abroad for a fortune, we're committed to keeping them here, where they belong. That said, the Seychelles government was extremely grateful for his archeological discovery. Between grant money, the funds to build the museum, and our individual bonuses, we've been well taken care of. I told Francois I didn't want any of it, but he said it was only fair I take something, given that I found the geyser. I've never been rich before, and it's strange to think of myself that way. But now, my new international bank account has more than seven zeros in it.

"I was thinking about *La Buse*," Zoe says, changing the topic. "How he didn't trust his crew and it led to his downfall. That's what Logan wanted to happen to me. He wanted me not to trust anyone. Sometimes I think it's worked."

"Lana?" I ask. She nods. We're both wondering if she killed Rick. No one will ever know what happened on that island when the two of them were alone.

"It was an empty island. And Lana was angry," Zoe says. "I can't help but wonder..."

"Me too," I tell her.

"I'm going to ask you something, and I need you to answer me honestly. I don't want to make La Buse's mistake, but I'm also not an idiot." She leans in, looking me dead in the eye, a fire burning in her irises. "Can I trust you?"

"Three weeks ago, no. But now you can," I say, drawing a line between the past and the present. She *couldn't* trust me before, it's true. I was buzzing around Mike, a bee with a misplaced center of gravity. But today, I'm a new woman. I've realized that being a bee means having super powers— the power to fly, the power to sting, the power to choose where flowers may grow. And I'm using mine for good from now on.

"I want to get him, Cassandra. I don't want to be the prey anymore. I want to be the predator. But to do that, I need resources. Logan seems to have unlimited funds, connections everywhere."

Now I understand what she's asking for: money. It's a new feeling. No one's ever bothered to ask me for money, probably because it was clear I didn't have any. I'm unbothered by it. Money means nothing to me. It's a number on a screen.

"I'll give you whatever you need," I say. "What do you have in mind?"

She reaches into her pocket and pulls out a small, gold envelope. There's no name on the front— just an address. It's the same P.O. Box number that was on the postcard. It's been carved into the envelope in a looping, graceful font, crafted with care, dripping with an irony that only Logan could appreciate.

"I'm asking Logan to go on a hunt of his own," she smiles. "This is the invitation."

"It's beautiful," I nod, happy to be a part of our secret game, our own little joke. "I certainly hope he accepts."

THE END.

TO CONTINUE THE ADVENTURE, order "The Trap is Set," the third and final book in the Predator / Prey thriller series! Available now in ebook, paperback, and audiobook.

MORE FROM VALERIE BRANDY

LETTER FROM THE AUTHOR

Dear Reader,

Thank you for dedicating your time to the world of the Predator / Prey thriller series! I'm a screenwriter and filmmaker coming to books from Film & TV, but one thing I love about books in particular, is connecting directly with a community of readers. It's very special to be able to speak with you and hear what you want from characters in our novels.

I hope you'll reach out to me by joining my mailing list at the link below! If you liked this book, continue with the next installment in the Predator / Prey thriller series, "The Trap is Set," which is the third and final book in the the trilogy. In addition, check out my Private Investigator Annie Hudson Real Estate Mystery Series, which starts with book one, "Murder Behind the Gates."

And if you want to read more from me in general, please keep in touch at the links below! I love hearing from readers, which makes all the work of writing worthwhile.

Warmly,

Valerie Brandy

Join the author's mailing list at:

www.valeriebrandy.com

ACKNOWLEDGMENTS

~

To everyone I thanked in book one. You have my continued appreciation, love, and dedication.

ABOUT THE AUTHOR

Valerie Brandy is a writer, director, and actress based in Los Angeles.

She began her writing career by selling a feature length screenplay at just 20 years old, becoming one of the youngest members of the WGA west at the time. She's since written for numerous film studios and television networks, most recently serving as a full time staff writer at Walt Disney Studios live action feature department, where she continues to develop new projects. Her work has been acknowledge by the Nichol Fellowships in Screenwriting, run by the Academy of Arts & Sciences.

Her directorial feature film debut, *Lola's Last Letter*— which she also wrote and starred in— was released in 2016 by Random Media and Sony's "The Orchard" after a successful festival run, premiering at the historic Chinese Theatre in Hollywood. The film received a five-star review from the Examiner, a special feature in Huffington Post, and a Best Principal Actress nomination from Los Angeles Film Review. Valerie shot the film in seven days with a cast and crew of just seven people. In their review of the film, Huffington post stated that, "... the key word in describing Brandy is *unflinching...*" Starpulse called the film, "... breathtakingly real and raw... Brandy is an important voice for her generation." *Lola's Last Letter* is currently available OnDemand at iTunes, Vudu, Googleplay, Comcast, Youtube, and many other platforms.

Brandy's second feature film, "A Unified Theory of Love," stars Richard Karn (*Home Improvement*) and Eric Isenwhoer (*Parks & Rec*), and is due to hit the festival circuit in 2024.

As an actress, Valerie recurred on FX's Emmy-winning show "Justified" as the manipulative Trixie. She received her B.A. from UCLA in three years, graduating as a prestigious Alumni Scholarship Recipient, and holds an M.F.A. in Film & Television Production from Asbury University, where she graduated Magna Cum Laude.

Brandy lives in the greater Los Angeles area with her smush-faced dog and snow-white cat. "Trail of Obsession" is her debut novel.